A Time of Lies

Kevin Kelley

A Novel by:

KEVIN KELLEY

DEDICATION

To Colleen Miller who got me writing, and Robert Morgan, whose eclectic Wednesday Night Writing Group kept me going. I am grateful to you all, and hope you are continuing to create.

CONTENTS

ACKNOWLEDGMENTS

Thank you, Chris Parks, for your guidance and encouragement.

1 CNN WASHINGTON DC - 2007

Christiane Amanpour: "Okay, Brandon, cameras are rolling. I know these lights are bright. Just look at me or into the camera and you'll be fine. In a few seconds, I'll get a signal to start. I'll make a brief introduction and then give you a chance to tell your side of the story. Are you ready?"

Brandon: "I think so."

Christiane: "All right. Here we go: ... Good evening, I'm Christiane Amanpour with a CNN exclusive interview. I'm sitting here with Brandon McCarty, brother of Lieutenant Christopher McCarty.

"Despite everything we've seen and heard about Lt. McCarty this month, Brandon remains convinced of his brother's innocence.

"Brandon, there's every indication your brother betrayed our country. Why should we believe what you have to say is anything other than family loyalty in the face of overwhelming evidence? How do you respond to that?"

Brandon: "Look, I understand why people are angry, I've seen the same footage, but they're wrong. They don't know my brother; they don't know the half of it. I know his heart, and I can tell you Christopher McCarty loves America and would never to do anything to harm it.

"Suddenly, he's accused of treason, his career and reputation are ruined; his wife and child are under siege. Our own mother can't even leave the house without reporters converging on her like a pack of wolves.

"It's completely unfair. No matter what you see in those videos. It's snap judgment, and it's wrong. I just wish people knew his side of the story."

2 SEPTEMBER MOURN - 2001

Christopher McCarty's second class at Darien High School had just started. The clock on the blue cinderblock wall read nine-twelve when three shrill blasts sounded over the PA system. An assembly was announced with attendance mandatory, no exceptions. "Good," he thought, "I'll miss calculus." He grabbed his backpack and joined the stream of students heading to the auditorium, surprised to see two teachers running to the theater. He stood taller, extending his six-foot height, scanning over other students' heads, then picked up his pace, weaving in and out of clumps of classmates, feeling tension roll through the hallway.

Students were barely inside when Principal Hanley spread his arms, hands flapping, urging silence from the podium.

"I know many of you have family working in the city. You should know there's been an attack on the World Trade Center."

Hanley explained what little he knew about the planes and the towers, and announced school was closed for the day. Chris sat for a few seconds, letting it sink in. He wasn't sure how near his father's office was to the World Trade Center, but he knew the Financial District had to be close. He launched out of his seat, running into the hallway, looking for anyone who could give him a ride. Mark Herndon had almost reached the parking lot when Chris poked him on the shoulder.

"Can I get a ride? I need to check on my mom."

Mark laughed. "Dude, relax. It's a day off! Let's go someplace fun."

"No! I can't. My dad works in Manhattan. I really need to get home."

"Sorry, I forgot. Come on."

A faint scent of breakfast still lingered when Chris opened the kitchen door: coffee, toast, and bacon. Scooter bounded into the room, skidding across the tile floor, wagging his tail and jumping up for his usual hug. It all felt comforting, until he saw his mother in the den staring at the television, a phone to her ear, her voice wavering:

"But somebody must know something!"

After a pause, she said, "Call me as soon as you know. I'm switching to my cell to keep our landline open." She looked up at Chris and beckoned him to her side.

"Oh, God," she said, reaching out, giving him a long tight hug. She stepped back, resting a hand on his shoulder, her eyes darting past him, as if willing her husband to walk through the door. "I've been calling him, but I can't get through.

"We don't know anything yet" ... still staring at the door. "His office is closing; everyone's being evacuated. They aren't sure were your father is. He's scheduled for a meeting at Cantor Fitzgerald." Her head turned toward the television, then snapped back to her son. "Christopher ... their office is in one of those towers."

Chris swallowed hard as he realized the implications. The room squeezed in. He looked at the expression on her face, clenched his fists and thought: *This is insane! Why would anybody do this? Who's doing this?*

He watched his mother sink into a chair, her eyes fixed on the television. She leapt when the phone rang. Chris thought it must be his dad. But it wasn't him, or his office. It was his aunt in Illinois calling his mother to see if she'd heard the news, calling to see if Tom was safe. His mother rushed the conversation to clear the line. It suddenly occurred to Chris that she'd get several such calls, and all he wanted was an

4

open line so his dad could get through. He checked to make sure his own cell was fully charged, then called his dad's number. No answer. He tried again.

They waited forty-five minutes, with no word. A reporter said people had been seen leaping from the upper floors. His mother stiffened her back and stood directly in front of the television, her fingers over her mouth, her eyes fixed. She reached back awkwardly, grabbing her son's hand without taking her eyes off the screen. Chris moved beside her, looping an arm around her shoulders, feeling helpless, not knowing how to comfort her, not taking his own eyes off the set.

Thick gray-white smoke streamed from the towers, billowing high overhead, while rescue crews rushed urgently about. Church bells tolled in the background. More news: The Pentagon had been hit. An airliner was missing over Pennsylvania and presumed down. All flights were grounded. The President was in Florida, reading to children at an elementary class. It felt surreal. Nobody seemed to be in charge; no one could explain a reason for the attack or even who the attackers were. He should be in high school preparing for gym; now he watched a nation under attack, perhaps preparing for war.

Just before ten o'clock his mother let out a shriek. The first tower collapsed, floor by floor, until its entire mass hit the street, spewing enormous clouds of heavy gray smoke. Concrete dust and debris flashed in concentric circles, encasing everything under a thick pulsing blanket, choking off air. Terrified people emerged from the smoke: gray ghosts, gasping for air, running for their lives. A woman fell onto the street. No one stopped to help.

Christopher's mother squeezed his arm tightly, turning to him, her mouth open, her eyes wide in horror. Flames and smoke streamed from the upper floors of the second tower. A reporter said, "There's incomprehensible mayhem in the streets; it looks like New York is in the midst of a nuclear winter."

When the second tower collapsed, his mother collapsed with it.

Noon came without a word. Christopher's brothers had each called. Ted, a doctor in Madison, Wisconsin, called from his office. He offered to drive straight home, since flights had been grounded. "Not yet," Christopher said. "I'm sure we'll hear something soon." Brandon, at the London School of Economics, with plans to follow his father into finance, called, expecting to hear his dad was fine, and was shocked to learn that might not be the case. Again, Chris said, "Let's just wait. I'll call as soon as I know something." Each brother spoke briefly with their mother, but she was too fragile to carry on much of a conversation.

Chris couldn't bear waiting. He grabbed a photo of his father from the grand piano, sliding the picture out of its frame, intending to run copies on the home printer. His hands shook; an image of his father lying trapped under concrete flashed in his head.

"Christopher, what are you doing?"

"I've got to find Dad. If he can't reach us, I'll find someone who's seen him."

He thought his father must be helping people, too busy to call. Besides, most phones were still down. Of course he'd be helping others. If nothing else, Tom McCarty had a strong sense of Catholic guilt that fueled a willingness to help others. He believed in the rewards of heaven.

She stood up, wringing her hands. "No. Stay! Please wait. He'll call."

"I can't just sit here, Mom. I've got to do something!"

He turned toward the door, but she blocked his way, putting both hands on his arms and locking his eyes with hers.

"Please, I need you here. I can't wait by myself." His mother sagged, and Chris had to keep her from falling. She steadied one hand on the piano as he helped her to the sofa. Scooter placed his head on her lap, his brown eyes looking up at her, concerned, his tail slowly thumping the floor, offering encouragement. She absently stroked his fur.

"It's okay, Mom. I'll stay. I'm sure you're right. Dad will be fine. He'll call as soon as the lines are open."

Something fundamental had changed. It hadn't occurred to him that his mother might need him. It had always been the other way around. Of course, he would wait with her for the call.

At six o'clock Chris knelt beside his bed, praying earnestly through tears, prayers interspersed with sharp bouts of anger, his fists pounding the bed, while light drained from the room. His mind swirled with images of his father trapped under twisted steel or, worse, scattering as ash, drifting over the city.

The call never came. His brothers returned home to Connecticut. His aunt flew in from Chicago and stayed nearly two weeks. His mother was too fragile to cope with even the smallest daily task. The memorial service was held at St. John's Parish. Tom had been an usher there every Sunday, and Chris had been an altar boy in middle school. Their church overflowed with mourners.

Monsignor gave a warm eulogy, speaking from the heart, of Tom's devotion to family and to the Lord. Chris was taken aback when the priest actually used the words, "Ashes to ashes and dust to dust." He didn't appreciate the phrase in this case. He thought of the enormous clouds of ash and dust spewing from the towers and thought, *"Part of that was my dad."* But then the priest said, "Take heart. We will all see Tom again. He is gone but a little while. As Jesus said in the Book of John, 'There are many rooms in my Father's house; I go there to prepare one for you.' We will see Tom again, waiting for us, fully restored, in the complete joy of heaven."

Of all the souls who lost their lives that day, 156 were from Connecticut. There were two services in Tom's memory and a host of group services in both Connecticut and Manhattan for all the victims. Christopher wished they would stop. He wished his family didn't have to be reminded of their loss every day. Not that he could ever forget, but they all needed space to recover.

He felt hopelessly lost. The sound of his father's voice came to him at odd hours, every day, like a tape recording playing endlessly in his head:

"Christopher, there's a reason people get discouraged with the world. They expect great things from it, and when it doesn't happen they give up. Don't assume the world will do great things for you. Expect great things from yourself, and make your world great."

His father's death created a deep void he began filling with anger and determination. Within days, one clear, overpowering resolve formed in Christopher's heart. He would not let this stand. He would devote his life to protecting his country. He became fully committed to getting into a military academy. West Point was closer to home, but he preferred the Naval Academy at Annapolis.

He began a new physical regimen. Already in decent shape from soccer, he dedicated himself to peak performance, waking at 4:30 each morning Monday through Saturday. At first he ran four miles, increased it to five and finally six miles a day. After school, he used the gym to bulk up, lifting weights, doing sit-ups, leg lifts, and push-ups. Each week he increased the number of reps, feeling his strength and endurance grow. If he made the Academy, he wanted to be prepared for all its physical demands.

Leaving the house early on dark, crisp mornings while the stars still sparkled made him feel alive. Scooter ran at his side, pulling the leash sideways whenever rabbits or squirrels darted from bushes. Toward the end of his run, lights would appear in some of the homes. Husbands and wives shuffling into the kitchen to start coffee, parents waking sleepy children. He felt the presence of his father, and a fierce determination to make him proud.

Principal Hanley, and half the faculty at Darien High, wrote glowing letters to their congressman and two senators. Nothing pleased an elected official more than nominating the son of a 9/11 victim to a military academy. Competition arose to nominate Christopher. Senator Blumenthal's staff was more efficient, and Christopher's nomination formally came from his office.

The senator made a special trip to Darien, appearing with Chris to announce the Naval Academy had officially accepted his nomination. Soon, Christopher McCarty would be a midshipman on his way to becoming either an ensign in the Navy or a second lieutenant in the Marines. Everyone felt so proud. No one could have predicted the path his life would take.

3 CHRISTMAS GIRL

Christopher applied himself, fit in well with the midshipmen, built a solid first three years at the Academy, and was eager to get his commission.

He needed a gift for his mother's birthday. She collected antique porcelain teacups and saucers, so he stopped at a little vintage store just blocks from the Academy. He picked up a dainty cup, turning it over to read the manufacturer's mark, and heard Sarah Brightman sing "Time to Say Goodbye" for the first time over the shop's sound system. The beauty of the voice captivated him. He couldn't catch all the words, but their emotion touched him. He stopped, dead still, devoting his attention to the song.

Several seconds passed before he focused on anything else. When he did, he realized a young woman was staring at him. She looked about his age, with bright green eyes and soft red hair. He thought, "She looks like Christmas." Seeing her face and hearing that music left him momentarily breathless. He blushed, embarrassed to be caught so lost in thought.

Chris wanted to know about the music but, more than anything, he wanted to keep her from leaving. He grinned sheepishly and approached her.

It turned out she knew all about the song, the singer, and the title. "Right," he thought, "she's beautiful *and* smart." He wanted to keep the conversation going, and asked if she'd help him find the CD at a store down the block. To his relief, she agreed.

They walked out onto the street down toward the marina.

"Thanks for doing this. I'm Chris."

"Maureen."

"I'm at the Academy." He immediately regretted stating the obvious.

"I figured." She swept her arm, palm up, indicating his uniform.

"Yeah, I guess so. What about you?"

"I'm at Johns Hopkins. "

"Good school. What're you studying?"

"Education."

"So, you'll be a teacher?"

"No, I'm studying concepts of learning: ways to make it more effective, more appropriate to the twenty-first century."

"You like Hopkins?"

"I do. But I wish it were here instead of Baltimore."

"Me too," he said a bit too emphatically. He put his arm gently on the small of her back and guided her into the music store. "I hope they have it."

"I'm sure they do. I'm just not sure what section it's in."

He stood behind her as she thumbed through CDs, captivated by her, by the color of her hair, by her scent, by the way she stood and moved. She reached up, brushing hair away from her face, revealing a long shimmering green earring. "She *is* Christmas," he thought again.

"Ah, here it is." She handed it to him, and he made a point to touch her hand.

Chris admired the picture of Sara Brightman on the cover.

"She's gorgeous. I can't believe I've never heard of her."

"What kind of music do you usually like?"

It turned out they had similar tastes. Chris started thumbing through the CDs stacked under the "T" tab. "Oh, nice! They have Traffic: *John Barleycorn Must Die.*' Do you know this?"

"I don't think so."

"It's great. You have to hear it. I think it came out in the late 60s. My music teacher turned me on to it. It's amazing."

He took it to the counter, paid the clerk, and handed her the CD. "I am glad I found this. I want you to have it."

"You don't have to do that."

"No, I want to. You should experience this. It's transformational."

"Thanks. I've always wanted to be transformed. I promise, I'll listen to it tonight."

She touched his arm, moving a finger across the insignia on his sleeve, and smiled "You know, they say: '*military life is to real life as military music is to real music.*'"

"Oh, a critic. You don't like the military?"

She blushed and pulled her arm back. "I'm sorry. I don't know why I said that. It's just something I heard."

"Great, I suppose next you'll say: '*a woman without a man is like a fish without a bicycle.*'"

"God, no! I'm not either of those. I honestly don't know why I said that. No one in my family has ever been in the service. Please, forget I said it."

"I think I can give you a pass. Fact is: no one in my family's been in the military either, at least not for a long time."

They talked about high school experiences. Each had disappointing prom dates; both had stories of really odd teachers. They laughed and speculated on the type of home-life those teachers must have had. Conversation stayed easy and light. He didn't want to tell her about his father. Tragedy isn't a good way to start a relationship. She might think he's damaged, or she might pity him. He wanted her to get to know him first. He wanted to get to know her.

They spent the afternoon walking the cobblestone streets, admiring boats bobbing at the docks, and talking about everything and nothing in particular. They returned to the antique store so she could help select the perfect teacup for his mother. She started laughing.

"What?"

"I'm sorry. I'm just not used to helping men choose teacups. It's actually very sweet. Just not what I was expecting."

"Too manly for you?" He gave her a faint fist bump on the shoulder.

"Yeah, that's it."

12

On the way out, he asked about her program at Hopkins. She reeled off statistics on the learning gap and how American students aren't developing skills for the new economy, but quickly changed the subject. She enjoyed his company and wanted to keep things light. "What do you want to do? I mean I know the Navy, but specifically?"

"Naval Intelligence. Counter-Intelligence. I want to know what's going on. I want to help stop disasters before they happen."

"Like 9/11?"

"Exactly like 9/11. But that's a ways away from now. I've got to finish the Academy first and then ..."

He stopped and checked his watch. "Damn! It's late. I've got to get back to the Yard." Chris looked at her with an expression that said, "*I would give anything to stay if I could.*"

Maureen smiled. "Duty calls. I understand."

"Can I call you?"

"You can."

A wide smile broke out over his face, and his eyes brightened.

"I will. I promise."

He turned to go, walking quickly before suddenly stopping and turning around.

"I don't have your number!"

She hadn't moved and stood with hands on her hips, looking at him with a smile that turned into a laugh.

"I know. Hand me your bag."

He held it out to her. She retrieved a pen and wrote her number on the side.

"Don't lose this."

"I won't. I wish I didn't have to go."

"Go. Go."

Chris gave quick salute, turned and started running to the Academy. He felt like kicking himself. Why'd he salute? That was lame. Why didn't he kiss her, at least on the cheek? He tightened his grip on the bag with her number.

Maureen watched him disappear, then raised the CD he'd given her, pressed it to her chest, and sighed. This was so unexpected, so nice. She walked back to her car nearly bouncing, thinking maybe he *will* call.

She had just left Mass Sunday morning when he did.

"I enjoyed yesterday," he said.

"Me, too. I'm glad you called."

"Well, I've been thinking: Navy's playing Notre Dame on Saturday. I'm wondering if you might like to come."

"That sounds fun." Her green eyes smiled. "I'd love to."

4 FOOTBALL GAME

Chris thought about her all week, wondering, hoping, really, how things might go. Maureen spent time deciding what to wear and checking the Internet to learn about Navy football. She liked football and regularly rooted for the Redskins, but didn't know anything about Navy's team.

They planned to meet at the Academy early on game day so he could introduce her to a couple of friends. She pulled up in her Toyota Camry, and Chris greeted her right where he promised to be. She wore a green sweater under a camel hair blazer with a Burberry scarf, tight jeans, and flat shoes. Her red hair, soft and shiny, fell just below her shoulders. He thought she looked beautiful and, again, thought she was a present he'd love to unwrap.

She met more of his friends in the stadium. They clearly liked Chris and enjoyed teasing him. They also clearly weren't used to seeing him in the company of a woman.

The game stayed close. In the fourth quarter Navy scored on a long pass from their own forty-yard line. The ball flew in a tight spiral to the wide receiver, who had faked outside and then cut sharply over the middle. He caught the ball in stride, twisted out of the grasp of a defender, and sprinted along the far sideline with two tacklers in close pursuit. One of them reached him at the two-yard line and lunged, but only managed to push him across the goal line.

The crowd erupted. Chris and Maureen jumped in place with both arms raised. He turned, and they hugged. He kissed her on the cheek. During the point-after he held her hand, and they leapt and kissed again as the ball split the uprights. Navy went ahead. They held the lead for their first victory of the season.

Afterward, he put his arm around her shoulder, weaving in and out of the crowd, heading to her car. He opened the door for her and went around to the passenger's side.

"What'd you think?" he asked.

"It was great fun! I loved it. Thanks for inviting me."

He looked into her eyes, reaching up with two fingers to brush hair away from her face, then held her cheek gently as he leaned in and kissed her lips. She put her arms around his neck, returning the kiss.

Chris pulled back to focus on her and softly said, "Hi."

"Hi."

"I've thought of this all week."

"I guess I have, too."

He kissed her again, cherishing the moment until someone pounded on the car window.

"Hey, you two, we're headed to O'Brien's for dinner. You should come. Unless, of course, you're getting a room somewhere."

They both blushed, turning to Nate, Chris's best friend at the Academy. Chris looked at her, indicating it would be her call.

"Why not?" she said.

The restaurant bustled, loud with excitement. Navy had been expected to lose. The victory had everyone stoked.

"We're a lot quicker than they expected," Nate said.

"And our defense is a stronger than last year," said Bill Ferguson, a tall midshipman with seductive dark eyes. Bill had a reputation as a ladies' man and had worked hard to earn it. He eyed Maureen with undisguised lust.

"What are you doing with this loser?" he asked, pointing at Chris.

"Leave her alone," Nate said. He turned to Maureen. "The only loser here is this idiot." He swiped good-naturedly at Bill with his napkin.

Bill backed it off a notch while still staring at Maureen.

"I'll tell you what. When you're ready for the best, give me a call." He smiled. "In the meantime, old Chris here isn't half bad."

"Thanks, Bill. I'm honored to have your approval."

"My pleasure, bro."

Their waitress, Susanna, had dealt with this crew before.

"Let me guess, Black and Blue burgers, medium-rare? "

They all nodded agreement. Susanna looked at Maureen.

"Guess I'll make it unanimous," she said. The conversation turned from football to life at the Academy. Chris and his friends were all in their First Year, the equivalent of senior year, looking forward to graduation and their commissions. They talked about their future and where they hoped to be assigned. By February they'd know their fate. Nate hoped for duty on a destroyer. Bill remained determined to get into Flight School. Chris said nothing had changed for him. He still wanted Naval Intelligence.

"Pencil-pushing desk work!" Bill said. "Sounds like dangerous work, sitting in your cubicle every day. You sure you're up to it? I'll think about you when I'm cruising Mach 2 over the Mediterranean."

"First of all, you have to get *into* Flight School, which is a big stretch, and, secondly, if you're ever flying over the Mediterranean it'll be because Naval Intelligence directs you there."

"Talk about big stretches: think how fat your ass will get sitting at your little desk reading memos all day."

"I might just come up with a whole new class of drones with idiots like you in them to push the 'Destruct' button if the computer fails."

"Real funny."

"All right guys," Nate said, "the Navy needs intelligence, and it needs pilots. I think it can accommodate both of you."

Chris had met Nate his first week at the Academy. Nate's grandfather had been a captain in the Navy, and his father had graduated Annapolis, now serving as an Admiral with the Pacific Fleet.

Nate might have adopted an air of entitlement at the Academy. But he didn't. He stayed steady and humble, worked hard, and took assignments seriously. If any one word described Nate, it would be *earnest*.

He helped guide Chris through some of the early traditions of the Academy and gave him pointers on what to expect. Nate learned early on what had happened to Chris's dad. He also knew that fourteen alumni from the Academy had lost their lives in the attack. Nate felt protective at first, though soon realized Chris was perfectly capable of taking care of himself.

The burgers were polished off and conversation had returned to football when Maureen reached out, squeezing Chris' arm for attention.

"I'm really sorry, but I have to be getting home. I'm staying with my parents tonight in Bethesda. I promised to go to Mass with them in the morning and then help Mom update her real estate brochure."

"Oh. I didn't realize." He pulled out his wallet and put twenty-five dollars on the table.

"Sorry guys. We gotta go. This should cover us. Let me know if it doesn't."

"You two behave yourselves," Bill said, still clearly interested in Maureen.

Chris pulled her chair back and guided her to the door. She reached down and took his hand in hers.

"Bill's quite a character," she said.

"I'd tell you he's harmless, but he's not."

"Well, the rest of your friends are nice. I like Nate. I can tell he respects you."

"He's a good friend. He also has access to a sailboat. His father's family has a home just up the Severn River. I think

18

we could talk him into taking us out next Saturday, if it's not too cold."

"Sounds nice. I'd love that."

"I'll check and let you know."

When they reached the car, he pulled her close. Chris kissed her lips, softly at first, and then more intensely. Her lips parted, and his tongue found hers. She leaned back, resting on the door of the car. He cradled her face in his hands, pulled his head back to look at her and gently kissed her lips, her neck, and ear before returning to her lips. Their tongues met again. His left hand slid down in a tentative caress of her breast but she quickly brushed it away. Chris pulled his head back again to look at her.

"A bit too soon, sailor." She smiled discretely.

"Sorry." He hesitated until she put her arms around his neck and drew him close.

He kissed her again, his hands around the small of her back. She pulled him into a tight hug and said, "I really should go."

"Do you have to?"

"I do." She gave him a coy smile, and they kissed twice.

"Sailing would be fun." She kissed his ear.

"I'll talk with Nate tonight."

"Let me know. I'll be with my parents all day tomorrow. My cell doesn't always get reception there. I'll give you their home number."

Maureen started the engine, then rolled down the window. "Go, Navy!" She smiled. He kissed her and stood watching her drive away until her car was out of sight.

5 SAILING

Chris persuaded Nate to take them out on Sweet Liberty, a blue and white 53-foot sailboat. Nate and his girlfriend, Janet, were already on board talking with a woman who looked to be in her mid-sixties.

"Permission to come aboard?" Chris said

"Permission granted. Welcome aboard." Nate held his hand out and helped Maureen onto the deck. Chris hopped on.

"Chris, Maureen, this is my aunt Barbara. She and my uncle own the boat along with my parents. They're very kind to let me use it."

"Pleased to meet you," Chris said. "We really appreciate you letting us take her out."

"Well, Nate's one of the best sailors you could have. He should be teaching it at the Academy. Nate, I know your father wishes he could be here to sail her with you."

"Yeah. It's more likely I'll join him on one of his ships in the Pacific before he gets a chance to sail with us here."

"The Admiral's very proud of you. He's looking forward to your commissioning at graduation. We all are."

"Thanks, Aunt Barbara."

"I should let you folks get underway. Nice meeting you all."

Fall leaves were already changing colors, green giving way to gold, orange, and scarlet. But the air remained warm. Temperatures would climb into the seventies with enough wind for a good sail, particularly out on the bay. Two seagulls glided above them as they cast off.

Chris and Maureen moved to the front of the boat to catch sun and talk. She wore jean shorts and a white blouse over a yellow two-piece bathing suit. Chris wore a Navy swimsuit and a gray Navy T-shirt. As the temperature rose he took off his T-shirt; Maureen slipped out of her shorts and blouse. She began applying sunscreen to her arms and neck, then handed the tube to Chris, turning her back to him. He squeezed the lotion onto the palms of his hands and gently rubbed it into her shoulders and back. The scent of the lotion and the touch of her skin excited deeper feelings than even he'd expected. She thanked him and settled back on her towel to catch some rays.

He turned sideways, propping his elbow on the deck and resting his chin on it, ostensibly to talk, but really to get a clearer view of her. She looked better than he'd imagined, a firm athletic body, smooth skin, covered with freckles. He liked them. Another feature that made her special. The sun brought out the highlights in her hair, her eyes sparkled. He was enthralled.

"Tell me something I don't know about you," he said.

She paused for a moment bringing a hand up to her forehead shielding the sun. "I've never been on a sailboat before."

"I know that. Tell me something meaningful."

"I'll tell you mine if you tell me yours."

"Agreed."

Chris paused for several seconds, then took a deep breath.

"You don't know about my father. He died on 9/11. He had a meeting at the World Trade Center when the terrorists hit, and never made it out. We didn't have a chance to say goodbye. One day he was here and the next he was gone. I miss him all the time."

"Oh my God! I had no idea." She placed a hand on his arm, turning to him and scrunching closer.

"Dad was a decent man, with a great sense of humor. He took good care of us. For my twelfth birthday, he took me on a trip, just the two of us. My brothers were already grown and out of the house. One day, out of the blue, he said, 'Chris, you and I are going on a vacation together.'" And we did.

"He had a business trip in Boston on a Friday. We drove up the day before and stayed at the Copley Square Hotel. I still remember it. Dad ordered us breakfast from room service, went to his morning appointment, and then came to take me on a tour of Boston. We went on a walking tour, following the Freedom Trail. The tour started at Boston Commons, went through the cemetery where Samuel Adams and John Hancock are buried, all the way out to Paul Revere's house and the Old North Church. He loved history. We had a guide, but Dad always had a few extra tidbits to tell me. It was great fun.

"The next day we drove the length of the Cape, out to the tip at Provincetown. We ate lobster for lunch. I'm not sure I'd ever had it before. Dad showed me how to crack the shells and get every bit out of them. We went to Chatham, spent the night there, and then the whole next day at the beach.

"He told me things about our family I never knew. My oldest brother got caught shoplifting when he was eleven. He paid a fine and it was taken off his record, but it still shocked me. Dad told me how he and my mother met at Georgetown. I felt grown up when he talked with me about those things.

"After 9/11, I couldn't bear the loss. I couldn't believe people were so filled with hate they'd kill innocent men, women, and children they don't know, that they'd kill a kind, generous man like my father. I didn't understand why we weren't able to stop them. There were clues, even memos warning about Bin Laden. Nothing prevented it. That's when I resolved to go into Intelligence.

"Most of my friends at the Yard don't understand. Only about one percent of midshipmen go into Intelligence. It's a Restricted Line career. I'll never fly jets off the deck of a carrier, never captain a destroyer or any ship. I won't lead men into combat, or command a submarine. Most Midis think it's a dead end. I think it's the best place to be to save lives, to head things off so jets don't have to take off with full payloads, so marines don't have to storm a beach, so Americans won't have to face another 9/11."

"What happened to your father, to all those people, is horrible. I can see why you chose Intelligence. You'll be good at it." She brought his arm closer, turned his hand up, and kissed his palm.

"I hope so."

They lay side-by-side, silently holding hands, feeling the warmth of the sun and the breezes that blew over them. The sails fluttered and rippled over head while lines clinked, as the boat gently slid through the water. He wanted to challenge her to reveal something about herself when Nate piped up, "Hey, Chris, did you say you brought lunch?"

"Yes, sir. Maureen made it. It's good stuff." He didn't want to move. It felt so peaceful lying on the deck, holding her hand.

Two hours after lunch they set course for home. Nate brought the boat up to that dock with expert precision. They tied her off. Nate returned the keys to his aunt, and he and Janet headed to his truck, arm in arm.

Back in her car, Maureen said, "We could have dinner at my place if you like."

"I like. That would be nice. Should we stop and pick up some food?"

"Sure, I sort of depleted my roommate's stash for our lunch today. We could get a nice bottle of wine, too."

"Great. I'm in."

When they arrived, he followed her up the stairs, she holding a grocery bag and he carrying the near-empty cooler. He took it to the kitchen and emptied the ice water into the sink. It was a modest apartment but tastefully decorated, with the scent of fresh candles. Maureen said her roommate was away visiting her family in Charlottesville.

"We have the place to ourselves. Do you like it?"

"It's very nice. You've got good taste."

"What I have is a modest budget."

"Well, you do wonders with it. My favorite part ..." he turned completely around scanning every part of the room "... is you."

Chris put his hands on her hips. "I liked being with you today." He drew her close and kissed her. She turned her head slightly and kissed him back. His lips gently brushed her neck, her lips, her cheeks, and her neck again. She tilted her head as his hands moved to the small of her back and pulled her close. His fingers moved up her spine, squeezing her skin as he went. He began massaging her shoulders and neck, then stepped back and smiled.

"*You* again," he whispered.

"Me again."

He slowly unbuttoned her blouse. She didn't object. Her yellow bikini top was under the shirt. He caressed her breasts on the outside of the suit, kissing her gently then slipping his hand underneath to feel her flesh. Their tongues entwined. He lifted her top up away from her breasts, then reached around back and undid it. He paused to take an appreciative look. Her breasts were firm, her nipples hard, and her skin showed a flush of color. She took a deep breath, causing her breasts to heave slightly. He leaned down and kissed them gently first one, then the other. She cupped his head in her hands and kissed the top of it.

Maureen straightened up, taking his hand in hers, leading him to the bedroom.

At the side of her bed she stopped to pull his T-shirt over his head. Chris had always been in good shape. The Academy had sculpted him into a hard, contoured athlete. He had a well-defined six-pack, strong arms, broad shoulders, and a firm chest. She thought he looked like a model in one of those firefighter calendars.

He lifted her, setting her gently onto the bed. Bending down to kiss her, his left hand reached to the top of her shorts. He undid the button, and pulled down on her zipper. His hand moved down between her legs, under her shorts, under her bikini bottom. He felt her raise her hips a bit. She reached down to pull her shorts off. He helped. She lay on the bed with only the bottom of her swimsuit on. He caressed her beneath it, gently probing with his fingers. He slid her suit down, raised her knees and lifted the suit up over them and down her ankles then over her toes. Chris discovered she was a true redhead. He buried his face between her thighs.

They made love all evening, dinner completely forgotten. Maureen put on some music. Returning to bed she rested her head on him, her hair splayed across his chest. His fingers stroked the back of her neck.

An old Art Garfunkel song, "Disney Girls," played on the stereo. He listened as Art sang, *"All my life I spent my nights in dreams of you."* And melted into blissful sleep.

Maureen awoke before six. She turned to watch him sleeping and smiled, tempted to wake him, but he looked so peaceful she let him be. Instead she quietly slid out from under the covers. She wanted a good run to settle her thoughts and quietly changed into her shorts, putting on her running shoes, and his Navy T-shirt, then left a note just in case he woke while she was out.

As she ran, her thoughts bounced back and forth from being giddy to wondering how this could ever go anywhere. He would be leaving right after graduation, probably assigned to a far-away place. If he did get into Intelligence, he might even be assigned somewhere she couldn't know about. It might be that the relationship was already doomed. But it felt wonderful. Maybe he'd be stationed nearby in DC or Langley, or with the NSA right here in Maryland. She picked up her pace.

Chris was still sleeping soundly when she returned. She made coffee, toast, and scrambled eggs, then brought breakfast into the bedroom, set it on the nightstand, and gently nudged his shoulder.

Chris awoke to the aroma of breakfast and the sight of her smiling face. "Good morning."

"Hi, sleepy head. I don't know how you take your coffee. Cream, sugar?"

"Just black is fine. What time is it?"

"Almost eight-thirty."

"Oh, my God! I haven't slept that long in years. How long have you been up?"

"Hours. I've already been for a run. Enjoy your breakfast. I'll be in the shower."

Chris sat up, sipped his coffee and took a bite of toast. He heard the water running in the shower, listened for a minute, smiled, tossed the toast back onto the plate and headed for the bathroom.

He saw her silhouetted through the glazed shower glass, her head tilted back soaking up the streaming water. He opened the door.

Maureen's eyes opened wide. "Excuse me?"

"I thought you might need help."

Chris took the shampoo off its rack, poured some onto his hands, and rubbed it in a circular motion to build lather. He rubbed the shampoo into her hair. His fingers massaged her head, first the top, then the sides above her ears, and then the back of her head and neck. He lathered her shoulders and then her breasts before reaching down below her waist. "It helps to be thorough."

Maureen reached for the plastic bottle of body wash and squeezed its liquid into her hands. "I should return the favor." And she did. They didn't leave until the water turned cold.

They spent the rest of that autumn seeing each other every chance they could. Sightseeing in DC, farmers' markets with fresh apple cider, pumpkins, and hayrides, dinners in Baltimore's Little Italy, or strolls around its Inner Harbor.

6 A GOOD IMPRESSION

Meeting Maureen's parents made him more nervous than he'd expected. His preference had been to meet for dinner at a nice restaurant in Annapolis. He'd feel more confident on home turf where the meeting wouldn't last much longer than the time it took to eat.

Instead her parents suggested Chris come to Bethesda on a Sunday to attend Mass and have brunch at Congressional Country Club. Maureen's mother and her family had belonged to the club for generations. Her father used it to entertain diplomats and other State Department officials. Very few officers at State ever had access to the Club on their own.

Opened in 1924, Congressional Country Club had hosted three US Opens, a Seniors Open, and a PGA Championship. Chris did some research and discovered seven presidents, Taft, Wilson, Harding, Coolidge, Hoover, Eisenhower, and Ford, had been members. Other notable members had included Vince Lombardi, John D. Rockefeller, Andrew Carnegie, and even Charlie Chaplin. The initiation fee was well over $100,000 and the waiting list nearly ten years long. It intimidated him more than a little bit.

They arranged to meet her parents at their church on Massachusetts Avenue: Little Flower Parish. Maureen explained that the real "Little Flower" had been a French nun, St. Therese of Lisieux, who entered a convent at 16 and lived only to the age of 24. Her writings, *Histoire d'une Ame*, condensed the essentials of her spirituality and sought to explain the purity of God's love.

More recently, Little Flower had become famous for its music. The Music Director of the Kennedy Center became a member of the congregation and directed its musicians. Sunday services were lifted on angelic tones, vibrating pure spirituality. Maureen cherished the church and felt fond of its priests. She hadn't found a church of equal quality in Baltimore and didn't expect to.

As they pulled into the parking lot Maureen saw her parents standing out front, talking with Father Ryan. Maureen had known him for years. He appeared to be in his mid-forties with dark wavy hair and smiling blue eyes. She always assumed Father Ryan would perform her wedding when the time came. Her dad enjoyed talking golf with the priest.

Chris wore his in uniform. He made a point to get out quickly and open Maureen's door for her. The morning air felt crisp, with gusts of wind sending leaves tumbling across the parking lot. He tugged down on his jacket to straighten any wrinkles, held his arm out for her to take, and escorted her to the church.

Maureen's mother, more petite, but with the same green eyes as her daughter, and shoulder-length blond hair, had an energy that radiated even when standing still. She burst into a bright smile and held her arms out wide, embracing Maureen in a fierce hug. Her father, a tall, heavyset man with freckles, short red hair, and enormous beefy hands, gave Chris a thorough inspection before extending his large right hand.

"Good to meet you, Christopher. I'm Brad," he said. "Maureen tells us you are in your final year. "

"Yes, sir, I am."

"Well, we're glad to meet you. Christopher, this is Father Ryan."

Chris shook hands with the priest who said, "Maureen is a special girl, son. I expect you must be special too. Welcome to Little Flower."

"Thank you, Father. Maureen loves your church."

"I would hope so! We're always glad when she can visit."

"We ought to head in," Brad said. "We'll take Holy Communion and then a nice brunch and a few mimosas at the club. Are you a golfer, Chris?"

28

"I play the Academy Club when I can, but we don't get many chances. It's nice, but it's a far cry from Congressional."

"That it is, Chris. Maybe I'll take you out one day."

"I would be honored, sir."

Mass was officiated by a visiting priest from Indonesia instead of Father Ryan. Chris strained to understand what the cleric said. Fewer and fewer Americans enter the priesthood each year. Celibacy is a hard cross to bear. But the music matched everything Maureen said it would. Chris thought they should charge admission.

After church Maureen's parents climbed into a Cadillac Escalade. Maureen and Chris followed them to the club in her Toyota.

"Tell me again where your family's been stationed?" Chris asked.

"Well, Germany, when I was an infant, then England, and then back to the States. In fifth grade, we moved to Brussels, and then one year in Prague."

"What exactly did your dad do in all those places?"

She shrugged her shoulders. "The usual, represented the United States, made friends abroad, reported back on trends and key people."

"You sure he's not CIA?"

"Very sure. He's State Department through and through."

"Where'd he go to school?"

"Undergraduate at Georgetown, that's where he met Mom. Then, Princeton, the Woodrow Wilson School of Public and International Studies."

"And your mother's a realtor?"

"Even with all our travel, she's got quite a network here for her real estate business. She grew up in Bethesda. Her grandfather had been a congressman from Ohio. Her dad, my grandfather, worked at the White House for President Kennedy."

"Okay. I'm officially intimidated."

"They will love you. You're already making a good impression. I can tell."

29

She drove out River Road for several miles and turned left into the entrance of the club, following the long driveway until the clubhouse came into view. It was a spectacular white edifice with a red tiled roof giving it a formal Mediterranean look.

Brunch reservations were for the Grill overlooking the golf course. Chris recognized two senators and a former Secretary of the Treasury.

Her parents were surprisingly easy to talk with. Maureen's mother, Karen, filled them in on the latest DC celebrity-class real estate sales. She urged Chris to buy a house the first chance he got.

"Real estate's the best investment anyone can make. You buy a place of your own, live in it two to three years, and trade up. Just keep doing that, and before you know it you'll have over a million dollars in equity. It's like being paid to live someplace. Renting's a dead-end street."

Chris didn't see how prices could go up forever. He wondered how anyone could even afford homes at their current value. But he nodded and smiled.

Brad asked Chris about his goals and became energized when Chris said, "Intelligence."

"That's a career with work that never ends. I know; I've gathered lots of intelligence at State. We know what we're doing. We understand people in our posted countries and their customs. All too often we pass intelligence on to Defense and watch them do exactly the opposite of what we recommend. Look at Iraq. Enough said. I hope you recognize valuable information when you see it."

"I hope so too, sir."

Chris explained his frustration over 9/11. Brad said how sorry he was about what happened to his father.

Brad's thick hands clapped Chris on the shoulders. "You know, we should definitely get you out on this golf course. I'll set it up."

Maureen smiled, knowing her dad had been won over.

"Now we need to have Maureen's favorite dessert!" Brad announced. "I haven't forgotten, Hon," he said and winked at her.

Dessert arrived: a chocolate cup filled with fresh fruit, topped with ice cream, and surrounded with a raspberry puree. Maureen and Chris shared it. Each bite tasted like love.

Back in the car Chris said, "I like your folks. How'd I do?"

She kissed him on the cheek, and patted the top of his hand. "You were adorable. You did great."

7 A CHRISTMAS GIFT

Chris went home to Connecticut a week before Christmas. His mother met him at La Guardia, along with Brandon who had returned from London, having accepted an investment banking position at JP Morgan. He would start in January and already knew he'd work most days from seven in the morning to midnight, crunching numbers on foreign acquisitions mostly in different time zones.

"You probably slept more your first year at the Academy than I will at JP Morgan."

"I doubt they'll have you running ten miles with 50 pound backpacks or doing 200 sit-ups. They probably won't be in your face screaming at you during meals and every time in between. I think you'll survive."

"You're both doing so well," his mother said from the passenger seat. "I'm proud of both of you. And Ted too: a doctor, an investment banker, and a naval officer. I wish your father could be here to see how each of you is doing. Chris, I have a little surprise for you when we get home."

"Yes? What is it?"

"A surprise."

What it was became apparent when they pulled into their circular driveway. A brand-new silver BMW Z4 convertible sat parked outside the front door with a bright red ribbon reaching up from each side to an enormous red bow on the top.

"I hope you like it. Brandon and I had fun picking it out."

"Oh, my God! Is that for me?"

"Surprise!"

"I'm stunned. What's this for?"

32

"For being you. You wouldn't let me buy you a car when you graduated high school, since you weren't allowed one at Annapolis. Now you're close enough to graduating that you deserve something special. You've worked hard. I want you to enjoy it.

"Besides, you saved me a fortune going to the academy. I think I'm getting off easy. You barely accepted any allowance at school."

"Yeah, well the Navy's paying me almost $1,000 a month plus tuition, room, board, and clothing. It wouldn't be right to take an allowance from you. In fact, I've been able to save most of my pay."

"Good. You can spend it on gas, and on that girl you keep talking about. How are things going between you two?"

"Things are good, very good in fact. You might even say I'm in love."

"I might say, or you might say?"

"Okay. I'll say it. I'm in love."

"Whoa, little bro, I haven't heard about this. Who is she?"

"Her name is Maureen. I met her in Annapolis. She's coming up for New Year's Eve. You'll get to meet her."

"I should hope so. Do you have a picture?"

"I'm not sure there's one that would do her justice. You'll have to wait and see her for yourself."

Chris left his suitcase in the front hall and accepted the keys from his mother. Scooter trotted in wagging his tail. He sat smiley-faced, raising his paw for Chris to shake, and got a long hug instead. His snout was turning white, and his eyes were beginning to glaze. Chris was struck with the realization that his dog was growing old.

Sitting in the driver's seat with his hands on the wheel, feeling the leather seats, and taking in the new car smell made him feel confident, secure. It felt good to be back home, but a bit strange. He rode by the high school, and then through the center of town. Despite the cold, he was tempted to lower the top. Just vanity, he knew, but it would be nice for some old friends to see him in his new wheels.

The town looked the same, but it didn't feel like his anymore. He'd already begun outgrowing it. He could never imagine what Darien would think of him in a couple of years.

Darien wasn't about the military; it's about money. Elegant estates, sheltered by broad trees and tall iron gates, were among the most impressive in America. Much of the wealth was earned on Wall Street. Generations of old money mingled with the new fabulously rich. Chris already missed Annapolis and Maureen. He thought about the money he'd saved and decided how he would spend a good portion of it

8 SANTA'S TOY SHOPPE

Maureen arrived the day after Christmas, taking Amtrak from Washington to Penn Station. There's no good time to be at Penn Station, but holidays are the worst, when it's jammed with frenzied people carrying too much luggage and too many packages. The station was a confusing mix of fast food places, junky little shops, lost souls searching for exits, experienced travelers pushing past the slower ones, and the homeless who seemed to never move. A black man stood inside the 34th Street entrance playing Christmas carols on a saxophone. The open case at his feet held six crinkled dollars and a few coins.

Chris worried he'd miss her in the crowd. When he finally saw Maureen, she was dragging a wobbly suitcase. One of the wheels had broken, so it tipped erratically from side to side as she struggled to maintain control. Her frustration turned to relief when she saw Chris. She let go of the handle; her suitcase toppled over. She stretched her arms wide and declared, "I hate this place! Some idiot knocked my suitcase right out the door when the train stopped. It smashed on to the platform; he stepped on it, then bounded off as if in a steeplechase. He never said, 'sorry,' never looked back. Now I can't get it to go straight."

"Welcome to New York, Mo" She punched him on the shoulder.

He picked up her suitcase and carried it three blocks through a freezing drizzle to his car. It barely fit in the trunk.

35

"Like the car?" he asked.

"Spoiled brat's car!" She lightly pinched his cheek. "I guess your mother loves you after all."

"Of course."

Chris held her door open and gave her a long kiss. She'd been so frustrated at the station they hadn't really connected until now. It felt good. Maureen felt whole again.

All the way up to New York she'd worried about making a good impression on Christopher's mother. From everything he'd told her she was a kind-hearted woman who must feel terribly alone with her husband gone and her sons all on their own.

Chris had told her his mother sets up a model Christmas village every year with houses and shops, a church, and a miniature skating rink, complete with skating figurines. Maureen found a model of Santa's Toyshop in Annapolis, complete with toys in its windows under a snow-covered roof, the same brand his mother collected. She emailed a picture to Chris who emailed back, "Perfect!" Now Maureen wondered if it had shattered in her suitcase.

Chris's mother, Anne, greeted them at the door with a warm smile. She showed Maureen to her room at the far end of the hall from Chris's bedroom.

Maureen unpacked, relieved to see her gift still intact. When she came downstairs and presented it, Anne's eyes lit up.

"This is so nice of you," she said. "Chris must have told you about my tradition. Every year I add a new house or building. It's probably silly, but I love putting up the Christmas village."

Maureen walked with her into the family room where the little town was displayed, and her heart sank when she realized Anne already had the exact same toyshop in her village. Her face flushed as she gave Chris a look that said, "She already *has* this!" He shrugged an "I didn't know" expression.

"Oh, you already have this one. I'm sorry. I'll exchange it for another."

"Nonsense! It's wonderful. You can never have too many toyshops. I'll always cherish it because it came from you. In fact, there's a gap over here it will fill perfectly. From now it'll be 'Maureen's Toy Shop.' Really, I love it. Thank you."

"I can exchange it if you like."

"I won't hear of it. No town is ever complete with only one toyshop. It's perfect. Truly, thank you, Maureen."

9 NEW YEAR'S EVE

Chris and Maureen spent New Year's Eve in Manhattan. They wanted to celebrate the New Year in the city while avoiding the crowd at Times Square.

Brandon recommended a popular club in the Village. It was packed with loud, happy revelers in funny, shiny hats and eyeglasses fashioned into the date of the New Year. Chris and Maureen squeezed through the crowd to the bar and waited a long time for the bartender to acknowledge them.

"What'll you have?" he finally shouted over the noise, his sleeves rolled up and his stomach protruding over his belt, straining the buttons on his bright red vest.

"A draft, Samuel Adams, and ..." He looked at Maureen.

"An apple martini."

He paused, his eyebrows raised in surprise. "... And an apple martini."

"Coming up."

The bartender returned with the drinks in surprising speed. He shouted to Chris.

"You military?"

"Annapolis. I graduate, get my commission, in May."

"No shit? You're a better man than I am. Don't go anywhere."

He prepared three drinks in shot glasses.

"Shooters! To thank you for your service."

They held their shot glasses high, including the bartender who yelled, "Go, Navy!"

"Go, Navy!" Chris and Maureen shouted, and downed the shots.

They watched couples in the crowd, speculating on what they did in real life, and how long they'd been together.

"That woman's a veterinarian," Chris nodded toward a woman with a pixie hairstyle.

"Oh, and why is that?"

"Look at the guy she's with. He has the face of a horse."

She laughed, "Yeah, maybe. See the guy in his forties with the woman in red heels?"

Red-shoes sat across from forty-something, her elbow raised with her chin resting on the top of her hand, looking intently into his eyes. He leaned forward, almost whispering in her ear. She laughed, tilting her head back, and then reached across, placing her index finger at the bridge of his nose, tracing it down to his lips. Smiling as he kissed her finger tip.

"What about him?"

"He's paying for her time."

"In that case, he's paying for a lot more than time."

Maureen held up her martini glass and clinked it against Christopher's beer.

A few drinks later Chris said, "We should dance."

Music pounded as lights pulsed over the crowd. They squeezed onto a corner of the floor and moved with the rhythm, dancing until Christopher's shirt was soaked with sweat. The drinks were having an effect. Chris felt happy, loose, like a civilian, enjoying a fuzzy, liquored-sensation of love.

When the music stopped Chris twirled Maureen close to him.

"I love you more than jelly beans!"

She burst out laughing. "Well, I love you more than Brussels sprouts."

"Love you more than Gummy Bears. LYMT Gummies!"

"Okay then, LYMT doughnuts."

She shook her head and laughed. People started chanting.

"Ten, nine, eight, seven …"

Midnight. They kissed and held each other, swaying gently.

"I can't imagine a better start to the New Year." Chris grinned.

A waitress passed by, carrying a large tray of peppermint shooters. They helped themselves, and Chris took a stagger step backwards.

"Hey, sailor, I think it's time we get you home," she said.

"Aren't you having fun?"

"The time of my life, but you need to get home."

She took his hand and steered him to the bar, where he paid their bill before being guided to the door.

"Are you all right to drive?"

"I'm fine. Navy strong!"

"Yeah, right!"

She helped him out onto the street and down the hill to the parking garage. The cold air felt like a slap in the face, and sobered him a bit. But, if the car hadn't been a stick shift, she'd have insisted on driving.

Chris wasn't familiar with Manhattan. He took several wrong turns before finally finding the right course. Their drive should have taken about an hour but instead took nearly two. Maureen kept nudging his shoulder and knee asking, "Seriously. Are you okay to drive? Are you staying awake?"

They arrived home at 2:46 AM. Maureen helped him up the backstairs to his bedroom. He grinned and pulled her in through his doorway.

"You know what would make this a *really* happy New Year?"

She gave him a gentle stiff arm and held a finger in front of her mouth to shush him.

"We'll wake your mother! I can't stay."

"Sure you can." He rocked sideways a few steps.

"Seriously, you know I love you. But not tonight. Besides, if I fall asleep here I'll never wake up by morning."

"Perfect."

"Yeah, perfect if you want me in trouble with your mom. Seriously, I have to go to my own room." And she did.

He pouted as she tiptoed out of his room and down the hall. "LYMT life," he whispered. Scooter padded in, walked a tight circle next to Christopher's bed, then lay down with his head on his paws, closing his eyes.

They each slept until nearly ten o'clock. Anne stood waiting for them in the kitchen. She'd been preparing a pancake breakfast with fresh fruit, eggs, and ham. Brandon had been sitting on a stool at the center island and got up to pour them coffee.

"Rough night?"

"Long night. Fun night. But I discovered I don't know my way around as well as I thought."

"You mean on the dance floor?"

"I mean Manhattan, getting to the Hutchinson River Parkway."

Anne stirred the pancake batter and asked Maureen how she liked her eggs. Maureen said any way would be fine and asked if she could help. While they prepared breakfast, Chris and Brandon had time to catch up.

"Chris, remember last summer, you said someone would interview us about you and your application for Intelligence? Well, no one has. Not Mom or me. Anyway, I thought you should know."

Chris felt a smile beginning to grow and quickly covered it with his coffee mug.

10 MARIA'S RESTORANTE

Back in Annapolis, Chris made reservations for two at Maria's Ristorante & Café on Market Street. He specifically asked for a table upstairs by the front window overlooking the marina with its Christmas lights still up. Once the reservation was made, he called her.

"We should have dinner Friday night. I know a great restaurant you haven't tried yet, and I know you love Italian."

"Sounds good. My class is over at four. I can meet you around six."

"Actually, I made a reservation for seven. We can have a drink first."

"A reservation? Sounds special."

"It gets really busy on Fridays. I thought I should make sure."

"I'll look forward to it. I haven't seen you enough lately."

"Yeah, me, either — you I mean."

Maureen met him a little after six. Parking was always a challenge in Annapolis. She found a spot four cold blocks from the restaurant.

Winter had fully descended on the city. Gray clouds had hung over Annapolis since early afternoon. Crisp wind played with Christmas decorations, causing the lights to flutter and sway. She cupped her hands and blew on them for warmth while her white breath danced and skated away on the wind.

Chris stood outside, and she was struck again by how good he looked in his uniform. She wondered if her roommate would be home later and whether she and Chris might have the place to themselves. It had been a long week. She looked forward to having some fun.

"Hi," she said laughing at herself. "I wore the wrong shoes! My feet are freeeezing!"

"Quick, inside. I'll warm you up." He wrapped his coat around her, and they went through the door with her tucked inside his arms.

The bar area was nearly full except for two stools close to the door. Those would have been their last choice, but they didn't have a choice and had to endure frequent drafts.

"I think we need Irish coffees," Chris suggested.

"Sounds perfect!"

The coffees arrived with generous dollops of whipped cream topped with drizzles of green Crème de Menthe. She wrapped both hands around the glass for warmth and took a sip.

"Just what I needed," she said. "It's been a long week."

Before their drinks were finished the hostess announced their table was ready. They followed her upstairs, and Chris made sure Maureen sat looking out toward the harbor. Snowflakes were drifting down over the boats. Several craft still had Christmas lights running up their masts and, although Christmas was over, it all painted a sparkling holiday scene. Chris reached down to touch the small box in his pocket, comforted to feel it there.

"This place is nice," she said picking up her menu. "Have you been here before?"

"Just once, with my mom during Parents' Weekend last year. Everything's good. I forget what I had, but I know it tasted great."

"This looks good." She pointed at her menu: "*rockfish sautéed in lemon, butter, white wine, and capers garnished with asparagus & pasta.*"

"That does sound good."

And it was. They shared a bottle of Italian wine, and Chris enjoyed chicken piccata. Throughout the meal, Maureen talked about how hard her week had been. She'd written two term papers, taken a psychology exam, and worked two nights at her tutoring job. She hadn't slept much and hoped to catch up over the weekend.

Chris barely listened. He kept thinking what he wanted to say and waited for dessert before he began.

"You know, if all goes well I'll have my assignment soon, maybe by the second week in February. I still think I'll get Intelligence. In fact, I'm pretty confident about it."

"I know," she said. "I worry about where they'll send you. Whether we'll be able to see each other."

"Me, too. There's no telling, I might end up anywhere. I've got my summer at sea and then by this time next year I could be halfway around the world. You'll be starting a job here, and I'll be absorbed with satellite photos, or communiqués, or whatever. We could lose touch, drift apart, get caught up in our own lives and our new careers. I don't want that to happen, Mo. I can't imagine a future without you."

Maureen looked nervous and took a long swallow of wine. She tilted her glass too quickly, sending a splash of white wine onto her blouse.

"Oh. Clumsy!" she said grabbing her napkin. "Sorry. I am still so tired."

He handed her his napkin and, when she finished dabbing her blouse, took her hand. "You okay?"

"I'm fine."

"Yes, you *are*, Maureen. You're wonderful. You know, you'll always be my Christmas girl; I don't ever want to spend a holiday without you." He reached into his pocket.

"We might not know where we'll be, but we know who we are. Whatever our future is, we should go through it together." He opened the box and held it out to her with a bright smile. "Maureen, will you marry me?"

She looked at the ring, and then at Chris, and then out over the harbor. Large flakes of snow fell faster now. She lifted her napkin and clutched it against her neck. Her eyes were damp. She bit her lower lip, staring down at the table.

44

"Oh, Chris I ... I can't. I am so sorry. I love you, but I can't."

He slowly lowered the ring box back to the table.

"I'm sorry, Chris. I didn't expect this, not tonight, anyway."

Chris hunched across the table toward her and whispered, "Are you saying no?"

She stared at him for a long moment, then slowly nodded her head. Chris looked furtively at the other tables then slid the box into his pocket. Light seemed to drain from room.

"We need to talk, but not here," she said softly. "Can we go someplace?"

Chris sat in stunned silence, then slowly looked up and motioned to the waitress, giving her the '*check*' sign, before draining his wine glass.

Neither spoke while the bill was presented and paid. They walked silently to her car while snowflakes intensified. Every few steps Chris turned his head toward her, but hers was down, her eyes fixed on the snowy sidewalk. She clearly wasn't ready to talk yet.

Once inside her car Chris said, "You have me worried, Mo. What's going on?"

She gripped the wheel with both hands and stared straight ahead.

He brushed snow off his shoulders. "Can you at least turn the engine on? It's freezing in here."

Maureen started the car. The radio blasted. She quickly grabbed the knob to shut it off.

She rested her elbows on the steering wheel and lowered her head into her hands.

Chris stared at her expectantly.

"Please understand," she stared out the windshield, "I really truly love you. You don't know how many times I've thought about us being married. It all seems so perfect."

"But ...?"

She turned to him. "But it's too soon. I'm not ready. Chris, I don't even know for sure who I am yet.

"You know all that hard work I had this week? I loved it. It was tough but I handled it well, and it felt good.

"I actually went to college to pursue something. Something I think I'll be good at. If we get married now, I'll never know."

"Maureen, you can still do all that …"

"You don't understand. Every year, I watched my mother follow Dad and his State Department career all over the world. Her life and her ambitions always came second to his. With the Navy, it's not just the travel; it's the whole Navy wife routine." She was staring out the window again.

"I sort of like who I am, who I'm becoming. I don't want to lose that. I know it sounds selfish … I can't believe I'm saying it. But I worry about it."

He took both of her shoulders into his hands until she turned and looked at him.

"You never said anything about this before."

"I know. I know, but it's been building. As I get closer to graduating, I just feel more and more that I must finish what I started. I have to know myself before I give myself to someone else." She lowered her head and her voice wavered. "Do you understand what I'm talking about? Do you know how hard this is for me? Can we please just go on the way we are?"

She leaned over, resting her head on his chest, sobbing quietly. Chris held her in silence for several minutes.

"I guess I can understand how you feel, but we can make it work. You'll still be you. I don't want to go off without you. I can't imagine us being apart."

"I'm sorry. I can't. I just can't."

He slowly stiffened and nudged her into sitting up. "I think you should drop me off."

They drove six blocks to the Academy gate. Chris looked at her for a long moment, hoping she would say something, change her mind, but got out in silence, with a strong temptation to throw the ring, box and all, as far into the snowy night as he could.

Maureen drove home, barely seeing the road through the snow and her tears. This was supposed to be such a good night. She'd looked forward to it all week. And he had proposed! How had she not have seen that coming? How could she have said no?

Her thoughts moved from one extreme to another like a shark swerving methodically back and forth. She had done the right thing. She had made the biggest mistake of her life. She knew she wasn't ready to be a Navy wife. She knew it would be a glorious adventure with her soul mate. Now she hoped her roommate would be gone so she wouldn't have to talk with anyone. She wouldn't be able to explain it anyway.

Maureen felt alone, in more ways than one. She tried to sleep, but her mind wouldn't let her. She got up and tried to read. It was useless; she couldn't concentrate. She opened her desk drawer, taking out a piece of lavender stationary and a pen.

Dearest Chris,

I hope you know how deeply my heart is touched by your proposal; how honored I feel.

Please forgive the way I acted. I just wasn't prepared tonight. I don't know why. Everything has been so special, so good. But somehow my internal calendar is set to a different schedule.

You are eternally precious to me. I never want to hurt you. But I need time, not time with anyone else. Just time to develop who I truly am. Please understand.

I pray we can stay together and work this out. Please be patient with me.

I love you.

> *Maureen*

The sun hadn't yet risen when she called Nate.

"It's Maureen. I need a favor."

"Maureen? It's early. What's goin' on? Are you all right? Is Chris okay?"

"We're fine. I need you to do something for me."

"Anything."

"I need you to give a letter to Chris for me. It needs to be this morning."

"You sound awful. Have you been crying?"

"You could say that. Chris proposed last night."

"So those are *happy* tears?"

"I said no."

"Oh, my God!" Nate sat up in bed. "He must be crushed. Why? What happened?"

"I'll tell you when I see you. I have a note for Chris, and I want him to have it first thing this morning. Can I bring it you?"

"Of course. Call when you're 10 minutes out, and I'll meet you at the gate."

Snow had drifted deeper overnight. The roads were glazed with patches of ice. Wind blew blinding gusts of snow across the highway. A few cars had slipped off the pavement. Maureen followed a snow plough most of the way into Annapolis, then called Nate.

"I think I'm 10 minutes away, but the roads are awful."

"Okay. I'll be right down."

She pulled up, swerved to a stop, and lowered her window as Nate approached.

"You look like hell," he said.

"I feel like it." She reached out, handing him the envelope.

"Can you make sure he gets it this morning?"

"Why don't you park the car? We can get some coffee and talk this through."

"You're sweet Nate, but I don't have the energy. I'm so conflicted right now I don't know what I'm doing. You know I love him. It's just too soon. Please, tell him I love him, and give him this."

"You two are perfect for each other. Let me get him down here and you guys can talk."

"I don't think I can right now. Please, Nate, can you just take it to him?"

"I will. He'll have it in ten minutes." He paused. "Is this likely to hurt him more?"

"No, I promise. I'm trying to make things better. I have to go. Thank you, Nate."

It was nearly noon before she made it home, where she collapsed onto her bed and fell immediately to sleep. The phone didn't ring. No one came knocking on her door.

11 LETTER RECEIVED

Nate took the letter to Chris' room, rapped on the door with the back of his knuckles, and opened it without waiting. Chris wasn't there. His bed was still stiffly made in precise Navy style. His roommate lay snoring in the other bunk.

Chris drove north on I-95 through blinding snow. He was seventy miles from the George Washington Bridge when his phone rang.

He looked at the number on the screen and ignored the call.

Ten minutes later it rang again.

"Yeah?"

"Chris, thank God! It's Nate. I talked with Maureen. Are you all right?"

"Don't want to talk about it."

"She loves you, buddy. Maureen gave me a letter for you. Where are you anyway?"

"Almost to New York."

"New York? Man, you've got to get back here, seriously. I know you're bummed, but you're in the Navy. You've got to report by 0100. Come read your letter."

"Did you read it?"

"No, it's sealed, and I wouldn't read it even if it weren't. Maureen wanted you to have it first thing this morning. I think she's been up crying all night. Look, I don't know what's going on, but I know she loves you. Get your ass back here so you two can make up."

"I just feel like driving."

"If you don't get your ass back here I'll burn her letter and you'll never know what she wrote."

"Read it to me now."

"No, way! This is between you two. But I'm telling you if you're not back by 2200 this goes up in flames."

"You wouldn't do that."

"I *will* do that. Get back here. Oh, and two words: *Make-up sex*. Think about it."

Chris drove another ten miles, his fingers clenched tightly on the steering wheel, before turning around at the exit.

The drive back was treacherous. His car wasn't designed for snow and ice. Visibility faded in and out through the blowing snow. Traffic snarled. A large semi in front of him slammed on its brakes and went into a skid. Chris, lost in thought, barely reacted in time. He swerved onto the shoulder and came to a stop. An old pickup truck behind him slid through the space he had occupied seconds before, nearly hitting the rear of the semi. Chris stiffened as he realized he'd almost been crushed. It took nearly the entire day to make it back.

He stopped first at Nate's room.

"All right, I'm back. Where's her letter?"

"It's in your room. I put it on your pillow. Thanks for coming to your senses. Do you remember you have an applied physics exam Monday morning?"

Chris grunted and headed for his room. He sat on his bed and read her letter. He read it again, folded it in half, got up, and placed it in his desk drawer.

He decided not to contact her. Maybe if he stayed away she'd realize how much she missed him. He vowed not to call, text, or email her for a while.

12 HOME INVASION

Maureen spent the next four days going about her schedule, checking frequently for any communication from him. She felt fragile and decided to call Nate the next day to make sure Chris had seen her letter.

Her phone rang as she walked to her first morning class, and she rushed to answer it.

"Mo, it's Dad. Something's happened, and I need you to come home for a day or two. We've been robbed. We need you to come see what's missing from your stuff. Mostly, I need you to comfort your mother. She's beside herself. She thinks it's all her fault."

"My God. What happened?"

"It's kind of embarrassing. Your mother went shopping at Nordstrom's in Tyson's Corner yesterday and stopped to use the ladies' room. While she was in the stall someone reached under and grabbed her purse.

"By the time she got out, the woman had disappeared. Karen didn't even see what kind of shoes she had. Anyway, she reported it to security, and they couldn't do much. They have cameras but they aren't trained on the restrooms. Security told her it'd never happened before, promised to do everything, but honestly didn't encourage her to think they'd find anything; said it might turn up in a trash bin but would likely be empty.

"Your mom was pretty shaken up. She had to take a cab home, and spent the afternoon canceling credit cards and talking to our banks. We drove back in the evening and picked up her car.

"Right after I left for work yesterday, she got a call from Nordstrom's. The security office said they had her purse, described it, and said the money and credit cards were gone but her driver's license, keys and pictures were still there. They asked her to come in at ten o'clock.

"When she got there, no one had any idea what she was talking about. The store hadn't found anything. They hadn't called her. She was pretty upset, and spent a long time arguing with them before she realized the thief had her keys.

"By the time she got home, we'd been cleaned out. The Millers, across the street, said a painter's van had been parked in our driveway for nearly an hour. They thought it odd when the garage door opened and they pulled inside, but never suspected a robbery. Their van must have been just down the street when your mother left for the store.

"Some of your stuff is missing, too. We just don't know for sure what it is. We need you to come home and go through things. Can you do it soon? We have to file reports with the police and insurance company."

"Holy shit! Oh, sorry, Dad. I just can't believe it. Of course I'll come. I have one class this morning and can be there by one."

"Maureen, I'm worried about your mother more than anything else. She's really shaken up, blames herself. When you come, no matter what you're missing, please act as if it's no big deal to you. Can you do that?"

"Of course. How are *you* doing?"

"I'm pretty shaken up, thank you. It's strange, feeling so insecure in my own home. I've got a security company coming tomorrow to install a system. All the locks have been changed, but I can't stop feeling violated. It's a weak, brittle feeling. Mostly, though, I just want your mom to get through this. It'll be good to have you here."

"Have you talked to Joan and Colleen yet?"

"Not yet, your sisters don't have much stuff here anymore, well, certainly not now!" He tried to laugh. "I'll call them in a bit."

Maureen was surprised by how normal the house looked when she pulled into the driveway. Logically, she knew it should look the same, but it didn't feel the same. Somehow, she just expected an outward sign of its violation.

She slipped her key in the front door but it wouldn't turn. 'Oh, of course,' she thought, and rang the bell.

Both her parents came to the door. Her mother's small frame seemed to have shrunk even further. After hugs and kisses Karen swept her arms into a wide circle and said, "Don't you think the house looks so much more spacious without ... all our belongings?"

Maureen stared from the foyer into the living room. Every painting missing from every wall. Empty spaces gaped where crystal vases and treasured sculptures had stood. A depressed ring in the carpet the only sign of the large hand-painted Chinese urn that had stood there. In the den, she saw a gaggle of electric cords where the home theater system used to be. The kitchen missed its Bose stereo that always rested next to the spice jars.

"All my jewelry, all our paintings, everything of value, all gone," her mother sighed.

"Well, it's all insured, or most of it anyway." Her father tried to sound optimistic.

"We can't replace those things, Brad! We spent all those years abroad collecting them from all over Europe. Places that are special to us, precious items ..." Her voice trailed off.

"I know, Karen," Brad said. "But think of the fun you'll have shopping for everything again."

"Oh, God! Don't even mention *shopping* to me!"

Maureen hugged her mother again. "We'll get through this. I am just glad you and dad are all right. You never know. The police might recover all of it."

"I doubt it," Karen said. "You know what I've been thinking? How do you prove you owned a painting? We

54

never photographed any of it, and now I don't know how to prove it's mine if they do find something."

"Here's a more pressing question: Did they clean out the refrigerator? I'm starving."

"I knew you'd be hungry. I was just making a Caesar salad when you arrived. Let's eat, get caught up on your life, and then you can see what's missing from your room."

Maureen and her dad moved to the kitchen while her mom set the table with the blue and yellow flower-painted plates she loved and pulled a large bowl from the refrigerator.

"Well, on a happier note," her father said, "how are things going with you and Chris? You know, we're very impressed with him."

Maureen clasped her hands together under the table. She clenched her teeth slightly, grimaced, and gently rocked in her chair.

"Chris and I ..." Keeping her fingers intertwined she raised her hands above the table and slowly rested them on the surface, her fingers spread wide. "We're fine."

"You don't sound fine. Did something happen?"

"I don't know. Well, actually, ... he asked me to marry him."

"You're engaged?"

"No, I turned him down. I think we're not speaking to each other now."

Her mother set the bowl on the table and sank into the chair across from Maureen. She leaned forward to look Maureen firmly in the eyes.

"When did all this happen?"

"Friday night. He took me to a nice restaurant, really quite romantic. Chris made the sweetest proposal and offered me a beautiful engagement ring. I was just too surprised. I said no. I think I broke his heart. I tried to tell him I'm not ready yet, but now he's not talking to me. I haven't heard from him all week."

"Oh, honey, have you called him?"

"I wrote him a letter. I just think he's too hurt to call. He'll come around. I think. Anyway, right now things are … tenuous. I guess that's a good word for it."

"I've an idea," her father said. "There's a dance at the club on Valentine's Day. It's only a couple of weeks away. I'll call him like I don't know anything and tell him the two of you are invited and …"

"Dad! I don't need an ambassador. It's something we've got to work out on our own."

She explained her feelings and how she'd been wrestling with everything. In the final analysis, she just wasn't ready yet and hoped he could be patient. After lunch, she headed up to her room with a notepad her dad had given her. She sat on her bed and looked around to see what had been taken, frustrated trying to remember what wasn't there. She really didn't care.

And then she realized what she missed, what had been missing all week: being able to share everything with Chris. Not just big things like, "Someone robbed my parents' house!" but ordinary little things. She'd never had a friend so close and so comfortable she could share everything with and not feel the least bit self-conscious. Certainly, he must feel it too. Certainly, he'll call soon?

She collapsed on her bed and fell asleep. Her mother came up around five, stood in the doorway watching her daughter, then flicked off the light and silently closed the door.

Maureen woke in total darkness, unsure of her bearings. When she realized she was home, she sat up and turned on the lamp. She looked at her nightstand and immediately realized something was missing: a picture of her grandparents in a silver frame. That picture had greeted her every day for nearly twelve years. Now it was gone. She didn't care about the frame, but cursed them for not leaving the photo.

She got up and started a careful search for any other items to catalogue on her note pad. Her high school ring from Walt Whitman was missing, along with a couple of necklaces and track medals she'd earned. They weren't valuable. She had no idea why someone would take them. Other than that, everything seemed to be in place.

Maureen spent the whole next day with her parents, talking about old memories. Every missing item had a story about where it had been found, how well her mother had bargained for it, how carefully they had packed it when moving from Belgium or Germany or wherever they'd been stationed. Maureen learned a lot about items she had taken for granted all her life. Items she would likely never see again.

The conversations seemed to help her mother. Over time she came to be more content with the experience of having selected various treasures and sharing them with her family.

"Oh, well, you kids got to enjoy them growing up." She gave a heavy sigh. "I guess your father's right. We can always replace things. We can't replace each other, and we're blessed to be together."

13 DO YOU LIKE COFFEE?

Chris immersed himself in studies and in his physical regimen. He ran the same distance around the Yard's outer perimeter, but with more speed and intensity. His sessions in the pool became contests to see how many more laps he could swim each night. He fought hard not to think about her.

As the days wore on, he began to falter and re-evaluate his strategy. What if she really wasn't missing him? What if she met someone new? By the end of the week he wavered badly. He sat at his desk slowly opening the drawer, staring at the letter for several seconds before reaching in and taking it out. He unfolded it, smelled the paper's faint scent, and read each word slowly and thoughtfully.

She picked up on the first ring.

"This is Starbucks calling. We were wondering, do you happen to like coffee?" Chris asked.

She stood and moved the phone from her left ear to her right, brushing her hair out of the way.

"As a matter of fact, I do." She remained completely still, anxious not to ruin a fragile moment.

"I thought you should know Starbucks has a pumpkin-flavored coffee with whipped cream. It's quite good."

"I *am* glad to know that ... I guess." She shrugged a *'where's this going?'* shrug.

He moved from his desk and sat on the edge of his bed.

"Well, it's a brand-new flavor. The company hired me to introduce it to our customers."

"I am sure you're doing a fine job. Starbucks is lucky to have you." A slight giddy feeling.

"Yes, well, they've asked me to invite people to try it with me, to evaluate your response."

"So, you're asking me for coffee?"

"It's my job, ma'am. Would tomorrow at 0800 work for you? I'll send a car and driver."

"That's very kind, sir, I shall await your carriage."

He hung up. Maureen stared at her phone. She held it to her heart, rose up lightly on her toes, spun around once, and fell back onto her bed.

Chris did a double fist pump into the air and went down the hall to tell Nate.

He pulled into the parking lot of Maureen's apartment fifteen minutes early and sat in his car, drumming the steering wheel with his fingers, thinking through what he wanted to say and how he hoped things would progress.

He started getting out just as her car pulled up next to his. Chris had assumed she had been in her apartment, and felt a flash of anger and jealousy, wondering if she was coming home from spending the night elsewhere.

Maureen got out carrying a cardboard tray with two large Starbucks coffees and two pastries.

"Hey, sailor," she said. "I thought it would be best to conduct our taste test in a home environment."

He broke into a broad grin, relieved. "I've missed you."

"I've missed you, too." She moved the tray to her side and they embraced.

"It's warmer inside," she said.

Chris took the tray and followed her up the stairs to her apartment.

She put Sara Brightman on the stereo and they made love while the coffee grew cold. It was deep caring love. He adored her. She thought he was the most precious gift ever.

They caressed and studied each other with deeply appreciative eyes. Every touch felt new and special.

She apologized for being so timid the night he proposed. He apologized for springing it on her so quickly. In the end, they agreed to put the question aside for a while. Not yet a yes, but certainly not a no.

Three weeks later Chris got the news he wanted. His assignment was finally official: The Office of Naval Intelligence. He had studied Mandarin at the Academy and become fairly proficient. His assignment would involve monitoring developments in the South China Sea. But first he would report to the Navy and Marine Corps Intelligence Training Center in Virginia Beach for more education.

The Office of Naval Intelligence, ONI, is the longest-serving intelligence agency of the federal government, dating back to 1882. It is now one of 17 agencies under the command of the Director of National Intelligence.

He called her with the news. She was happy for him, and glad to learn he'd be stateside a while longer; but she wondered if it marked the beginning of the end of their relationship.

Chris called his mother and left a message on her machine, then called Brandon in Manhattan.

"Brandon, I thought you'd like to know your little brother has officially been accepted into Naval Intelligence."

"Congratulations, Chris! You've wanted that for a long time. I'm proud of you. Dad would be too."

"Yeah, I miss him every day."

"Well, you're doing great. It's odd, though; nobody ever contacted me for a background check. I guess they know all they need to about their midshipmen."

"Actually, Brandon, you did have an interview."

"Nope, no one ever talked to me at all. I don't think anyone contacted Mom either."

"Yeah? Tell me if this rings a bell: Just before you left London, you're at a coffee shop and a young woman, looking like a student, is pacing around checking her watch. She's frustrated and annoyed. Asks if you've seen someone and describes him. Says it's her brother. He's supposed to meet her but he's always late."

"That sounds very familiar."

"She plopped down next to you and started talking about her brother. Asked if you had any siblings. You two spent 45 minutes talking and by the time the conversation ended she had all the information she needed."

"Are you shitting me? I remember her. She gave me a fake phone number."

"Yep, that was your interview. Mom probably met someone at a store or hair salon who wanted to chat about her grown children."

"Un-fucking believable, I'm blown away."

"But you can't tell anyone. I wouldn't know anything about it except they needed to interview me about something you told them."

"I didn't say anything bad about you. I'm sure of it."

"You told her about Coach's Jeep."

Brandon burst out laughing. "Oh, my God, I did tell her that!"

In Christopher's senior year he and the rest of the soccer team arranged to "borrow" their coach's old red Jeep one Friday night. They spent all Saturday carefully taking it apart, and all Sunday carefully reassembling it in the school gym. It was a senior prank, but their coach didn't see the humor in it. In fact, he pressed charges.

Parents, and their lawyers, eventually persuaded Coach to drop his complaint. A rumor held that a large sum had been raised as "reimbursement for expenses" to sway his decision.

"The Navy didn't care about it too much. But, please don't tell anyone about your interview. I don't want to get kicked out of Intelligence before I even begin."

"I promise."

"I'm serious!"

"Okay. I seriously promise to keep it to myself."

"Thank you. Not even with Mom."

"Okay. Not even with Mom."

"How's JP Morgan?"

"Sucks. They have me doing meaningless grunt work until two o'clock every morning."

"Well, stick it out. You'll be worth a few of million before you know it."

"I'd settle for a few nights' sleep at this point"

"You'll be at graduation, right?"

"We'll all be there."

14 CATCH ME FIRST

Chris and Maureen fell back into a comfortable caring relationship. Through mutual agreement, they concentrated on the present without worrying about the future.

By the last week in March it hardly seemed they'd been apart. On Saturday Maureen met Chris early for a long run. They began in the Yard running along the Severn River, then in a big loop out King George Street to Rowe Boulevard, taking them outside the city before cutting over to West and heading back downtown. They raced each other the last quarter-mile with Chris staying just ahead of her.

She stopped abruptly at the square, bent down with her hands on her knees, breathing hard, her chest heaving. "Whew, need to catch my breath." They were directly in front of Maria's Restaurant. She smiled. "We should go here again."

"Aren't you afraid I'll propose again."

"Maybe I want you to."

"Be careful, I just might."

"You'll have to catch me first." She bolted past him toward the Academy gate, not just running, sprinting full speed.

Chris grinned, taking up pursuit only to discover she outpaced him. He kicked into high gear, taking longer strides, pumping his arms. Maureen shot through the gate onto the academy lawn, turning sharply to her right toward Farragut Field. Chris closed the distance between them, shouting, "You know I'll catch you!" She laughed with the little breath she had left and turned back to gauge his progress. As she did, her right foot stepped into a low patch and she tumbled full speed, turning part of her momentum into a forward roll.

Chris was immediately at her side, down on one knee reaching for her and asking, "You okay, Flash?"

Maureen grimaced, reaching for her ankle. "It's swollen; I don't think I'll be running for a while."

He began to help her up, but stopped.

"You know, I'm on one knee already, and you did say if I caught you …" He panted heavily. "Mo, I'm sorry, but I still want to marry you. If the answer's no, I won't ask again, but I am asking now. Will you?"

"You don't give up, do you?"

They were married the day after graduation at the Naval Academy Chapel. Maureen's favorite priest, Father Ryan, drove up from Bethesda to officiate, and they joined a conveyor line of brides and grooms that day. The Academy allowed each wedding party to use the chapel for precisely forty-five minutes, after which they must immediately clear out for the next happy couple.

Their honeymoon needed to be brief. Chris had a short window before reporting for his summer shipboard assignment. They flew to St. Martin, spending two days on the Dutch side and two days on the French side. Chris's brothers had given them a gift of sailboat racing. A local company acquired yachts that had competed in previous America's Cup competitions. Once the races were done, the ships were immediately outmoded, as the newest technology was incorporated into the next ones. The boats were built only for speed, with no amenities, so their resale was limited.

The company let tourists try their hand at racing under the supervision of a trained crew that shouted orders to novices, directing them to turn cranks, pull ropes, and lean one way or the other. Chris was impressed with Maureen's agility as she took easily to the tasks. Their boat cut through the Caribbean, searching angles to cut off wind from their competitors' sails. They were surging into first place when their mainsail suddenly ripped, settling the boat back into the water, allowing the other yachts to slip swiftly ahead. Chris had to swallow some pride, but still enjoyed the experience. Sunshine, gentle waves, and fruit-flavored drinks created the ideal backdrop for a honeymoon.

Just four months later, Maureen discovered that a baby was on the way. It wasn't the news she expected. She felt fragile, unready, and, to be honest, robbed of her independence. Her idea of young married life hadn't included a child for at least five years. Chris felt buoyant, a little nervous, but delighted at the thought of a child—their child. She harbored a slight, silent grudge that he was a touch too Catholic. The baby arrived in February, two weeks early, but very healthy. They named him Thomas Joseph McCarty, after Christopher's dad. Maureen's mother started calling him T. J., but to Mo he was always Joey. And Joey stuck.

Intelligence training in Virginia lasted another two months with intensive instruction in a wide array of disciplines: computing and electronics, anti-air, anti-surface, anti-submarine, amphibious and strike warfare training, followed up with counterintelligence, strategic intelligence, air defense analysis and combat mission planning.

Short trips home to see Maureen were welcome, but busy. He studied long into the night after Joey fell asleep, sometimes not crawling under the covers until Maureen was dreaming soundly. She felt cheated by his absences, confined by her role as Joey's primary caregiver and, more often than not, lonely.

His next assignment lasted two months on an operational fleet tour, where his education was constantly tested and refined. Even though Muslim terrorists had killed his father, Chris came to believe China posed a larger threat to American security. He had spent two years in intensive study becoming fluent in Mandarin, while studying every aspect of Chinese military capabilities.

By the time his training ended the Defense community had become increasingly worried by the escalation of China's military capabilities. They were building a major aircraft carrier, developing missiles capable of striking US ships from great distances, and mastering stealth technology to effectively cloak their submarines.

His next assignment wasn't in the South China Sea, but rather the Sea of Japan. A major US aircraft carrier had been on joint maneuvers with Japanese and other US ships when a Chinese Song Class submarine surfaced nearby. It had been following the fleet so silently the Navy's concern went on high alert.

Chris had been newly promoted to Lieutenant, and assigned to the Kitty Hawk in the Seventh Fleet to brief Naval commanders and to monitor developments across Asia. His son was now three years old. Christopher had been in Japan barely three months when everything changed.

15 PLUCKED FROM THE SEA

Lt. Christopher McCarty hurried across the aircraft carrier's deck, bending under the strong wash of the helicopter's blades, nearly slipping on the damp deck before throwing his duffle bag aboard and casting an eye on the dark clouds building to the North. Winds were picking up, with waves white-cresting and gaining speed. He climbed aboard, giving a thumb up to indicate he was the last passenger strapping in.

Two sailors already occupied the rear of the craft. Chris felt comforted to see Calvin Jackson at the controls. Calvin had spent a long career as a chopper jockey. He'd grown up in the poorest section of Detroit, where staying out of gangs constituted a near miracle. But he'd managed to avoid them, escaping Detroit entirely by joining the Navy just before Desert Storm in 1990. Chris often heard Calvin say, "Don't just call me African-American 'cause I'm Detroit-American, and that's a whole other side of tough." Then he'd flash a broad joyful grin and break into a classic Motown refrain. His boisterous laugh could raise anyone's spirits.

Their helicopter lifted slowly, swaying as it rose. Chris looked down, watching the lights of the aircraft carrier fade and disappear beneath the rain, like a whale plunging deep into the sea. Six minutes into the flight they hit a solid wall of water; large sideways sheets forcefully slapped the windows, while lightning pierced the dark sky on all sides. Fierce winds pushed relentlessly against them, forcing Calvin to use all his strength to maintain control.

They bounced left to right and back again, a plaything in the wind. Chris clenched both hands tightly around his harness. Water sprayed through the top of his window seals, splashing him in the face. He closed his eyes and bent as far into the cabin as he could. His only thought, in between prayers, was, *I'm glad Calvin's at the stick.*

Twenty minutes into the flight, a bright light flashed below them. A blast at the rear of the craft forced their chopper up, hurtling it erratically higher. An instant sparkle of electric static was quickly followed by flames and a pungent odor of oil and smoke. The helicopter's nose tilted toward the sea, spinning around and round in a downward cycle. Chris felt his stomach rising into his throat. He shut his eyes tight and gritted his teeth. The last thing he remembered was saying his prayers, knowing the water was about to rise up and capture him. Then he felt nothing.

Christopher woke slowly, his mind thick and clouded, as if a spider's web had been spun around his brain. His head throbbed. He tested his senses, gingerly clenching his fingers and gradually releasing them, vaguely aware of voices around him. They weren't speaking English. It sounded Asian, but not Mandarin and not Japanese. He had good language skills but strained to identify this one.

His eyes opened slowly like a newborn puppy's, moist and goopy, blurred vision slowly revealing two men in white jackets arguing among themselves, unaware he'd awakened. The room felt cold with a strong antiseptic smell. Someone's hand touched his shoulder.

A woman's voice at the left of his bed spoke in English, "Good evening, Lieutenant McCarty." A soothing, almost joyful voice. "We are so happy you are with us. We feared you would perish like the others."

He turned toward her, sending a sharp pain up his neck and shoulders. A pretty woman, with smiling eyes and flowing black hair, stood next to him, wearing a dark blue dress with a white floral design that wove its way around her. The silk collar riding high rested just under her chin.

"My name is Soon Yi," she said. "You are safe now. We will see you fully recovered."

"Where am I?"

"You are in our finest hospital. You will have very best treatment."

"What city?"

"Our capital city, Pyongyang. You are honored guest of The Democratic People's Republic of Korea."

"North Korea?"

"We prefer to think there is only one Korea."

"How ... Who perished?"

"Your helicopter crashed into the Korean sea. Patrol boats of the People's Navy saved you. Our Great Leader, Kim Jong Il, is proud to have rescued you. It is through his grace you are alive and safe with us." Chris tried sitting up but immediately felt sick to his stomach. One of the men in white extended his palm, placed it on Christopher's shoulder, and gently pushed him back down into the bed.

"You must rest," Soon Yi said. "You must get strong."

He shivered, feeling weak, cold, and sweaty at the same time. The woman nodded toward the doctors. Chris saw one of them plunge a needle into the IV connected to his left arm and then felt as if he were drifting slowly down while the room faded into darkness.

Nine hours passed before Chris awoke. Soon Yi had changed clothes but remained with him. She wore a green dress that fit tightly around her small body. The scent of fresh gardenias drifted from her smooth skin.

"Good morning, cowboy," she smiled. "Glad you awake now. Perhaps today you gain strength."

He still felt as if his head had been wrapped in gauze, his throat harsh and dry like he'd eaten sand, his lips parched and cracked.

"Water. Please, water," he rasped.

"You are honored guest. You may have what you want,"

She clapped her delicate hands twice. A nurse appeared. Soon Yi spoke to her, and the woman quickly produced a pitcher of water and a glass. She poured it and held it to Chris' lips. It dribbled down his chin. He took it from her with a shaking hand and brought it to his mouth. The water was metallic with an aftertaste like aspirin.

"You will be reunited with your family soon. Good news! You are bridge between my country and yours. Our Dear Leader called your president. In no time, you will be home, and our countries will find a pathway to peace. We show good faith, and your leader will show good faith to The People's Republic of Korea. Yes?"

Chris seriously doubted that. North Korea had long been a rogue nation. Technically it was still at war with the United States, and had been since 1950. The Armistice of 1953 didn't officially end the conflict, and Kim Jong Il used every opportunity to convince his population that America remained on the verge of attacking them.

His people scavenged and starved, while Kim Jong Il pursued a "Military First" policy. Nearly 25% of the country's economy was devoted to defense. He maintained the fourth-largest army in the world, with almost a million soldiers on active duty or reserve. Kim aggressively pursued nuclear armaments along with an ambitious space program.

Official reports confirmed Kim loved American movies, American basketball, and American pornography most of all. US Military Intelligence had reason to believe that Kim Jong Il had become the world's largest counterfeiter of American currency. China and South Korea each confirmed he had circulated over forty-five million in counterfeit $100 US bills.

Soon Yi lowered her voice, explaining in hushed tones that the Dear Leader had grown weary of constant tension with the United States. He had been considering an overture to the President through the Chinese ambassador to the United States. Now, she said, he would help a young Navy officer regain his health and would reunite him with his country. Surely that would crack the ice and allow a form of détente to occur. It had worked between Russia and the United States. Kim Jong Il looked forward to more peaceful relations with the West.

Chris had seen intelligence photos of Kim surrounded by "pleasure girls" at a karaoke party in one of his mansions. Other photos showed him hosting gambling parties with large bricks of $100 bills at every table. He also knew a recent famine had killed at least 10 percent of the population, and family incomes had dropped to only 8 percent of that enjoyed by South Koreans. Farm production plummeted, and fuel consumption sank. All the while Kim partied and indulged his fantasies.

Like his father before him, Kim was worshipped as a living deity. For him, the country was one big playground. His Japanese chef escaped the previous year, reporting the lavish lifestyle of the Kim family. He told of extravagant feasts while peasants scrounged for grass and roots to eat.

If Kim had truly experienced a change of heart, Chris realized it could lift millions of people out of oppression and poverty. It seemed unlikely, but US Intelligence on North Korea remained spotty at best. It wasn't easy to keep tabs on such a secretive state. He realized this was a rare opportunity to gather information, an inside look at the Hermit Kingdom.

Over the next two days, his health improved considerably. He walked the hospital corridors unassisted, but always with Soon Yi or a doctor at his side, and always under the watchful eyes of armed soldiers. Staff members bowed reverentially as he passed. He felt them staring and knew they were bursting with curiosity at seeing an actual American, a treacherous imperialist, in their midst.

16 RED CROSS VISIT

The third morning, Soon Yi arrived with a soldier holding a large breakfast tray.

"American breakfast," she announced. "Eggs, ham, toast, and coffee. Everything you like."

Chris sat up. Until now, he'd eaten only flavorless gelatin, bland rice with peas, or a bitter soup. The eggs were cold, and the ham tough, but it was still an improvement.

"You enjoy! Today you have special visitor!"

She explained the Red Cross had arranged an observer, Mr. Brandt, to check on his health and to verify that he was being well treated.

"It's the request of your president." She smiled. "We are happy to show how well you are cared for."

At nine o'clock a puffy, middle-aged man, in a rumpled suit, arrived at the hospital. He appeared to be European, and spoke quietly with an accent that might have been German, asking how Chris had been treated. Did he need anything? Had he been told the terms of his exchange?

Chris said he'd been told only that he would be released soon and returned to his family.

"They told me about negotiations with the president. Do you know where that stands? Does my wife know I'm okay?"

"You're a chess piece being played on an international board," the man explained. "We believe Kim Jong Il is thinking of his legacy now."

He lowered his voice almost to a whisper.

"His health is failing. He'll soon turn the country over to one of his sons. It seems he's not sure how strong any of them are. Kim wants an opening with the West to bring in more aid money and more food. That will ease the path for whichever son he chooses. The passing years are nudging Kim to soften his stance."

"They send me home, and Kim's a hero?"

"Kim's claiming he practically plucked you from the sea and nursed you back to health himself. He's still bargaining though. He wants several North Korean operatives released from South Korean jails. That's the easy part. He also wants your president to fly here personally on Air Force One to pick you up and to thank him publicly."

"So, I'm not going home?"

The man laughed, "You catch on quickly. Don't be too concerned. They'll work something out. Perhaps your Secretary of State will come instead. It just takes time. Can I truthfully report that you are being well cared for?"

"So far, no complaints. Can I call my wife?"

"I am told that may be possible by tomorrow, next week at the latest."

"Can you get a message to her? Let her know I love her and that I'll be home as soon as possible? Maybe you can have the State Department call her? Her father's a career diplomat with State."

"I can certainly convey all that." He hooked a finger under his collar, stretching his neck as if the shirt was strangling him and straightened his tie as he stood.

"Thank you for coming. Let me give you her number."

For the first time, Chris felt optimistic. Forces were at work, deals were being struck, and he would make his way home. He sat up in bed with his knees raised, his arms folded over them, slowly rocking back and forth, anxious to get home.

Soon Yi returned with a soldier who held Chris's uniform and shoes.

"All pressed and shined." Soon Yi smiled. "Good as new, yes?

"You are strong enough to see our glorious city today. We made special preparations. When you are dressed, we will see a children's show at our national garden."

After she left, the soldier stiffly placed Chris's folded clothes on the chair by his bed, nodded, turned, and marched briskly out of the room. Chris swung his feet over the side of the bed, sitting for several seconds looking at his uniform and his polished shoes. Even his underwear and socks had been cleaned. It would feel good to get out of his hospital gown, to wear his uniform, to be in the United States Navy again. His confidence rose.

Once dressed, he wasn't sure what to do. Could he just walk over, open the door, and stride into the corridor? Should he wait for someone to come and escort him out? *"Hell,"* he thought. *"I'm an officer in the United States Navy. I'm not waiting for anyone."* He opened the door and stepped out into the hallway.

Soon Yi waited with two soldiers. She had changed into a flowing, pink, kimono-style dress. A pink flower in her hair perfectly matched the dress. She gave a slight bow, accompanied by smiling eyes.

"You are handsome soldier," she said.

"And you are a beautiful hostess," he replied, immediately regretting his choice of words. He wondered if "hostess" might be a derogatory term. If so, Soon Yi didn't seem offended. He also wondered why he felt a sense of euphoria, and why everything seemed just slightly out of synch.

They walked out into a clear sunny day. A Mercedes awaited them at the curb. One soldier opened the back door nearest the curb, while the driver quickly got out and opened the other back door. Chris and Soon Yi took their places in back. The driver returned behind the wheel, and the other soldier joined him in the front seat. Kim Jong Il's picture, prominently displayed, stared at them from the dash.

"You will see our beautiful gardens and see a children's dance."

He wondered if she ever stopped smiling.

They drove down an eight-lane boulevard, the streets nearly empty of traffic. Enormous government buildings, intended to inspire awe, instead looked old, tired, and unwelcoming. North Korean flags dominated every building, and enormous statues along the road glorified Kim Jong Il.

Billboards carried the Dear Leader's picture, depicting him instructing engineers or advising farmers. The cult of personality was meant to convey Kim as an expert in every conceivable profession.

Chris recalled a news story of Kim's being a great fan of Tiger Woods. It was reported that the Supreme Leader took up golf and remarkably shot thirty-eight under par in his first outing. In fact, he shot five holes-in-one. Several of his security guards had attested to the feat. Not bad for a man who stood five-feet-two and wore platform shoes. It was just another example that Kim was brilliant at everything he did.

People along the sidewalks looked thin and harried, casting furtive glances at his car, as if it might pull over at any minute and haul them away. Chris tried his best to take everything in, to commit as much as possible to memory. Their car turned into a long driveway and passed under an intricate ornamental gate. They'd arrived at Pyongyang's botanical gardens. Spring cherry blossoms, pink and white, were in bloom. Yellow daffodils popped up in front of vibrant green grass.

A group of fifty young children stood in neat rows in front of the main building, wearing brightly colored costumes that gave a slight carnival air to the assembly. But the children stood perfectly still, almost at military attention, staring straight ahead.

Soldiers quickly opened doors for Chris and Soon Yi. A viewing stand across from the students overflowed with people who appeared to be government officials. They rose in unison and bowed a formal welcome toward Chris. He awkwardly returned the bow.

Soon Yi guided him to turn and face the students. Two small girls, about the age of six, approached, carrying a ring of flowers. They handed it to Soon Yi, who smiled and bowed. She turned to Chris and held the lei up to place around his neck. He removed his cap, bending down as she slipped the flowers over his head. To his surprise, she gave him a soft kiss on each cheek, while polite applause rose from the viewing stand.

She took his arm, escorting him up to the center seats reserved for them. The audience remained standing until Chris and Soon Yi sat. Music began playing from speakers above the children, who immediately began to perform. Their arms shot up. They twirled and leapt. Boys and girls moved in complete precision with grace and energy. Chris was enchanted, at first.

As the dance continued, he wondered how children so young were trained to move in complete unison, more synchronized than a military unit. What could have created such exactitude? How much had these children gone through before this was drilled into them? The dance lasted thirty minutes, uninterrupted. Every child smiled intently throughout. *They're automatons, robots,* Chris thought. He despaired their loss of freedom.

When it ended, the audience applauded vigorously. Chris wondered if some were responding to their own children. Soon Yi took his arm and introduced him to several officials. Each one seemed happy to see him; none spoke English, but all smiled and bowed, indicating they were honored to have him there. Chris tried his best to be a good ambassador, to leave a good impression.

Soon Yi led him on a stroll through the gardens. She tucked her arm under his and talked about the garden's history, showing areas dedicated to different plants, and explaining the park's constant use. Teachers brought students year-round to learn about nature and to study the different trees and flowers. She paused under a cherry tree and lifted her nose up to the blossoms, inhaling deeply.

"Ah, so good! You like?"

He reached up and gently brought a branch close to his nose.

He couldn't smell anything, and doubted that she had, but said, "Very nice."

Chris asked about her life and her family. Soon Yi paused. Just for a moment, her smile was gone. She said she'd been trained in languages, hoping to be considered for the North Korean delegation to the United Nations. She would be their interpreter and would bring much honor to her family. Beyond that she had little to say about her parents, only that they lived further north with her two younger brothers. He was surprised she asked little about him. There was little he would have told her.

A breeze swept up, blowing streams of blossoms like snowflakes. She held up her arms with open palms to catch them. Soon Yi giggled as she collected blossoms from the air, then stopped and placed a handful in his shirt pocket.

"So you don't forget me."

He smiled. "You, I will always remember."

Chris motioned toward a flowerbed, pointing to a purple tulip. "May I?"

She nodded approval so he gently picked it and placed the flower in her hand.

"For happy memories," he said. Once more, the world seemed slightly out of kilter, but pleasant.

Chris sagged slightly, suddenly very tired, feeling drained and in need of rest. She understood without being asked, and raised her arm, her finger tracing a circular motion. The Mercedes appeared promptly. On the way to the hospital he again asked permission to call his wife, but was reminded it would have to wait until the Dear Leader had finished his negotiations with the president. She assured him it wouldn't be long.

His neck and shoulders ached as he climbed back into bed. Chris hoped he wouldn't have to bow to anyone for a long time. A throbbing pain pulsed on the left side of his head. He pressed his hands against his temples, massaging them in a circular pattern. It didn't help.

An older, frail-looking nurse entered with tea and slices of oranges on a green plate. She set them on the table beside his bed, then took a thermometer from the pocket of her white frock. Without speaking she took his temperature and listened to his heart with her stethoscope. He stared at the poster on the wall showing chambers of the heart and the circulatory system. She seemed satisfied with results and bowed herself out of the room.

Chris woke sluggishly. He had slept soundly and only slowly regained his bearings. His eyes focused on the empty teacup and he wondered if he'd been drugged. There was no way to gauge the time or how long he had slept. His watch and wallet hadn't been returned to him.

A thin fluorescent bulb blinked sporadically, perhaps dying, in his windowless room. It could have been day; it could have been the dead of night. He got out of bed and realized his uniform and shoes were gone. Standing in his boxer shorts and T-shirt he approached the door and slowly turned the handle. He assumed it would be locked and jerked it open with more force than needed. A young female nurse gasped at the sight of him. Her eyes grew wide. She placed her hand in front of her mouth to stifle a giggle, then turned quickly and hurried to the nursing station.

He looked down, realized he was in his underwear, and slowly backed into his room, brushing the door shut with his arm. Within a minute a young doctor appeared. He extended his arm, pointing at the bed, directing Chris to get under the covers. Chris pointed to his own wrist then lifted his palm up in a questioning fashion. The doctor shrugged. Chris repeated the gestures. A glimmer of recognition came over the physician and he held his arm out so Chris could read his watch: Eight Twenty AM. Morning. He must have slept fourteen hours.

The doctor pointed to the bed again. Chris climbed under the covers and gave the doctor a look that said, *Fine! Are you happy?* The physician nodded contentment and left.

Chris got out of bed and paced around the room. He used the bedpan to relieve himself. His back was stiff from too many hours in bed. He arched and stretched, then flexed every muscle he could. He stretched through the pain and decided he had recovered well enough for push-ups. He had to stop after thirty. He felt out of kilter, as if disconnected from his body. The sit-ups would have to wait.

Soon Yi arrived an hour later, breathless and excited to explain that Chris would be attending a state dinner with Kim Jong Il himself. Chris raised his eyebrows, stunned. He wondered if she was playing with him. She assured him it was true, that a great honor would be bestowed upon him. He thought about Maureen, and felt an urgent need to call her. Again, they told him it would have to wait a day or two.

17 JAPAN CALLING

Maureen had just pulled into the garage of her Virginia home. She balanced two bags of groceries and leaned against the door so she could turn the handle without having to put the bags down, then gave the door a quick sideways push with her hip. It swung open just as her cell phone buzzed. Groceries were quickly deposited on the counter and she retrieved the phone from her purse.

"Hi, this is Maureen."

A woman on the other end explained she was calling from Japan. She told Maureen that Chris was still on assignment at sea but would be getting some R&R in ten days. Chris had asked her to call Maureen and make all the arrangements so she could join him for a brief vacation in Tokyo.

"The Navy will fly you, space-available, to Japan and provide all your lodging and meals. He would have called himself, but he's off site and isn't permitted to communicate. I'm sure you understand."

"Tokyo? When? Yes! I mean, I think so. I have to see if I can get time off. Our son's in preschool; is Chris expecting Joey to make the trip?"

"That's your decision, but I think he's hoping for a second honeymoon. He may want you all to himself," she giggled. "Tell me about your boy."

Maureen talked about Joey, and how quickly he was growing. "Chris has missed so much."

"His leave begins in ten days and he has up to two weeks' free time available."

"Oh, my God, this is so quick. Yes! Tell him yes … I think. Let me talk to my office about getting away. I also need to talk to my parents about our son. When can I get back to you?"

"I can call tomorrow, at this same time, if you like."

"Yes, that'll be fine. Same time tomorrow."

As soon as she hung up she thought: *I should bring Joey. He's hardly seen his father at all.* But the thought of a romantic getaway, just the two of them, some adult time, was hard to resist. She would have to think that through.

Her manager might not give her the time off. She'd have to settle that before saying anything to Joey or her parents. It was exciting to think of being with Chris again. Maureen reached into the groceries, pulled out a bag of Doritos, and tugged from each side to open it. The first chip nearly reached her mouth when she stopped. *I can't be eating,* she thought. *I've only got a few days to get myself in better shape.*

Maureen's boss resisted the idea, but relented when Mo promised she'd work straight through Christmas with no time off. She also agreed to limit her trip to eight days.

With that settled, Maureen called her parents. Joey was still so young. The trip might not be all that meaningful to him anyway at his age, and he would have fun with his grandparents. They welcomed the chance to have him all to themselves. Maureen hoped they truly understood how much energy it takes to keep up with a four-year-old boy.

That evening her phone rang right on time. The Japanese woman said all the details would be taken care of. Most likely she would be flown to San Diego for the first leg of her trip and then transfer to the longer flight to Japan. The woman asked if Maureen had any allergies or food restrictions. She asked for contact information for the person they should call if an emergency arose. Maureen provided all of that and got assurances she would have the final details within a day or two. When the call ended, she tapped the Photos button and swiped through pictures of her and Chris at Annapolis, in New York City, and St. Martin. She lingered longest over a picture of Chris asleep on the sofa with baby Joey in his arms.

Maureen woke at five the next morning to get in a run while her son was still asleep. After dropping Joey at kindergarten, she started thinking about her wardrobe, deciding to spend lunch hours shopping for an outfit or two. She hadn't paid attention to fashion in a long time, at least not her own. At a stoplight, she tilted the rearview mirror down to look at herself, fluffed her hair out with her fingers, and decided to call her salon as soon as she got to work.

Another call from Japan came the next night. The woman talked with Maureen for over half an hour, describing the accommodations in Tokyo and the attractions the city had to offer. Since their time would be limited, Chris had asked the woman to determine what Maureen would most like to see and do. Maureen said she really didn't care what they did as long as they were together. She couldn't help getting excited as the woman talked of all the possibilities they might explore. She explained that Maureen would need to fax a copy of her driver's license and passport to the base at San Diego so she could be quickly transitioned for the flight to Japan. She gave her the fax number, and Maureen happily complied. The woman confirmed that a car would be sent to pick Maureen up on the morning of her departure.

18 DINNER WITH KIM

Christopher had been given his uniform again, freshly cleaned and ironed. His shoes had a bright coat of polish, and his belt buckle had been freshly shined. Soon Yi waited for him in the hallway. She wore a more formal gown, and seemed nervous. Chris was surprised to feel so calm about such an important meeting. Things felt a bit out of whack, floating, and he wondered if he'd been sedated.

"You are only American to meet Precious Leader since your Secretary of State, Madame Albright's official visit back in 2000."

Chris knew about that trip. It had been preceded by a trip to Washington by Kim's chief deputy. Talks were held on providing aid to North Korea in exchange for their abandoning their nuclear ambitions. Madeleine Albright had flown to Pyongyang ten days later to encourage a nuclear-free Korean Peninsula. She carried a personal letter from President Clinton and held two days of talks and open ceremonies aimed at improving relations. The efforts looked promising at first, but North Korea proved intransigent. Madeleine Albright later recalled she'd worn particularly tall high heels to appear taller and intimidate Kim, but he had worn higher heels and they were equal in height—on equal footing, so to speak.

Chris still wasn't the slightest bit nervous about meeting Kim. He wasn't sure he believed the meeting would actually take place. But he thought he should be feeling some anxiety, and felt suspicious of his own tranquility. Nevertheless, he resolved to stay sharp, eager to use his intelligence training to gather all information possible from any such encounter.

The Mercedes awaited them at the curb. A group of cameramen gathered around, taking still shots and video as he and Soon Yi walked from the hospital to the car. Bright lights and the whirring sound of cameras assaulted them. Chris remembered seeing some of the same videographers at the children's performance.

The ride went quickly. Two police cars with lights flashing preceded them as they sped down nearly empty streets. He thought he should see lights coming on in more of the buildings, but most remained dark. They pulled up to a large concrete building that stood out by being brightly lit like a Hollywood opening. Two rows of soldiers stood at attention along each side of a red carpet, stretching from their car up the imposing steps to the massive double doors of the building. As he stepped from the car the soldiers saluted in unison. Chris hesitated, studying them. The hats above their rigid salutes looked like muffin tops. He glanced at Soon Yi, who nodded encouragement and he awkwardly returned a brief salute.

Soon Yi took his arm as they climbed the stairs. Halfway up, she placed her right hand on his upper arm, turned slightly toward Chris and gave him an exuberant smile, like a child excited by a gift. She briefly rested her head on his shoulder. He paused a half step, stiffened a bit, and continued on. Once inside, two men in heavily decorated uniforms greeted them. They saluted Chris and waited patiently until he returned the courtesy.

"The Supreme Leader awaits you," one said in halting English. Chris doubted the man understood the words he said.

"I am looking forward to meeting him." He received a blank stare from each of them. They clicked their heels, made a smart turn, and marched down the long corridor in slow, goose-step fashion. Chris and Soon Yi followed. When they came to another set of large doors, two guards saluted and immediately opened them, revealing an impressive room lit by rows of sparkling chandeliers. Chris eyed banquet tables occupied by stiff military officers and official-looking party leaders. As they entered, someone spoke quietly to Soon Yi. She nodded and bowed, then told Christopher she would be waiting for him after dinner.

A soldier led him to the front of the hall and up a short set of stairs to a platform and a place of honor at the center of the main table, next to two empty chairs. The whole assembly rose as he approached. A red velvet curtain opened behind Chris, and Kim Jong Il himself stepped out, standing right next to him. The room erupted in prolonged applause. Chris couldn't help snapping to attention. Although the curtain was red, the sight of Kim at five feet two wearing platform shoes got Chris thinking of the *Wizard of Oz.*

Kim basked in the enthusiasm for a full minute before holding both arms up to signal silence. He turned and, instead of bowing, reached out and grasped Chris by the hand. Chris found himself bowing as they shook. A man at Kim's right spoke in English, welcoming Chris. He explained that the Great Leader had a message for him. He then turned to Kim who spoke in Korean. His message, as translated, stressed he was glad to have rescued an officer of the US Navy and, even though The Democratic People's Republic of Korea represented the strongest military force on earth, it could also be benevolent.

He said he understood Christopher had seen some of his capital city, their beautiful gardens, and talented children. He hoped that Chris would enjoy his stay. Chris smiled and said he was grateful to have been rescued. "Your gardens are quite beautiful," he said, "and you have been most gracious to me."

Kim settled into his chair, and everyone sat in unison. A waiter appeared with a bottle of Hennessy cognac. Chris recalled a footnote in an intelligence briefing that Kim spent up to $800,000 a year on Hennessy at over $600 a bottle while the average North Korean lived on $900 a year. He had been Hennessy's largest customer for the past ten years. Kim drained his glass, which the waiter immediately refilled.

Chris took mental notes of everything: the number and rank of officers, the security detail around the room, the bureaucrats and the level of deference each paid to one another. Kim asked Chris questions about his family and about his service in the Navy. Chris deflected the questions as best he could by talking about his medical care and how kind the doctors and nurses had been to him.

Kim persisted. He bragged about the North Korean Navy.

"We still have your intelligence ship." Kim boasted through his interpreter.

Chris felt stunned. *What ship could they have?* They certainly couldn't have his last ship, the *Kitty Hawk*, and the ship he had been heading for, the *USS Patriot*, was nowhere near Korean waters.

"Your Navy surrendered without a fight. I have personally pissed on the deck of your ship." Kim laughed loudly.

Chris thought, "This guy really *is* crazy."

"Perhaps you would like to visit her. She is docked right here in Pyongyang on the Taedong River."

Chris relaxed, realizing Kim had been bragging about the *USS Pueblo*, which North Korea seized in 1968. It had indeed been a US Naval intelligence ship, intercepted in international waters by two North Korean sub chasers, four torpedo boats, and the threatening presence of MiG-21 fighters. Two Americans had been killed by gunfire from torpedo boats. The remaining eighty-two members of the crew were captured and held in prison camps for eleven months before being marched, single file, over the bridge to South Korea, a span North Koreans call the 'Bridge to Nowhere.'

"It is one of our most popular tourist attractions," Kim said. "Perhaps you would like to visit it."

"That was a long time ago," Chris said, smiling nervously to the interpreter

"Yes, and our military is much stronger now." Kim smiled back.

The meal dragged on with several courses of fish, meats, wines, and pastries. As it drew to an end, Kim stood, raised his glass and spoke loudly in Korean. Just before tilting the glass to Christopher it sounded as if he said the words, "Maureen" and "Joey."

The interpreter conveyed Kim's wishes that Chris would enjoy his stay in their country. He praised Chris for responding so well to North Korean healing and hospitality. Kim hoped his wife, Maureen, and his son, Joey, would be happy to see him again soon.

Chris rose on slightly shaky knees, concerned that Kim knew the names of his wife and child. He raised his glass and thanked the Dear Leader for his hospitality. "I am pleased and grateful for all you have done for me."

After dinner Kim exited to a loud ovation. Chris was escorted down a long corridor to a room at the rear of the building. Only one soldier and the interpreter accompanied him inside. It was decorated as an ornate bedroom. They offered him a cigar and cognac, which he declined. Two young women, perhaps not yet 18, were ushered in and seated on a long red sofa. They wore matching silk dresses and orchid corsages on their wrists. They smiled, though their bodies were tense.

"They are for your enjoyment," the interpreter offered.

"Very kind, but I must decline," he said firmly, shaking his head, and stepping back toward the door.

"You should enjoy all our country has to offer. It is a gift from our leader. Something you should not decline."

"I'm grateful, but my health is still poor. May I return to the hospital please?"

The interpreter flashed a mix of disappointment and anger. He grumbled something with a menacing tone to the soldier, who then showed Chris back out into the hallway.

The following afternoon, Soon Yi took Christopher to an opera performed with great energy. Chris had never been a fan of opera. He recalled his high school performance in *The Pirates of Penzance*. That had been fun. This sounded excruciating. He didn't understand the language. Their music seemed discordant, and his back pain grew worse with every song. He was relieved when intermission came—hoping the show had ended—but Soon Yi assured him there would be more. She also told him he would be introduced to the audience at the beginning of the next act. "We are proud to have you here. Our people are eager to see a real American."

Despite the late afternoon, Chris noticed, again, that lights weren't coming on everywhere. He heard a lone generator sputter to life next to the theatre. When they returned to their seats the interpreter from the state dinner awaited. He explained that the opera director would make some brief comments welcoming him and that it would be polite for Christopher to rise and acknowledge the audience. A bright smile and a happy wave would be appropriate.

The interpreter had barely finished his briefing when a man at center stage addressed the audience with authority and enthusiasm. The interpreter explained that the audience was learning Kim Jong Il had rescued Chris. The Dear Leader wanted him to enjoy the best of Korean culture.

The audience rose, erupting in prolonged applause, all eyes directed on him in his box. Chris rose dutifully, smiled broadly, and waved cheerfully, but felt foolish. He wished he could return to his hospital bed, ached to be back in America, to be home.

19 QUESTIONS IN THE NIGHT

At four o'clock in the morning a swift-moving caravan of black SUVs raced through the streets of Vienna, Virginia, converging on Maureen's home; bright lights, red, blue and white, flashed through the neighborhood. A SWAT team, in full battle gear, surrounded the house, while a squad of eight men and two women stormed the front. A battering ram crashed through the wooden door, splintering it open. Agents rushed inside, guns and flashlights sweeping every room.

Maureen sat up in bed, startled and afraid. Before she could move, three agents burst into her room. They pulled her to her feet and screamed at her that she was under arrest. She heard boots clomping throughout the house.

"What are you doing?" she pleaded. "My son's asleep!" She tried to wrench her elbow free but couldn't escape the firm grasp of a female agent. Cuffs were slammed onto her wrists.

"Maureen McCarty? Mrs. Christopher McCarty?"

"Yes! What's this? What are you doing?"

"Maybe you want to tell us about your husband."

"Tell you what? He's not here. My husband's in the Navy, serving in Japan! What the hell's going on?"

"You tell us, lady! Why is your husband betraying our country?"

"Are you nuts? He's a military officer. He's *protecting* the country. Where's my son?"

"We have him. He's safe, and we're taking you into custody."

"Custody? No! Tell me what's going on. You've no right to take me and my son. This is a huge mistake!"

"You're the one who's made a mistake, lady. Just so you know, we're going to tear this house apart. Everything in here, everyone you know, anyone you've ever talked to, and any email or computer you've ever touched is ours. Put her in the car."

"You can't do that! You don't have any right to barge in here …"

"In the car!"

She planted her feet and twisted her body to escape the agent's grasp, but only ended up wrenching her arm.

"I'm in a nightgown, you goon!"

"Should have thought of that before you turned traitor."

They'd already agreed to take her out in whatever she wore. It would make her more vulnerable, giving them more control.

"Where's my son? You have to let me see Joey!"

"When you start cooperating we'll think about letting you see your boy."

Maureen was hustled out of the house and into the back of one of the SUVs. A smaller group had already descended on her parents' home. Other teams were converging on Anne McCarty's home in Connecticut along with the homes of each of Christopher's brothers. No one spoke to her on the ride into DC, nor would they answer any of her questions. She cried and fumed, and prayed.

Crossing the Potomac over the Memorial Bridge, she stared at the Jefferson Memorial brightly lit against the dark night, a sight that had always made her feel patriotic, but now made her nervous and queasy. At the DC field office, a parade of agents led her down a long hallway into a conference room.

"This is an enormous mistake! Call the Office of Naval Intelligence. They'll tell you my husband's on duty—serving this country. His father died in the World Trade Center, for God's sake! How can you be doing this?"

An agent forced her into a chair and reached for a remote control on the conference table. He clicked the television to CNN.

Maureen was stunned by what she saw: her husband in a garden with an attractive Korean woman. She kissed him on both cheeks. They were watching a children's performance. She saw them sitting on bleachers surrounded by North Korean officials, smiling and applauding. Her husband and the young woman seemed to enjoy cherry blossoms together. The woman put petals in his shirt pocket. Chris offered the woman a purple flower. The film showed Chris in a crowded theater, smiling and waving to a standing ovation. Next, it cut to Christopher in full uniform, saluting a double line of North Korean soldiers. The pretty woman at his side, smiling and resting her head on his shoulder. Finally, her husband seated at a banquet with the actual leader of North Korea, offering each other toasts, with Chris smiling throughout.

"Your husband has defected to North Korea. We know you have plans to join him."

"This is nuts. That video is a fake. If you knew my husband ..."

"We have a translation of Kim's speech. He's welcoming your husband to North Korea, saying how happy he is that a naval officer is willing to leave his own country behind for the glory of life in The People's Democratic Republic of Korea. He's naming you and your son as eager to join them in Pyongyang."

"That's absurd!"

"And I suppose all your phone calls from North Korea were absurd too?"

"What calls? I've never talked with anyone from North Korea. That's bullshit!"

"Your phone records say otherwise. We know you're planning to leave the country."

Maureen remained speechless for a full minute, remembering her calls from Japan, watching the screen and hearing reporters talk about her husband, speculating on why he'd betray America. The video clips began to roll again in an endless loop.

"Would you like some water, Mrs. McCarty?"

"I'd like to see my son! Now! I have a right to see my son."

"We'll see. Why don't you tell us what you know?"

"Know? I don't know anything. We are going to meet in Japan. He has a leave coming up, and I'm going to join him in Tokyo. Please, you have this all wrong." She buried her head in her hands. Her elbows rested on the table and she appeared to shrink down into it.

"I want to call my parents. My father's an officer with the State Department."

"No calls just yet. We'll see." The agent's eyes were on her breasts that were barely covered by her thin nightgown.

"Can I please at least have a blanket or a coat ... and some coffee?" She folded her arms across and chest and turned sideways to obscure his view.

"Sure." He motioned with his hand, and an agent left the room.

"Let's start at the beginning. Now, why don't you tell us where you and your husband met?"

"Where did we meet? We met at the US Naval Academy, for God's sake. All he's ever talked about is how he wants to protect America. You have this all wrong. If he's in North Korea, he's been kidnapped!"

"He doesn't look very kidnapped to us, Mrs. McCarty. He seems quite happy as a matter of fact. Look, let's not play games here. He's obviously defected. You can either help us, or you can spend the rest of your life behind bars."

"Jail? I haven't done a goddamned thing. This is so stupid!"

"When's the last time you heard from your husband, ma'am?"

"Three weeks ago, maybe two, I don't know. He was fine. We mostly talked about our son. He said food on an aircraft carrier is surprisingly good, and we talked about his mother and my parents. That's it! No big secrets, nothing conspiratorial."

A man arrived with a blanket, a Styrofoam cup of coffee, two packets of fake cream, a packet of fake sugar, and a red plastic stirring stick. She wrapped her fingers around the cup as if it were a prized possession. The agent draped the blanket over her shoulders.

"We understand. You're young, you're in love, you have a little boy, and maybe your husband convinced you he's doing the right thing. But it's over. You're not going anywhere and, based on the woman he's with in those pictures, it looks like he's not exactly waiting for you."

20 AN OFFER TO SERVE

Chris, in pain and exhausted after the state dinner, reviewed every second of the event, wanting to be as clear as possible during his debriefing. He assumed he'd be questioned on board a plane bound either for the States or Japan. He was focusing on whether Kim showed any signs of illness or infirmity as the same frail nurse arrived, bringing tea and orange slices. Chris looked up and smiled but vowed not to touch anything she brought. He wanted his mind as sharp as possible.

He had a hard time getting to sleep, wondering if he might actually be playing a small role in improving U.S.-North Korean relations. He thought of the few peasants he had seen, frail and downtrodden. If North Korea rejoined the real world, their lives could be greatly improved. He held that thought until sleep finally came.

Within minutes, four soldiers, two on each side of his bed, woke him abruptly. Soon Yi, reached down slapping his shoulder.

"Wake up, American. It's your time to serve."

Chris rolled over, raising his arm to block any other blow. He sat part way up and turned to see her, freezing as he realized it was Soon Yi, dressed in a military uniform. Her hair was drawn back tightly under her military cap, giving her stern expression an even more austere look. He flinched involuntarily, moving back away from her. *She's an officer, about mid-rank,* he realized.

"Our Supreme Leader has an offer for you."

Her facial expression remained strictly cold and official, the delicate, pretty, Soon Yi completely gone.

Chris sat up to evaluate her new look. He had a sick feeling in his stomach as he realized she had been playing him. He tried to remember if anything he'd told her could have been inappropriate or dangerous. Nothing significant stood out.

"An offer from Kim Jong Il?"

"And from all the citizens of our great Republic." She looked smug.

"What kind of offer?"

"We offer you our sanctuary and asylum from your country in exchange for information about your navy."

Chris laughed. "What are you, nuts? I don't want sanctuary here. I want to go home, and I certainly don't have any naval information to share."

"Too bad. Perhaps you change your mind today."

"And why would I do that?"

She looked at one of the soldiers who held a bundle of clothes, which he placed on the table next to the bed.

"Get dressed. We have something to show you." They turned and marched out of his room.

Chris looked at the clothes. They were typical dark North Korean style. The pants were too short, ending well above his ankles. He put them on, along with a pair of sandals, and opened the door to the hallway. Four soldiers standing guard outside his room escorted him down the corridor, up a flight of stairs, and into a medical library. Soon Yi waited for him at the door, signaling the guards to place him in a chair at the end of a table. They took up positions standing immediately beside and behind him. Soon Yi turned on a television, its video paused on a picture of him toasting Kim Jong Il.

"Now, this is where you choose the rest of your life. Your country already sees you as a traitor. Your wife's been arrested. You have no way to leave our country, and only one way to live."

"What the hell …?"

"Let me show you what your country has been watching." She pressed the remote, activating the video. He watched scenes of himself apparently enjoying North Korean hospitality. He winced at pictures of Soon Yi kissing his cheeks, and the image of her bestowing cherry blossoms and flowers on him. Next, he saw himself getting out of a Mercedes and saluting a line of North Korean soldiers. Then video of him cheerfully waving to an enthusiastic audience, that gave him a standing ovation. Finally, footage of him dining with Kim Jong Il, exchanging toasts with each other.

At the state dinner, Chris had felt responsible for representing the United States favorably. He wanted to convey a sense of professional friendliness showing respect for his hosts. Now, on screen, he looked like an over-eager new convert enjoying the company of North Korea's top leadership. He could be heard clearly saying, *"You have been most gracious to me."*

"We have explained to the world that you seek asylum here. Look! Our Gracious Leader is welcoming you to The Democratic People's Republic of Korea, and you are smiling and toasting him. You even toasted when Leader Kim raised his glass to the destruction of the United States."

"I did not!"

"Oh, but you did." She pressed the remote control and the film backed up to the point where the dinner toasts had begun. "Here, this is the toast. Do you see your smile? The whole world has seen it now."

"No one will believe that! It's pure nonsense."

"They already believe it. The whole world believes it. Kim Jong Il has told the world press of your long conversations and all the information you have shared with him. He's happy to grant you and your family protection from the American government."

"That's total bullshit! Maybe you've forgotten that the Red Cross interviewed me. Their observer knows I didn't defect. He knows this is a lie."

"Oh, Mr. Brandt, yes, I forgot. He had a nice talk with you. You gave him your wife's phone number, so very kind of you. We have spoken with her several times. Several calls from our country to your home; what will your CIA make of that I wonder? The Red Cross has never been here."

Chris' hands felt moist and clammy. He erupted in a ferocious anger.

"You can't get away with this! There's no way people will believe it, certainly not my wife, certainly not my government. I demand to call my State Department. I am an American citizen and an officer in the United States Navy! Believe me there will be major consequences."

"Consequences? Will America launch an attack against the invincible Korean military, for a *traitor*? Will they risk that against one million Korean soldiers? I think not. Mr. Christopher, you are here for life. You must decide how long that life will be. Allow me to show you something else."

She pressed the remote control and Chris saw a convoy of black SUVs, lights flashing, pulling up to his home in Virginia. The film quality wasn't as good as the other footage, probably shot by a cell phone. He watched as the door to his house shattered and agents streamed in. The film paused and then his wife, in only her nightgown, was paraded out in handcuffs and pressed into the back on an SUV. An agent emerged with Joey in her arms, and they disappeared into another vehicle.

"Your wife looks quite beautiful." Soon Yi handed Chris a copy of Maureen's passport and driver's license. "Yes, very attractive. Too bad your house is not secure. It's so easy to find. We may want to visit with her if the CIA turns her loose. If you give us no choice, that is. Maybe we talk to your little boy, too."

Chris shot up, trying to stand, but the soldiers pressed him firmly back down. He forced his arms up, trying to loosen their grasp. "Get your goddamned hands off me!" Two soldiers slammed him down with heavy thrusts on his shoulders. He put both hands on the table and tried to quickly push himself out of the chair, only to be forced down again. A guard placed his hand firmly behind Christopher's head forcing it onto the table. Chris turned so he was lying on his ear, glaring across the table's surface at Soon Yi.

"You have a choice. We offer you a life here, a good life, with a home and a garden. You will be honored guest, a hero who has chosen Korea over America. You will be allowed to live freely and openly and will only have to pose for photographers and answer some questions we have about your navy."

The guard loosened his grip, allowing Chris to sit up, while others held him firmly by his shoulders.

"This is bullshit! You can't be serious."

"Your other choice is something I believe you Americans call *enhanced interrogation*. Your family will be in danger. We have ways of reaching out, and your country is so open." She smiled coldly. "It is your choice."

"And if I cooperate you'll parade me in front of cameras like a monkey for the rest of my life. No thanks!"

"Too bad, I had grown fond of you. Perhaps you still can change your mind."

She signaled to the guards who hoisted him out of the chair. He twisted sharply, trying to free his arms, but they roughly subdued and handcuffed him. A doctor approached carrying a hypodermic needle and, with no apparent emotion, punched the needle into Chris' arm, depressing the plunger. Just for an instant, Chris saw something different on Soon Yi's face. It looked like shame. Chris felt a momentary nausea, his knees buckled, and he blacked out.

21 BOXING IN THE DARK

He awoke on a cold concrete floor wearing only his boxer shorts, in a room hopelessly dark. Chris could barely sense the outline of a metal door to his left. He steadied one hand on the ground and struggled to his feet, leaning on the solid immovable door. He felt along its surface and realized there wasn't a handle or a knob on his side. Turning inward, he tried to make out the contents of the room. His eyes adjusted to the darkness just enough to see the shape of something low against the back wall. He bent down, reaching out his arms, slowly sweeping them back and forth. His groping hands encountered a thin, lumpy mat. It smelled of urine and mold. He began methodically searching along the walls to determine what else could be there. The only other feature, an open hole in the floor about the size of a soft ball. From the smell, he realized it was to be his toilet.

Chris felt despair mixed with fear. More than anything else, he felt ashamed. How could he have been so stupid? A trained intelligence officer falling for that crap about improving relations between the US and North Korea! Chris realized he'd probably been drugged to some extent ever since arriving in Pyongyang.

He slid into a sitting position with his back pressed against the wall, his elbows resting on his knees. The video images ran through his head in an unending circuit. Most painful of all were the pictures of Maureen being led from the house in handcuffs, and little Joey disappearing into a black SUV. He had caused that. He had let himself be used, and now she and his son would pay the price, probably for the rest of their lives.

And then he thought of his mother. My God, what must she be thinking?

She had been so proud of him, and now she too would have to endure this. He had to find a way out, a way to tell everyone that this was all a lie. He wanted to cry but instead knelt and began to pray.

"Heavenly Father, I need Your help. I thank you for my family, for my wife and son. I pray that You comfort and protect Maureen, Joey, and my mother. Please, Father, if it is Your will, Lord, I ask that You give me strength and wisdom to withstand what is ahead of me, and I pray that You provide me a pathway home."

While making the sign of the cross, a priest's voice came to him as it always had after confession, admonishing him to say four Our Fathers and three Hail Marys. So he did. The prayers helped restore a tiny degree of reason and courage. In the quiet darkness, he heard his father's voice again: *"Expect great things of yourself and make your own world great."* That seemed hopeless here, but he resolved to survive this, no matter what.

Chris stood and felt his way to the door. He pounded on it, loud and hard. "Hey, who's out there? Let me out. Hey! I'm awake in here."

No one replied. Over the next several hours he repeated the drill. Pounding on the door, shouting for help. No one answered. No one came. His throat felt parched and his stomach empty. There wasn't a sink in the cell. He searched in vain hoping to find a water source, but found none. Eventually he collapsed onto the mat and fell asleep.

Chris dreamed he attended the state dinner with Kim Jong Il again. Only this time, when Kim raised his glass, the ceiling shattered and US Special Forces descended on ropes, tossing smoke grenades and firing machine guns into the crowd. Kim's head exploded. The room went deathly quiet, but then music began to play. North Korean children danced into the room, jumping and twirling. They smiled sweetly at Chris and beckoned him to follow out into a garden bathed in sunlight, flowing with cherry blossoms and butterflies. Maureen sat on a bench beneath a cherry tree holding Joey on her lap. His son looked up squealing with delight. He broke free from Maureen and ran into Christopher's outstretched arms.

When he opened his eyes, they were wet with tears. He stared into the blackness, feeling an urgent need to escape, not so much from the cell, but from himself.

Hours ticked by in silent darkness. He heard his own heartbeat and felt blood pulsing in his veins. He should have been hungry but wasn't. After so long without food, the body seemed content to abstain. Thirst became another matter. He probed the walls with his fingers, desperate to find moisture, hoping a trickle of water would dribble down from the ceiling or pool up from the floor. He found nothing but hard cold dryness.

Chris was on all fours, probing a corner, when he heard footsteps outside his door. He turned as it clanged open. Bright light from the hallway flooded his eyes. He shielded them with his arm as he stood. Three dark silhouettes in the doorway came into view.

A general flanked by two officers stood, evaluating Chris. The officer crossed his arms in front of his chest, covering an impressive display of medals and ribbons. His face reminded Chris of something his father once told him during a hunting trip. Animals of prey have large round eyes on the side of their heads to watch for predators. Predators have eyes in the front to focus on what they want to kill. This general was clearly a predator, and his eyes were focused sharply on Chris.

The officer surprised him by speaking in English. "Our country has offered you great honor. You have insulted us and offended our Dear Leader for no good purpose. You must know you cannot leave Korea. We offered you a life here. Perhaps you can still have it. Perhaps not."

"I'm a citizen of the United States of America and an officer in the United States Navy! I'm entitled to rights under international law."

"You're entitled to nothing. You're under the supreme law of the Democratic People's Republic of Korea. International law has no place here. We can do whatever we want to you."

"I have nothing to say."

"Allow me to be blunt, Officer McCarty. Kim Jong Il has told the world you've sought asylum here. It suits his purpose to embarrass America, and he wants only to film you from time to time attending public events. I want only the most basic information about your military. Information you can easily provide. In exchange, you can live. Perhaps someday your wife and son can join you here."

"Allow *me* to be blunt. Everyone in your country has lied to me from the moment I woke up in this fairyland. Everyone! I've no reason to believe anything you say and no reason to satisfy your Little Leader's whims."

The general looked at the officer on his left and nodded. The soldier struck Chris so quickly he couldn't react. Blood began to trickle from his lips. The general barked an angry order to the aide and Chris thought he would be hit again. Instead the general lowered his voice and explained, "He isn't to hit your face. We want you looking good. But he will hit you again, somewhere else, if you insult Chairman Kim."

Chris stepped back rubbing his arm against his lips. "I would look better if I had some water. Kim might be angry if you allow me die of thirst and starvation."

"You will have all you want to drink, anything you want to drink, if you cooperate. Or you can waste away in darkness. A simple decision, really, don't you think?"

"You're right, General. It *is* an easy decision. Don't let the door hit you on the way out!"

The general stiffened and started to say something, but thought better of it. He turned and left, with his aides in close pursuit. The door banged shut. A loud click confirmed it was securely locked. Darkness swallowed the cell again.

Chris lowered his head onto his chest, clenched his fists, and began to slowly bang his forehead with them. Then he let out a loud, angry scream and punched the air in fierce rapid jabs, a boxer fighting himself in the dark.

Ten minutes later he heard someone at the door. A metal grate slid open just above floor level followed by a scraping sound as a tray slid into the cell bearing a bowl of rice and a bottle of water.

Chris grabbed the bottle and downed most of it in a single swig. He stopped, deciding to save the last little bit, then sat with his back resting on the door, holding the bowl on his lap and scooping the rice into his mouth with his fingers. The rice was cold and stuck together like starchy glue.

He remembered an old joke: *The food in this place is terrible— and the portions are too small.*

Chris heard his father's voice again: *"Make your world great."* If he could have shot himself right then, he would have been happy to put a bullet through his head. He fell onto the thin mattress, curled into a ball, and cried himself to sleep.

Chris slept fitfully until something tickled his cheek. He woke but didn't move. He felt it again and sensed eyes were watching him. Very slowly he opened his own. He couldn't see anything. Then something cold and wet touched his arm. He jerked back as a large wet rat scampered over his bare chest back into the sewage hole. Chris sat bolt upright, breathing hard, staring into the dark nothing, his despair complete.

22 THE PRESS

Maureen had been questioned for twelve hours straight. She finally got permission to call an attorney who arrived and bluntly told the authorities to *"either charge her or let her go."*

The lead agent just laughed. "You don't understand, counselor. We don't have to let anyone go. We classify her as a terrorist—she never sees the light of day again—end of story! We allowed you here so you can talk some sense into her. Let her know there's no use in stalling. She has to cooperate with us."

Reports from the Office of Naval Intelligence coupled with findings from field interviews and naval officers were casting doubt on Chris' actions. There didn't seem to be any clear motive for him to defect. The Navy admitted they'd lost a helicopter and had been conducting a quiet search so as to not alert the North Koreans. They believed the chopper, and all on board, had been permanently lost and were preparing to notify next-of-kin.

Nevertheless, the phone calls Mrs. McCarty received from North Korea certainly indicated a conspiracy. After much internal discussion, they decided turning her loose and keeping her under surveillance would be more productive. Bugs were planted in her car, her office, and her parents' home. Tracking devices were attached to her cell phone, her watch, and even sewn into each purse she owned.

Two officers were assigned to drive her home. They escorted her to the basement and down a long brightly-lit hallway with highly polished floors to a room that looked like a child's nursery. Joey sat on a small blue beanbag chair in his Spiderman pajamas while a woman read to him from *Winnie the Pooh*.

"Hey, Buddy." She smiled through her exhaustion.

His eyes lit up and he bounded into her arms.

"We'll drive you home now, ma'am. He's been treated well."

She gave him an ice-cold stare.

Joey slept on his mother's lap in the back of the SUV while Maureen sat in stunned silence, trying to digest all she'd been through, trying to understand how they could be so wrong about Chris, how they could have gotten those pictures of him. She closed her eyes and sank into the leather seat with her head tilted back on the headrest, then fell heavily to sleep.

"Whoa, lady, you might want to wake up. Looks like you and the kid are about to be TV stars."

Maureen opened her eyes and realized they were almost at her house. Only it didn't look like home anymore. TV vans with ten-foot antennas and communication trucks crowded the street; klieg lights were casting an eerie yellow-green light onto her lawn and front door. A cluster of microphones nestled on stands near the front of her driveway.

As the SUV approached, more lights came on. Reporters rushed from vehicles like racehorses out of the gate. They swarmed her car, slapping the windows with their palms. She began to understand why they were called "the Press."

"Why'd your husband defect? What does he have against America? Do you agree with your husband, Mrs. McCarty? Did you know he was doing this?"

Reporters surrounded the SUV as it came to a halt. The driver pressed the horn and tapped the gas to disperse them from the front of the car.

"Oh, my God! You've got to help us get inside. Please, I can't get through them with Joey in my arms."

"We'll take care of it, ma'am." He turned on the siren and smiled as the crowd momentarily leapt back. He pulled onto the lawn, as close to the house as possible; then the two officers jumped out, opened her car door, and helped her exit. Maureen still wore only her nightgown. She held the blanket around her, with one hand clutching it to her chest. In her other arm, she held Joey up against her shoulder. "Stay close and keep your head down," they instructed and then blocked a pathway to her front door. The glazed-glass storm door had been locked, the wooden door behind it still splintered and crushed. Maureen realized she didn't have her keys. She slumped while hoisting Joey further up on her shoulder and screamed at the agent.

"We're trapped! Damn it! Do something!"

Questions were shouted from all directions as reporters surged closer. One of the agents with his back to her, facing the crowd, pulled a set of keys from his pocket and held them high for Maureen to see. She grabbed them in one swift motion, losing the blanket in the process, then quickly unlocked the glass door, pushed the broken front door open, and slid inside.

Joey stared, wide-eyed and frightened. Maureen carried him into the den, set him down, then sat on the sofa holding him and trying not to cry. "Hush, hon. It's okay. Mommy loves you. Let's get you some hot chocolate, then a nice long nap."

Her home phone rang. Maureen put Joey down and held his hand as they headed into the kitchen. She picked up the phone, assuming it would be her parents. Instead a reporter from *The Washington Post* said, "Mrs. McCarty, our readers will want your side of the story. What can you tell them?"

Maureen hung up. The phone immediately rang again. She reached behind the base unit and unplugged the cord from the wall.

"Joey, would you like some little marshmallows in your hot chocolate?"

"Yes, please." She brushed the top of his head with her hand, then knelt and looked him in the eyes.

106

"You're a good boy, Joey. I am so proud of you." She kissed his forehead and gave him a long desperate hug.

His voice, soft against her shoulder, asked, "Mommy, is Daddy a bad man?"

23 MARLA'S NEWS

Marla Jackson is the epitome of a dedicated military wife. She'd moved seven times with Calvin, always living on a Navy base, always volunteering to help military families navigate the ins and outs of service life. She raised their two sons nearly on her own while Calvin attended flight school, learned to fly choppers, and deployed to Desert Storm, Afghanistan, Iraq, and now the Pacific Fleet in Japan.

She and the boys would have joined him in Japan, but Raymond still had another year of high school and Spencer had just started Duke on a partial basketball scholarship. The boys had attended eight different schools in six different states. She wouldn't consider another move until Raymond was firmly settled in college.

Getting him there would be a challenge. His older brother was bright, sociable, responsible, and athletic. Moving from school to school had always been a relatively smooth transition for Spencer, even when he and his brother were the only black kids in class. Raymond, on the other hand, was chubby, introverted, and awkward. Forming friendships had never been easy for him and, the few times that he had, were followed by another move to another state. The friendships never followed.

If Marla wasn't on him constantly, Raymond would hole up in his room listening to music, playing video games, and ignoring his homework. He had the ability to stretch out on his stomach in bed, headphones on, belting complex rap riffs, while deftly evading cops in "Grand Theft Auto." College remained only a dim hope on the horizon, but Marla would never give up on him.

Marla balanced her time with military precision. After getting Raymond fed and off to school each morning, she'd drive to the base library, where she hosted a group of volunteer wives in the basement collecting and sorting items for packages they'd send to soldiers on deployment. That would be followed by a quick bag lunch or a stop at the food court in the PX, and then a two-hour support group for both wives and husbands whose spouses were in combat theaters.

Marla had a special ability to give encouragement and hope, along with a realistic view of what families could expect of military life. She taught them various shortcuts and work-arounds to deal with the complexities of life on base, and ways to cope with the loneliness. She offered herself freely, which often encouraged people to call at all hours for help and private consultations.

Saturdays were taken up with laundry, essential chores, and mapping out Raymond's school assignments for the coming week. Sundays, she would drag him to church, which he hated, except for the part where his mother sang in the choir. She had a strong, clear voice with emotions of pure joy in the Lord. The congregation treasured her, and Raymond always felt a special pride in hearing her sing. It made up for the sermons and the fact that he had to wear a tie.

Sunday nights were always reserved for writing to Calvin. Not just emails and not just Skype, because those were regulars, but actual hand-written letters he could touch and fold and re-read wherever he happened to be. Marla and Raymond wrote from San Diego, and Spencer kept up the tradition, writing every week from Duke.

Marla sat composing her letter, agitated over an argument she'd had with Raymond. He'd been blaring music at the kitchen table when she heard the lyrics: *"I like to do the bitches; oh, I like it in their britches."* Marla slammed a hand onto the desk, launched herself out of the chair, and grabbed his iPod from the counter. She fumbled to turn it off, growing angrier as she realized she couldn't find an "off" button, and ended up throwing it across the room onto the sofa, demanding that Raymond shut it off.

Nothing made her madder than music or videos devaluing women. Raymond retrieved it, shut it off, and stormed into his bedroom, slamming the door. He fumed in his room while Marla fumed at her desk. Finally, she shook her head, pushed herself away from the desk and went to his room. She knocked on the door, then slowly entered and sat on the edge of his bed, her arm around his shoulders while they had a stilted, awkward conversation about respecting girls.

She returned to her Sunday night letter, waiting to calm down before writing the next line. Marla never wanted to convey anything that might cause Calvin worry, so she decided to write about the blossoms that were just budding on the lemon tree behind their small home.

The doorbell rang. Marla was accustomed to Navy wives showing up at all hours, sometimes in tears, needing help. She took a deep breath, rose slowly from her desk and approached the door, adjusting her hair on the way.

She managed an encouraging smile as she turned on the porch light and opened the door. In front of her stood a Navy captain, at attention holding his hat stiffly under his left arm. To his left the chaplain—her minister—stood with his hands clasped, his fingers entwined.

The captain spoke softly, "Mrs. Jackson. We have some news about your husband."

"Marla, it's not necessarily what you think," the chaplain said quickly.

They explained that Calvin's helicopter had gone down in the Sea of Japan. Every effort was being launched to find and rescue him. The chopper had gone down in a bad storm. It may be that they were blown far off course and could still be found. But she should know, it had been four days. His chances were slim.

Her knees wobbled, her hands went instinctively to her face, shielding her eyes, and she stumbled forward into the chaplain's arms. He braced her silently for several seconds and then said, "Marla, I know you believe in the power of prayer. It's time we talk with the Lord."

He helped her back inside, guiding her to the couch, but she gently pushed him aside and slowly weaved down the hall to Raymond's room, almost in a trance. He lay on his bed with headphones on. She slowly lifted them from his head. Raymond started to swipe her away until he saw her face and sunken posture.

"Baby, your Daddy is missing." She took his hand and led him back into the living room. The two of them knelt in front of the sofa with the minister, who led them in prayer while the captain stood awkwardly just inside the door. When he and the chaplain left, Marla started to tell Raymond that everything would be fine, but her voice trembled, and cracked. She wanted to encourage her son, but gave up all pretenses and collapsed, crying, in his arms.

24 FRIENDS REUNITED

Chris shivered, phasing in and out of sleep, when his cell door clanged open. Two soldiers grabbed him by the arms and hauled him into the corridor. He twisted, lifting his shoulders, trying to free his arms, but a guard jammed a metal rod into his ribs. His legs buckled as hands squeezed his armpits and lifted him forward. Soon Yi, dressed in her military uniform and looking very serious, asked if he had had enough time to change his mind

He boiled with rage, rage at Soon Yi, rage at the whole country of North Korea, and rage at himself. His Intelligence training, however, had taught him to stifle emotion. Chris was schooled in resisting torture—withstanding it really—and burying all traces of anger or fear.

He stared at her in silence, inhaling to catch his breath.

"Do you have anything to say?"

"Yes. How can you be doing this? How do you live with yourself?"

He thought he saw the briefest flicker of guilt. "You have much to learn," she said. "I think we'll start your education now." She nodded to the guards, who again grasped him by the arms and dragged him down the corridor to a solid door at the end.

Soon Yi used a large key to open it, and the guards shoved Chris inside. He fell forward, injuring his wrist and scraping the skin off his left knee. Soon Yi followed him in.

"I believe you know each other."

Christopher began to adjust to the darkness, sensing someone else in the cell. He could make out a man's head and realized it as a shape he recognized. He knew this man, but wasn't quite sure who he was. And then Calvin spoke.

"Holy shit! They told me you were alive, man. But I didn't believe 'em."

"Calvin, my God, I thought you were dead. I thought you died in the storm."

"A storm I could've flown through. We were hit by a rocket. I think they had a small boat with a rocket launcher. I don't know how they tracked us, but they did."

"Is anyone else alive?"

"I don't think so. They said you were alive, said you were defecting—which I *know* is total bull crap. They haven't said anything about anyone else."

"Are you two having fun?" Soon Yi asked.

The soldiers pulled Christopher to a standing position. Calvin remained seated awkwardly on his mat.

"So, I see you *are* friends," Soon Yi smiled. "Let's see if you are good friends."

The guards lifted Calvin to his feet. He screamed in pain.

"Oh, yes, your leg is broken. You might want to have that attended to, or you will surely lose that limb.

"You see, Officer McCarty? You are familiar with our excellent medical care. We can save your friend's leg, or it can fester and rot. You decide."

"Prisoners of war are entitled to rights under the Geneva Convention!"

"You're wasting time." She nodded at the guards who dropped Calvin. He shrieked as he collapsed onto the floor. "How would a pilot fly without a hand? I wonder. He seems to favor his right one. I think he will miss it when it is gone." She spoke to one of the soldiers, who drew a machete from a sheaf at his waist.

"Can you see what the major is holding? He won't hesitate to take an American hand. He rather enjoys it. If you like, we can put the hand in your cell to keep you company. A memento, so to speak. Yes?"

Chris stared hard, evaluating her. He'd been trained that threats like these were used to induce cooperation but rarely carried out. In this case, however, he had no doubt the North Koreans would relish a chance to hack an American apart, piece by piece.

The guards lifted Calvin again. He yelped in pain. They pushed his back against the wall and hoisted his right arm so that it rested against the wall at shoulder height. One guard held the arm firmly in place. Calvin turned his head away. The guard swung the blade.

"Wait! Hold it! Jesus Christ! Leave him alone. What do you want from us?"

The blade stopped an inch from Calvin's wrist.

"We want something only from you, Christopher, just you."

"Let him go. Easy! Put him down easy, and we can talk."

She spoke to the guards, who gradually released their grip, guiding Calvin slowly down the wall. The major looked disappointed as he slid the machete back into its sheaf.

"I'm okay, Lieutenant. Whatever they want, don't do it."

The guard bent and slapped Calvin. Blood trickled from just below his right eye.

Chris lurched toward him, but the guards blocked him. They turned him and dragged him out of the cell. He heard the metal door slam behind him as they forced him back to his cell. She stopped them just outside his door.

"We only ask a small thing. Leader Kim would have you talk to the news agency. You tell them how happy you are, and Calvin keeps his limbs. If that is too much for you, we will give parts of him to you, one piece at a time."

"I tell them I'm happy, and you agree to release Calvin. He goes home, and I talk to your press."

"Please don't assume to set terms. You're lucky we don't slice him to pieces in front of you. We will be back tomorrow to hear your answer. That might be too late for your friend's leg. Maybe not, we'll see."

The guards pushed Chris back into his cell, and the door slammed shut.

25 NEW HOPE

Reporters set up permanent camp outside Maureen's house. Her boss left a message. Maureen would remain on unpaid leave for the foreseeable future. No neighbors offered food or comfort. Perhaps they didn't want to fight through the reporters. Perhaps they wished she'd get the hell out of town. Death threats arrived by mail, email, phone, and by bricks aimed at her window.

Every so often she'd attach the phone cord to make a call on her land line. She called her parents who were also besieged, her mother nearly frantic. Her father seemed defeated but supportive.

"I know, Hon. it doesn't make sense. Your mother and I want to believe he isn't doing this. It's just that those pictures ... well, how do you explain the pictures? I mean, my God, he's toasting Kim Jong Il. The State Department and the CIA have grilled me non-stop. I think your mother's losing it."

"Come on, dad. Those pictures can't be real; probably Photoshopped. He must've been set up somehow, or brainwashed. You *know* Chris. You know this is wrong. It's just wrong! I hope you told them that. I hope you made it very clear."

"Of course I did. We both did. What can we do for you, Mo? You should come home, bring Joey, and stay here with us."

"Are the reporters still at your house, Dad?"

"We're under siege. Every time we open the door we're hit with a barrage of questions and an explosion of flashes.

They're like animals, really. They've no regard for decency, no respect."

"Maybe they'll get tired in a day or two, or another big story will break. If that happens, we'll come up."

"Do you have enough food? "

"Not much. It's running low. I hate going out in public. Joey's going stir crazy. He can only watch Sesame Street so many times. I can only read him the same stories over and over again … He asked me if his father is a bad man. It's breaking my heart."

"Well, you've got to get him out of there. You could go stay with your sister Joan. She and Ed would love to have you. I talked with her today. The CIA and the Navy have questioned her, but the reporters haven't latched on to her. I guess, since she uses her married name, the press hasn't made the connection."

"I couldn't do that to them. They've only been married three years, and I'd end up bringing the whole traveling circus with me."

"Seriously, think about it. They've a nice secluded home in Bucks County. They're on ten acres. Joey could run around; no one would know who he is. You'd both be safe and out of the way until this gets sorted out."

Maureen pictured her sister's house. It was an old stone colonial on farmland just outside New Hope, Pennsylvania. Joan adored the natural beauty of the place and its rich American history. George Washington had crossed the Delaware not far from her farm. Vice President Aaron Burr had lived in New Hope, as had author James Michener. Student radical Abbie Hoffman, who blazed so much controversy in the 1960s, took his life in an apartment in New Hope.

Her farm sits on a rolling green hill surrounded by a short stone wall. An apple orchard occupies one acre, and a rustic wooden barn shelters two very spoiled horses. It's an ideal country setting just 40 miles from Philadelphia. Maureen had to admit it would be the perfect hideaway.

She had a strong need to hide. Pictures of her were in every newspaper and magazine imaginable. A British tabloid ran the picture of Maureen in her nightgown with her hands cuffed behind her back. The headline read: *'American Traitor's Wife Apprehended.'*

Pictures from her high school and college yearbooks were on popular display, as were pictures of her returning home, her eyes flashing anger and her lips and jaw held tight as if she hated the world. There were interviews with neighbors and with college friends. Most said she seemed so normal, but kind of quiet, aloof. It's always the quiet ones.

After three more days with no let-up, Maureen devised a plan. She went online and purchased two airline tickets to Orlando, then called her office, telling them she was taking Joey to Disney World in case they might need her back at work. She called Robin who usually babysat for Joey.

"Just wanted to let you know I'm taking Joey to Disney World to get him out of here and give him a break. He needs some fun. Anyway, I wanted to let you know so you'd be free to sit for someone else if anything comes up."

She told her the date she'd be leaving, and how long she'd be gone. She even made of point of telling her which airline they were taking. Then she called her father again.

Four days later she awoke at five o'clock and got Joey out of bed. He was a sluggish lump, too sleepy to get out of his pajamas. She reminded him they were going on a special trip, and he came out of his haze. After breakfast of Cheerios and cinnamon toast, she gathered two suitcases she'd already packed: Joey's being bright red and blue with a smiling Nemo fish on the back, and hers a large black suitcase with a yellow ribbon around the handle. It belonged to Chris and held more than her usual bag.

An hour later a Lincoln town car pulled in front of her house. Its license plate read 'Airprt 4.' The driver had a hard time getting close to the house and called to let her know he'd arrived. She asked if he could come in to help with the bags, wanting the driver to put them in the car before she and

Joey made a dash for it. It turned out to be a good precaution. They barely made it in before being surrounded by reporters and photographers.

For the first time, she felt a little sorry for them. It must be hard to camp out on someone's yard for weeks at a time waiting for a fleeting glimpse of them, and frustrating to jostle each other in a mad competition for so little purpose. At least, she thought, now that I'm leaving town they can all go home.

Some would go home; others ran to their cars, following her all the way to Dulles Airport. They took turns pulling up beside her with video cameras rolling. She had Joey lie down on her lap, and kept her head turned away from the window. Once at the terminal, Maureen got out, holding Joey's hand while the driver pulled their bags out of the trunk. She tipped him well for having had to put up with her carnival act. Reporters emerged from their vehicles and started gathering around her.

"Are you joining your husband?"

"Where are you off to, Mrs. McCarty?"

"Have you and your husband been talking to each other?"

"Please, we just want some time to ourselves." She held her hand up, waist high, in an abbreviated 'stop' sign. Then she and Joey rushed into the terminal. Their boarding passes had been printed at home, so she held Joey's hand tightly and speed-walked directly to the security line. Reporters could follow only to that point, and occupied themselves shouting questions at her. Other passengers pointed at Maureen, some whispering to each other, some joining the reporters in shouting questions.

Joey clung to her, peering out from behind her legs.

Once in the concourse she took Joey to the women's room. They ducked into the large handicap stall with their luggage. Maureen explained that they were playing a trick on the reporters and would wear pretend costumes "just like Halloween." Joey liked the idea.

Maureen opened her large suitcase. A smaller, floral print one was tucked inside. It contained a gray wig, large glasses, clunky shoes, an ill-fitting dress, and an old woolen sweater. She just needed a little bend in her back to complete the image of a much older woman. Joey transformed into Batman, complete with cape and mask. She put his Nemo suitcase into her smaller floral print one, and they emerged, grandmother and grandson, off to see the world.

Maureen kept a hand on Joey's shoulder and ushered him past Gate C-7 with its sign for Orlando. They continued to C-12 and joined the passengers heading for Philadelphia. She felt sure someone from her office, or her babysitter, would soon have reporters searching Disney World for her.

Joan and Ed were at the airport to meet her, Joan on tiptoes trying to see over the crowd of new arrivals. An old lady with an odd little boy in a Batman costume approached.

"You seem like such a nice couple. Can you tell me how to get to New Hope?"

Joan's eyebrows shot up. "Oh, my God! Is that you, Mo?"

Maureen smiled triumphantly. Joan and Ed hugged her, then Joan bent down and hugged Joey.

"My very own caped crusader. Are you protecting your mom, Joey?"

Joey gave a bashful nod. He wasn't sure who Aunt Joan and Uncle Ed were.

"Our car's in short-term parking," Joan said. "Did you check any bags?"

"No, we're good. Let's just get out of here."

"Of course." Ed lifted Joey up on to his back, piggyback style, and then grabbed the handle of Maureen's suitcase. "Let's go fight crime," he said, and Joey let out a giggle.

26 UNFRIENDLY PERSUASION

It had been a long full day since he had seen Calvin. Chris remained isolated, thirsty, humiliated, and angry. His food had gotten worse. A bowl of thin cornmeal mush had been slid into his cell with a tin cup of warm water that tasted like iron.

He tried yelling to Calvin at the top of his lungs but, if the pilot heard him, he didn't reply. Chris resolved to build his strength. He stretched and did modified jumping jacks because the ceiling sloped too low for arm extensions. He followed up with lunges, push-ups, squats, and sit-ups. His strength was sapped by lack of food and sleep, but his determination remained solid. He firmly planned to do more each day.

He tried to recall each conversation he had had with Soon Yi. She must be the reason they had a picture of Maureen's passport and driver's license, she and Mr. Brandt—whoever the hell he really was. Voices from the hallway and the sound of loud moaning brought him to his feet.

He heard the key in his door and shielded his eyes as it opened. Two soldiers were holding Calvin by his shoulders. Calvin's feet dragged behind him as they pulled him into the doorway of Christopher's cell. He seemed barely conscious. Soon Yi and the general stood at the doorway.

The general spoke. "Time to decide, Christopher. Do we leave your friend here in pieces, or do you come into the daylight and make a statement to our reporters?"

Chris had considered this carefully. He'd given careful thought to how he might communicate in public. "I will appear before your press only as long as Calvin is alive. If he dies, I'm done. And if medical treatment is withheld from him, I'm done."

"You're a sensible man. We'll keep him alive because the Dear Leader has put his faith in you." He spoke in Korean, and one of the soldiers nearly sprinted out of the cell. When he returned, he carried a stretcher. Calvin whimpered in pain as they laid him on it and carried him the opposite direction from his own cell.

"Tonight, you return to the hospital. In four days, you will appear before cameras to thank Kim Jong Il and the Korean people. You will publicly embrace your new life here, and you will condemn American imperialism."

Chris grunted. Soon Yi stepped forward holding a pair of handcuffs. She signaled for Chris to turn his back and then she gently cuffed each wrist. "You made the good decision," she whispered.

During the next four days, Chris was returned to the hospital where he received three full meals a day and remained on an intravenous drip to keep him hydrated. Nurses sedated him at night to assure him plenty of rest. He bathed, shaved, and received a military haircut. His uniform, belt, and shoes were cleaned, pressed, and shined for his big day.

Soon Yi arrived in the morning with a script for him to read. "You must read exactly what is written, nothing else.

He silently read what had been prepared:

My name is Lt. Christopher McCarty. I am a trained Intelligence Officer of the United States Navy. My country sent me to spy on the Democratic People's Republic of Korea.

America stands in perpetual vigilance to strike your country at the first sign of weakness. Only your late Marshall Kim Il-Sung, and your Supreme Leader, Kim Jong Il, have been able to protect you. They have held you in their loving embrace and shielded you from attacks by the American military.

I am here to renounce the treachery of imperialist America and to offer my affection to the people of Korea. I have come to know your Dear Leader as a brilliant and generous man who is shaping Korea into the richest, most powerful country on earth.

I renounce the American government, with all its aggression, and seek asylum in your beautiful land. I hope to learn at the feet of Kim Jong Il, and to show my love for all Koreans.

He read it a second time. "May I have some time to practice this? I will talk slowly and clearly so every word is understood."

Soon Yi nodded approval. "We leave in one hour." She left him alone to study his words.

While Chris studied, he practiced slight movements with his fingers and his wrists. He felt ready by the time she returned.

He went before the cameras as the epitome of a spit and polish US Naval Officer, only this American officer stood flanked on both sides and from behind by rows of North Korean military leaders in stiff formal uniforms. They were assembled on the steps of an imposing concrete and marble building topped with several North Korean flags and an enormous picture of Kim Jong Il staring down on the gathered crowd.

Chris stood behind a podium with his prepared remarks in front of him. He squinted in the bright lights of the cameras, and cleared his throat as the cameras rolled and clicked.

"My name is Lieutenant Christopher McCarty." He spoke slowly with the cadence and accent of Forest Gump. "I am a trained intelligence officer." Again, it could have been Tom Hanks reprising his famous roll. You could almost sense he'd mention, *"Life is like a box of chocolates. You never know what you're going to get."* Soon Yi interpreted for the audience. She looked at him uncomfortably but felt too intimidated by her surroundings to interrupt. She had never heard of Forest Gump, but knew he conveyed falseness.

As he spoke he began to make subtle movements with his hands. To viewers who had never seen sign language the movements seemed meaningless. But Maureen would

123

recognize them. She would get his message. No one who knew Chris would believe he spoke from the heart.

When he finished speaking, a general strode to the podium, saluted, and then hugged Chris. He stepped back, saluting again, holding it, while Chris hesitated. Soon Yi gave him a look and used a karate chop motion against her right hand. Christopher understood she meant Calvin and returned the general's salute. Soon Yi smiled.

27 THE NEXT VIDEO

Maureen enjoyed the open scenery of the Pennsylvania countryside while Ed drove them to New Hope. Nature bloomed proudly, with hyacinths, daffodils, and forsythia flashing pink, white, and yellow against a lush green background.

They pulled into the long driveway leading to Joan and Ed's home. Maureen had forgotten how scenic it was.

Joey had fallen asleep in her lap. "Hey, Buddy, time to get up. We're here." He rubbed his eyes and looked out at the open fields and the apple trees in bloom. He pressed the button to open the window and breathed in deeply, enjoying the fragrance of the fresh farm air. Joey smiled broadly, reminding Maureen of her childhood dog who loved to stick his head out of car windows into the wind. She hadn't had any childhood thoughts in a long time.

Ed pulled the car up to the detached garage. "Hey, Joey, do you like horses? We have two of them in the barn. Want to see?"

"Real horses?"

"Real horses. Come on, I'll show you." He reached his arm back and waited for Joey to run under it. Ed guided him to the barn where two horses stood in stalls staring at them. Joey wanted to touch them but felt nervous and clung to Ed's pant leg.

"This one's Commander. He's a boy. And this one is Daisy. They're brother and sister. Do you want to feed them?" Joey looked eager and nervous at the same time.

"Here." He pulled a small apple from a tin pail across from the stalls. "Let me show you. Hold your hand flat, like this, with your fingers down. Just hold it still, and the horse will take it from you." He demonstrated with Commander.

"Now you can feed Daisy." Joey did as instructed. He turned his head away and stiffened his arm as Daisy's head approached his hand. Joey closed his eyes. Then he let out a laugh. "It tickles," he said. "I did it! Did you see?"

"You were great, Joey. Let's see how your mom's doing." The boy wiped his wet hand against his jeans, then held it out for his uncle to take. "Then can we come back and feed the horses again?"

Joan enjoyed showing Maureen around her home, decorated in authentic early colonial style. Maureen could imagine George Washington standing in the living room.

"Sis, I can't thank you enough. You've no idea what a zoo my house has been. We've had reporters roving all over the lawn, taking pictures through every window, and shouting at us whenever we go out. Joey gets terrified. You're so good to put us up. Really, you've no idea."

"You and Joey are always welcome here. Stay as long as you like. I can't imagine how hard this has been on you. It's all so strange. Anything you and Joey need, anytime."

A black Lincoln Town car turned into the driveway and sped to the front of the house. Two FBI agents got out and approached the open front door. Maureen and Joan were halfway up the staircase when they heard men on the front steps.

One of the agents rang the bell, as the other stepped through the open threshold. "FBI agents, Mrs. McCarty! We need to talk. Now!"

Maureen's shoulders tensed. She looked up at the ceiling muttering, "Jesus Christ!" and tightening her grip on the railing. Her posture slumped as she turned and stepped slowly back down the stairs.

"I'm not doing anything wrong. I just need some peace for my son. Please don't take us away."

"We don't care where you hide. You can stay here as long as you like. But there's something we want you to see. You might want to sit down."

"How'd you know where to find me?"

"We'll always know where you are, ma'am. Please have a seat." He motioned toward the sofa in the den. The other agent went to the car and retrieved a laptop computer.

He came back in just as Ed and Joey returned from the stables. They all entered together. Ed looked confused and guilty. He wondered if he'd be in trouble for harboring a fugitive.

"You can all watch this," the lead agent said. He placed the laptop on the coffee table and turned it on. The next pictures were of Christopher speaking from North Korea.

At his first words, Maureen stifled a laugh. "He doesn't mean any of that. He's trying to tell us it isn't real."

"How so, ma'am?"

"How so? He sounds like Forest Gump for heaven's sake! That's not his real voice. He doesn't mean any of that. That's not how my husband talks."

"Mrs. McCarty, your husband is denouncing the United States. He's claiming we sent him there to spy on them and he's saying he wants asylum in North Korea."

"Wait! Back it up. What's he doing with his hands?" She shifted forward on the sofa and leaned in, focusing on the screen. "What's that? Can you slow it down?"

The agent backed it up and slowed down the motion.

"There! See what he's doing? That's sign language! It's an L."

As they concentrated on his hand movements, the agents had to admit he seemed to be signaling something.

"That's a Y."

They ran the film over until she could clearly decipher all of it.

"It's a thing we do. LYMT means 'Love You More Than.' It's sign language; he's spelling LYMT life! That's what he's saying. Love you more than life. He wants us to know he's being forced to do this! He's saying he loves me."

The agent stood. "Maybe he wants you to join him."

"No! He'd never want that. He's been tortured or something. He doesn't mean a word of that speech. I think he means more than just me; I think he means he loves America more than life."

The agents looked at one another. Maybe she had a point; maybe she's fooling herself.

"We'll take this to an expert in sign language. You might be right, but you might just be reading more into it than is really there."

"No, I'm not at all. Listen to his voice! That's not how he talks. You've got to get him out of there."

The agent snapped the laptop shut. "We'll take that under advisement. Enjoy your stay here. Don't even think of leaving the country."

"Oh, for God's sake! I'm not going anywhere. Please, you've got to get him home!"

"We'll be in touch." And with that they were gone.

Maureen sank onto the sofa, her hands on her knees. She looked back and forth at Ed and Joan. "You both know Chris. He doesn't sound anything like that. He and I used to do that LYMT thing all the time. He's trapped. You saw that right?"

They agreed it wasn't his voice. "I don't know anything about sign language," Joan said, "but he's obviously signaling something."

28 LITTLE SOON YI

Soon Yi and three soldiers escorted Christopher back to his room. She waited until the troopers were stationed outside before saying, "You may have fooled them for now, but if you keep this up you will be executed along with your friend."

"Is this your idea of military honor? Are you proud of this?"

Soon Yi flinched ever so slightly. She knew her life and military career stood in stark contrast to Christopher's, even though she'd been born to a favored class, a gift of birth. Her grandfather had fought against the Japanese under Kim Il-Sung. His actions placed the whole family firmly in the "core class."

From the time she was four years old, she had been taught to bow before the photograph of the Great Leader. Kim's picture occupied a place of prominence in her living room. The government provided the photograph to every home, along with a special cloth for its care that her mother used daily to clean the glass. It could never be used for anything else. Soon Yi learned to bow before the image and thank him for all the blessings he bestowed on her and her family. He remained their protector and provider. Everything flowed from his wisdom and grace.

The Great Leader had developed an ironclad caste system. He commanded the very top. Below him were fifty-one levels of subservience. Those levels fit neatly into three broad categories: the core class, the wavering class, and the hostile class.

Her grandfather's heritage had placed the family in, but certainly not at the top of, the core class. Soon Yi's family status insulated her from the plight that befell other classes. Most importantly, it offered possible entry into the Workers' Party—the pathway to respectable jobs and a good life.

The bottom rung, nearly 250,000 people, in the hostile class, were relegated to slave labor camps. The group consisted of anyone whose family member had helped South Korea during the civil war, as well as intellectuals, Buddhists, Catholics, gays, pro-Japanese sympathizers, criminals, and anyone who showed the slightest disrespect of Kim.

Upward mobility was impossible. The only movement within the class system was down. Any perceived slight of the Great Leader, any sign of resistance, was met with immediate and permanent punishment. It wasn't enough to punish only the offender. Laws stipulated that any infraction required the punishment of three generations. An off-hand remark could plunge an entire family—grandparents, parents, and children—into work camps, or to serve as target practice for firing squads.

Every neighborhood had its Inminban Committee with an elected leader to spy on every neighbor. Children learned from the first day of elementary school to report any mention of disloyalty in their family or among their friends. Records were kept on everyone. Inminban members paid unannounced visits to their neighbors at all hours to see if anyone had slipped away from their designated place, or if any home contained even the slightest hint of outside influences. Once cast into the hostile class, the offender and family remained there for life.

Soon Yi learned to accept this as the right and proper order of things. After all, every blessing flowed from Kim Il-Sung. He was their great protector who kept the American military at bay. He provided wisdom to the farmers, guidance to factory workers, encouragement to laborers, and leadership to the military. Posters everywhere proclaimed his benevolence and his fatherly love for his people. Every student learned that Korea remained strong while other countries wallowed in poverty. The poorest, most despicable place on earth, they learned, was South Korea, which suffered under the control of the CIA and the imperialist American government.

Soon Yi's earliest memories were of living in an apartment in Chongjin, a port city 250 miles northeast of Pyongyang, known as the City of Iron. The Japanese occupation in the early 1900s had transformed the city from a peaceful fishing village to a major industrial complex. They developed the port for trade with their homeland in Japan, built steel factories, metal fabrication plants, and machine shops, and mined kaolin for use in paint and concrete.

After Japan lost the Second World War, it was forced to give up its territories. A US State Department officer, Dean Rusk, proposed an arbitrary division of Korea along its thirty-eighth parallel. Russia was granted the North for their "sphere of influence," and America the South for theirs. Russia quickly agreed, and within months had troops stationed in Pyongyang.

When Soon Yi was a little girl the city bustled, alive with activity. Smokestacks from busy factories streamed black clouds of ash that blew inward from the sea. The air was alive with pounding metal, sounds of active industries, and bustling rail yards.

Each morning, her mother walked Soon Yi to school, holding her hand while teaching her songs in honor of Kim Il-Sung. It was a happy time. Her mother would bend down to one knee and hug Soon Yi before heading to her job at the clothing factory. "Make me proud, little bee," she always said, straightening Soon Yi's uniform, "make me proud."

Soon Yi determined to do just that. She listened attentively to her teachers, learned quickly to memorize the heroic exploits of Kim Il-Sung and to literally sing his praises. She understood her duty to be ever vigilant for any signs of disloyalty. On Wednesdays, the class stayed at school an extra hour to confess any sins or failings on their part, or on the part of neighbors and family. Soon Yi would confess to not working hard enough; she promised to do more for the Democratic People's Republic of Korea. One afternoon she cried and admitted she had spilled rice. The Great Leader, in all his kindness, provided food to the people, and she had spilled a portion of his gift.

On her eighth birthday, Soon Yi's father surprised her with a bicycle. The inmates of the Chongjin Political Prison Camp had made it, but Soon Yi didn't know about such places or their harsh conditions. Had she known, she would have assumed the prisoners deserved their fate. She loved her bike and quickly mastered it with a little help from her father. She was forbidden, however, to turn the corner of her street and admonished to always stay in plain sight. So, she rode back and forth on the unpaved road in front of her apartment, and pedaled slowly to school while her mother walked briskly at her side.

Her father was a quiet man who kept mostly to himself. His position as a manager of the steel plant afforded him a level of status and respect. The job required him to leave home before sunrise and often kept him at work until well into the evening. His position enabled them to attain some luxuries: a radio, a carpet on the living room floor, beds with linens, and even a camera. At night, her father smoked cigarettes and stared out toward the ocean beyond his factory. She often thought he yearned to be at sea, off exploring the world.

Her two little brothers didn't come into being until her ninth year. Twins were far from what her mother anticipated, but twins they were nevertheless. Soon Yi was expected to provide a good amount of their care and attention. She accepted those responsibilities willingly and doted on them with love and good humor. By North Korean standards they were a happy and dutiful family.

They were also entirely ignorant of changes in the rest of the world. Contact with the outside remained strictly forbidden. Radios and televisions were tuned to receive only the propaganda broadcast constantly by the government.

As a result, they had little appreciation of how much their government relied on China and the Soviet Union for aid. Ever since the Korean War, it had been in Moscow's interest to provide vast amounts of assistance to the government in Pyongyang. Rail lines were built. Constant shipments of coal, iron ore, rice, wheat, and, of course, armaments flowed into the country. By the time the Soviet Union dissolved in 1991, it had neither the interest nor the ability to prop up North Korea. Their shipments evaporated quickly.

With disruptions in supplies, trains ran only sporadically. Without coal, the power grid mostly went down; without power, and lacking iron ore, the steel mills fell idle. The clothing factory where Soon Yi's mother worked became less and less active. North Korea slowly shut down. Food began to disappear.

By then, Soon Yi had been selected to attend the best school in Chongjin. Her family connections, spotless record of loyalty, and her sharp mind had served her well. She would be prepared for a position in government. Certainly, she would be accepted into the Workers' Party. She applied herself to studies with rigorous discipline, always careful to show the greatest loyalty to, and enthusiasm for, Kim Il-Sung.

She hadn't expected to fall in love. Indeed, she didn't know a single boy who sparked her interest until Kun-Woo Jiang. Soon Yi had been sitting on bench waiting for a bus and reading her biology book. She didn't see the young soldier when he approached, but became aware that someone paced back and forth near her. When she looked up, he had stopped pacing and stood at what the military calls 'Parade Rest' with his arms behind his back. He smiled.

"So, you're learning biology, very commendable."

She blushed, and returned to her reading while brushing hair behind her ear with her fingers.

"I suppose you are an intellectual. Perhaps you know philosophy and math? I'm a great learner myself."

She squirmed a bit. He looked handsome, but far too brash. She bent her head closer to her book.

"Would you like to know what I want to learn most of all, more than anything in the entire world?"

She glanced up as if to see if he was really talking to her.

"I want to learn your name. I am Kun-Woo Jiang."

She looked left and right and then met his gaze and blushed again. To his surprise, she stood up and took a step toward him.

"Well, Kun-Woo Jiang, I'm … late for class." Her bus arrived, and she hurried past him, climbing onboard, not looking back, but with a satisfied smile on her face.

She thought about him when she walked to the stop the next day, but almost turned and walked away when she saw him standing near the bench. Something about him made her very nervous, nervous and giddy. She steeled herself, took a deep breath, and sat down.

"I spoke much too brashly yesterday. Please forgive my arrogance." He handed her a small bunch of wild flowers he'd hidden under his coat. "I wasn't sure what to say; I just wanted to speak with you. May I sit?"

Soon Yi nodded silently, keeping her eyes down on the flowers in her hand, quietly inhaling their fragrance. They sat without speaking for a full minute.

"Do you always make fun of girls who study?" almost a whisper.

"No, truly, I was impressed. I just didn't say it very well. I think it's great that you're in school. I studied at the University of Technology too before joining the Korean People's Army."

"What did you study?"

"Mechanical Engineering: I loved it."

"But you joined the People's Army?"

"My parents fell on hard times. I need to help them. Besides, the army gets first priority on food, clothing, medicine, everything. It's an honor to serve. What do you study?"

134

"I'm concentrating on languages. Russian. I hope to be a diplomat."

"A diplomat studying biology? Sorry, I sound arrogant again. I don't mean to. The fact is I miss school. I miss the learning, miss my friends, and miss all the possibilities that learning offers. You're lucky to be a scholar."

They met nearly every day on the same bench, arriving earlier and earlier to spend time together. He guarded a factory at night, and gladly gave up sleep to spend time with her, to see her smile, to look into her eyes, and to hear her voice. She had a sly humor that came out in subtle ways. He marveled at her wisdom, her poise, and her beauty. Kun-Woo Jiang was captivated.

After three months, they had still not held hands; he would never dare touch her, though he burned to. Public displays of affection were forbidden in North Korea. They took enough risk just walking together as a couple, unchaperoned. He felt content just to spend time with her. They arrived early enough to take long walks. He showed off his knowledge of military affairs, and she talked about her family and how she wanted to someday send them post cards from exotic cities around the world. She would represent Korea to the world. Someday Korea would be united, and she would welcome the poor people of the South into her country.

It was a nice dream, but conditions deteriorated rapidly. Smokestacks rarely spewed soot into the air anymore. Electricity sputtered out most of the time. It would come on for an hour or two in the morning and perhaps two hours in the evening. With factories idle, work units were sent into the countryside on "make work" assignments or to help labor in the fields.

No work eventually meant no pay. Soon Yi's mother lost her job first. Her father kept his, but wages were only promises. Government stores held meager supplies in the best of times and now were nearly empty. What staples could be found were priced well beyond the means of most.

Her mother rose early each morning, walking miles into the countryside in search of food. She wasn't alone. As more and more people began to forage, she had to walk significantly farther for only the slimmest of food. Often tree bark and grasses supplemented whatever edible root or plant she could find. Those long hungry treks made a dramatic difference in her physically. She and her husband were shrinking in size and in spirit. She often went without so that her children would have something in their stomachs.

The most shocking event occurred on July 8, 1994. To the utter disbelief of almost everyone, Kim Il-Sung died. The army went on high alert; people went into fear and mourning. Life being already so hard, it would be unbearable without their Great Leader. At least the majority held that opinion. A certain number, however, no longer had faith in Kim Il-Sung, though they dared not show it. They hoped his son would be open to change and reform. Instead, Kim Jong Il became even worse. He declared a "Military First" policy, diverting more resources away from citizens. Starvation claimed lives at a ruthless pace. Kim Jong Il proclaimed that only two meals a day should be eaten so that the people could prove their self-sufficiency. He assured them conditions were far worse in other countries.

Soon Yi persuaded Kun-Woo to help her family. He began smuggling food for her. A famine that would eventually take the lives of up to two million North Koreans had gotten the attention of the world. The United States and international relief agencies began sending large quantities of food, some of which arrived regularly at the port of Chongjin. None of it made its way to the ordinary people.

Sixth Army Corps, including Kun-Woo, loaded the crates and sacks directly onto army trucks. Only members of the military or government officials ever consumed the food. Kun-Woo would secretly siphon off pockets full of rice or corn from a sack and smuggle it to Soon Yi for her family. If caught he would be executed, no questions asked. Her young brothers learned from other children who would often run behind a truck to slit the sacks with sharp sticks. They would gather whatever grain fell and rush into hiding.

Kun-Woo wasn't the only soldier diverting food. The practice became more wide-spread until one night in the fall when the entire Sixth Army Corps, 3,000 men and women with a number of tanks, trucks and other vehicles, was removed overnight. The whole army was purged, replaced by the Ninth Army from Wonsan. Kun-Woo disappeared with them that night. Rumors revolved around conflicting theories: the army had been assigned to the border with South Korea, the soldiers were in concentration camps for "re-training," or their officers had all been executed. No one knew for sure.

Soon Yi felt desperately sad. She'd never told her parents about Kun-Woo. They wouldn't approve. Now she had no one to talk to about her deep loneliness. She doubted her parents would last much longer without his help.

North Korea's policy of Military First turned out to be her saving grace. The army constantly looked for more recruits, especially from the educated youth of their most loyal class. Soon Yi could join the army, where food would be sufficient and where she would have a chance to help her parents and little brothers. It might also the one place she could find information on Kun-Woo.

Her training consisted of weeks of hazing by older soldiers who were mostly uneducated and cruel. Her first assignment was to patrol the rail depot at night. Starving people, often the sole surviving members of their families, clustered at the station hoping a train would arrive, hoping it carried food. Night temperatures often fell below freezing. Nearly every morning a person or two would be found dead. Soon Yi's detail collected their bodies, heaved them on to wagons, and transported them to group graves. It was numbing work in more ways than one. She never complained, never shirked. She also never lost an opportunity to search for clues to Kun-Woo's whereabouts.

One December evening, just after dark, she noticed something out of the ordinary at the depot. A man moved slowly, pushing a cart with three large trunks, each placed at an odd angle so that none completely covered the one below. The man was dressed well, as if on holiday, though his clothes hung loosely around him. As she passed, he gave her a broad nervous grin. She wondered how anyone could own three trunks of belongings.

Soon Yi walked several paces before turning around. "One moment," she said, approaching him again. "Your travel papers please."

The man fumbled for papers in his pockets, then turned and ran at full speed down the platform. Soon Yi blew her whistle. A pair of soldiers looked up to see the man running directly toward them. They tackled and straddled him as he lay on the ground. Soon Yi approached, stooping down until her lips rested just above his ears. "You will learn to obey the People's Army!"

While soldiers held the man in place, Soon Yi went back to the cart and trunks. She undid the ropes wrapped around each one, and carefully lifted the lid. The top trunk held a young girl, perhaps four years of age. The next, a boy about six, and the bottom trunk held a woman, around twenty-five years of age. A whole family, packed and ready to go.

Once out of the trunk the woman cried and begged leniency for her children. She admitted they were trying to reach China. "But only for food! We love Korea; we only need to feed our children."

That admission provided all she needed. Soldiers quickly handcuffed them and led the family from the platform. She personally delivered them to her supervisor who praised her for her vigilance. The family would disappear. They would live only as long as they could work in one of Korea's most oppressive labor camps. Her superior kept each of the trunks for himself.

With that single act, Soon Yi had earned the trust of her comrades. Two weeks later she was ordered to give a report to the assembled company at their monthly loyalty meeting. She stood on a small platform inside the assembly hall. Her colonel praised her for her vigilance and asked her to explain the capture. She hesitated and spoke softly at first. But her confidence grew and she ended up giving a cogent, articulate presentation describing what had attracted her attention and how she suspected disloyalty. A general visiting from Pyongyang stood in attendance. He smiled, impressed by her presentation, deciding he could find a good use for her in the capital city.

29 A SHOPPING TRIP

After appearing before the cameras, Chris spent five days under guard at the hospital. The small antiseptic room squeezed in on him, tighter every day. His only solace was his confidence the Forest Gump act must have convinced the Navy and his family he acted under duress. But he wavered, less sure his sign language had been effective.

Early on the morning of the sixth day Soon Yi, her sternness overlaid with an air of gloating, had him escorted to a room down the hall. Calvin lay in a bed with a cast on his leg. The cut under his eye had healed somewhat, and he looked comfortable. She whispered to Chris: "We keep our promise. You keep yours."

"I don't know what you did, Lieutenant, but you sure got their attention." Calvin held his hand up making a wide circle to indicate his new surroundings. "I might keep my leg after all."

Chris went to his bedside and grasped Calvin's hand in both of his. "We're going to get through this. Stay strong." The pilot's face was gaunt, his eyes bloodshot and sunken.

"I'm hang'n in there. What the fuck's this all about anyway?"

Chris cocked his head toward Soon Yi. "I'll have to tell you later. In the meantime, get better. We need each other. It's complicated. But we're screwed for the time being. I don't think anyone's coming for us. Are they feeding you?"

140

"If you can call this pitiful slop food. At least it's better than that prison crap."

Soon Yi took Chris by the elbow and led him back to his room.

"We have kept our agreement. Your friend is safe, for now, for as long as you cooperate. But, no more funny-talking. You pull that trick again, and Calvin won't think anything is funny ever again.

"Much is planned for you today. We take you shopping and then a little sightseeing. Think of it as something Calvin would want."

They drove Chris to Pyongyang's Department Store Number One. It was a large building in the city center with glass windows running up and down the eight-story facade, giving it a modern feel. The store was brightly lit, spotlessly clean, with highly-polished floors and efficient escalators. The shelves were full of every imaginable consumer good, all arranged in meticulous fashion, as if someone with OCD had been in charge of placing every item in its exact right place. Well-dressed shoppers drifted from counter to counter, visiting every floor. Chris was taken to a shoe department where his feet were measured and a pair of brown shoes selected for him. Next, they took him to the third floor and selected a white shirt and a gray suit that fit just a bit too tight for him.

Chris recognized the same people, with the same shopping bags, going up and down escalators, visiting the same counters over and over again. He noticed they weren't buying anything. They were play-actors, only pretending to shop. Department Store Number One suddenly took on the appearance of a museum, portraying a store, not actually being one. He realized it was another part of Pyongyang's propaganda to the outside world. He also knew that every minute of his shopping spree had been recorded on camera.

"Now for some fun," Soon Yi announced. "You will be reunited with your Navy." She let out a small laugh as if delighted by an inside joke.

He soon realized what she meant, but it wasn't the least bit funny. They drove a short distance to the river and up to the USS Pueblo. Chris sat in the car, staring straight ahead, his hands clamped on the seat in front of him. A soldier opened his door, but Chris didn't move.

"No thanks. I'm staying put. I don't need to see it."

Soon Yi placed a hand on his shoulder and gave him a firm push. "You will tour the boat and you will look content or Calvin will pay the price. Get out."

Chris took a deep breath, gave her a frigid stare, and slowly climbed from the car. A group of school children in uniforms waited in line to board one of Pyongyang's most popular tourist attractions. Soldiers escorted him to the front of the line and up the gangplank, where he was greeted on deck by the same general who had visited his cell. The general gave a broad smile with his nicotine-stained teeth and made an exaggerated gesture welcoming Chris to the ship. The students gaped and pointed at him as they talked excitedly, some jumping up and down, at seeing a real American, the one from State Television, who had fled his country for Korea.

Chris knew the Navy still listed the *USS Pueblo* on active duty status, even though it had been dry docked in Pyongyang since 1968. He noticed that the ship's side closest to shore had been painted and well-maintained, while the other side had been left to rust and decay. The ship had been built in 1944 as a cargo ship. It was fitted with intelligence-gathering equipment in 1966, but hardly state-of-the-art. Nevertheless, Korean guides enjoyed showing off "an armed spy ship of the US imperialist aggression forces."

A camera crew followed the activity as Chris toured every compartment of the ship. They led him from bow to stern and down below, then posed him next to a bulkhead pockmarked with bullet holes. Each hole had a red circle painted around it so none would be missed. They were marked to show the lethal capabilities of the North Korean Navy. Next, photographers filmed him standing by a mounted machine gun. Cameras followed as he climbed down to the communications center with its floor-to-ceiling electronics and monitors. His last cell phone had far more computing power than the entire room, but the Koreans were proud to have captured an American spy ship. Finally, they took him into the galley where he received lunch with a portly admiral who smiled constantly but never spoke. All great footage destined for the world's news services.

Afterwards, he and Soon Yi were being driven back to the hospital. She smiled and said, "You did well."

He turned to her. "My son is three years old! Those videos are likely to be the only thing he ever knows of me. Do you have children, Soon Yi?"

She looked at him, considering what he said for several seconds before slowly shaking her head.

"My wife will have to live with this for the rest of her life. Have you ever been married, ever been in love?"

She turned away looking out the window and said slowly: "I have been in love. Not married, but I have been in love."

"Why would you do this to me? I've never even had a bad thought toward Korea."

"You forget. We are at war."

"War? The last act of aggression, after the Pueblo, occurred when your MIGs shot down an unarmed US reconnaissance plane 90 miles offshore killing 31 Americans. That was in 1969 for God's sake! The only invasion you've had from the United States is the massive amount of food we sent you. Do you even know about that?

"That store you took me to, it isn't real, is it? What else in this country isn't real? You must know it's all a fraud. Why do you think you're not allowed to know about the rest of the world?"

"Stop this talking! You can't change your fate, and neither can I, not you, not your friend, Calvin. None of us. You must make the best of it. Your life before is completely over."

30 A MOON DANCE

She *had* been in love. *I'm still in love* she thought, after Chris was returned to the hospital. Soon Yi sat silently in the car, thinking back to her time with Kun-Woo.

She had discovered where he'd been assigned now, but had only seen him once briefly. He'd been punished for diverting food from the army. After two years of hard labor in a re-education camp he'd been released, assigned to guard a rail yard in Pyongyang and load cargo onto cars when available. He was reminded, in brutal fashion, that coal is of vital importance, warned any theft on his watch would result in punishment far more permanent that what he'd endured in hard labor.

Soon Yi's life had changed so much from the time he'd been taken away. It started five years ago. The speech she'd been ordered to give, after capturing a family at the station, attracted the attention of a high-ranking officer. General Sung Moon had been standing in the back of the troops. He was captivated. Soon Yi had spoken with growing confidence, articulate, loyal, graceful, and attractive. The general made a quick decision to transfer her to his district.

Before she could contemplate the implications, military police packed her and put her on a bus for Pyongyang. She had fifteen minutes to say goodbye to her parents and brothers. She knew it would be a long time before she saw them again.

Her bus arrived at Pyongyang in early evening. Soon Yi turned her head in all directions, impressed to see lights from some of the tall buildings reflecting off the surface of the

144

Taedong River. Streets were wide and clean. Trolleys were filled with people, and shops stocked with more goods than stores in her hometown. The air felt cleaner than she had experienced in Chongjin. Everything seemed bigger, fresher, more exciting than what she had left behind.

Her living quarters were also a pleasant improvement. Instead of sharing a cot in an open barracks, the army assigned her a small apartment of her own in a building close to the Ministry building. Her room had an electric hot plate. She could heat water for tea, even cook rice when it was available.

Soon Yi reported for duty the next day and, instead of ordering her what to do, a portly colonel asked what she wanted to learn.

"I want to serve Korea by learning other languages. My dream is to represent our country as an interpreter at the United Nations. I want the world to know how wonderful Korea is."

"What languages do you speak?"

"I've learned Russian and have developed good skills with it."

"But you don't know English?"

"No, it's not allowed."

"It is if you want to interpret for our mission at the UN. General Moon has ordered that you be given the opportunity to follow your goals."

"That is very kind of the general. I am thankful for his generosity, but I've never learned a word of English."

"You will start today." The colonel handed her an address and told her how to take the trolley to Kim Il-Sung University, the school that educated Korea's political elite along with its Foreign Service and intelligence officers.

That first day overwhelmed her. The university was a sparkling white complex sitting prominently on its own hill. It contained computer labs, classrooms, large auditoriums, and recreational facilities, even a world-class swimming pool. Soon Yi's head turned repeatedly as she studied her new surroundings, evaluating other students hurrying to their courses. She smoothed the front of her uniform with one hand while the other reached up to straighten her hair. Most students appeared more prepared, more educated, and more focused than Soon Yi. She felt exhilarated to be back in school, nervous but fiercely determined to succeed. She looked at her assignment slip to confirm the room number, then raised her head, pulled her shoulders back, and strode as confidently as she could into the class. The professor took her slip, studying it silently, then stared at her for a long moment, as if she might be a threat to his authority. He slowly raised his arm and, without a word, pointed to a desk in the back row.

General Moon stayed away until the end of her second week in school. When class ended for the day she was ordered to appear in the office of the president of the university, and arrived to find the general sitting comfortably on a leather sofa, smoking a thin black cigarette. Soon Yi bowed discreetly and waited for him to speak.

"I understand you're doing well in class and that you've shown promise in your studies. It's important that you develop all the skills necessary to represent Korea to the world."

"You are very kind, General. I have wanted to thank you for my transfer. I am grateful for the opportunity."

"If you're to represent Korea to the world you need to learn more than language. You must learn social skills, decorum, the ability to listen and observe. You must learn to dance. Do you dance?"

"I have never had occasion to learn."

"We will correct that Saturday night. There is a party at one of Kim Jong Il's homes. The High Commander himself will be there. It's to honor the top military leaders who protect our southern border. I will be your escort and your dance instructor. Please be ready by 1800 hours."

"Yes, General," she stood awkwardly silent, heart racing, not sure how to respond.

146

"What should I wear?"

"Your prettiest hanbok, of course, and please do something with your hair; also remember that makeup is not forbidden in Pyongyang."

Her heart sank. The hanbok is a traditional silk formal gown worn at festive occasions. She didn't own one. Even if she did, she wouldn't have had time to pack it before being rushed from home.

Soon Yi bowed her head, lowered her eyes, and sighed. "I am sorry General. I don't own one."

The general smiled, opening a briefcase from the table in front of him. "I thought as much." He took a piece of paper and held it out to her. "Go to this shop. They will be expecting you, and I will be expecting you to choose the prettiest dress in the store. Remember, we will be guests of Kim Jong Il himself. You are meant to look your best."

"Yes, General, certainly." She bowed and backed out of the room. He drummed his fingers on his knee and smiled to himself as he watched her go.

The party took place in an opulent mansion. Every top military leader was in attendance. Tables were laden with food. Wine and cognac were plentiful, and flowers overflowed ornate crystal vases. Other tables had been set for gambling: roulette, poker, and black jack. Young women in skimpy silk floral dresses stood at each table.

Soon Yi gasped when she saw the abundant displays. She thought she should be thrilled to see so much food. Instead, she felt repulsed. One table held more than her family would eat in several years. She guessed they would throw out more food than her family would eat in months.

An orchestra performed from a balcony above the large room, playing the finest music she had ever heard. Suddenly the orchestra stopped. A brief silence followed by the first chords of the national anthem filling the hall. Everyone stood at attention, eyeing the main entrance, and were thrilled when Kim Jong Il strode into the room.

Soldiers saluted. Women bowed their heads. Tears of joy and smiles of adulation appeared on the faces of men and women alike. Soon Yi felt a shock, like electricity running through her core, her heart beat accelerated, her body trembled, and tears fell uncontrollably from eyes, cast down, fearing to look at the majestic presence of the Supreme Leader. The man she had been taught to adore. Kim raised his hand in a jovial wave that the crowd greeted with prolonged, enthusiastic applause.

Kim was handed a glass of cognac which he raised, offering a toast to the commanders of the southern front who helped him protect Korea from the imperialists who crouched just below their border, ready to spring at any sign of weakness, eager to devour his people. His remarks were followed by another round of energetic applause.

He beckoned one of his aides who signaled two soldiers guarding the entrance. They exited briefly and returned carrying large metal attaché cases that they placed on a table in front of the Dear Leader. He stood aside as a general approached to unlock each case. Once unlocked, the general saluted and backed away. Kim reached in and withdrew two large stacks of new $100 bills, crisp US currency. He gestured to the young hostess at the closest table and handed her two stacks. Each table had a hostess and each in turn received two bricks of $100 bills. The bundles likely represented $25,000, so that every table had $50,000 as its bank. Kim joked about using America's money: "We will make far better use of their currency than those greedy capitalists ever did." No one dared not to laugh.

The guests broke into several small groups, gathered around tables where lively gambling was encouraged with free-flowing liquor and flirting laughter from young women dealing cards and spinning roulette wheels. The largest buffet stood against one side of the room where guests could dine at their leisure. Waitresses circulated the room, offering endless drinks.

The band resumed playing from the balcony, transitioning from classical music to more festive songs as the evening progressed. A marble dance floor toward the back of the hall remained empty until Kim suggested its use. It immediately filled with soldiers and their dates. Soon Yi had been standing behind General Moon while he played poker. When Kim suggested dancing, he placed his cards face down and turned to her. "Now I will teach you to dance."

He took her arm and escorted her to the dance floor. Soon Yi's heart raced. She had never danced with a man before, and now she would be dancing for the first time, with a general, and in front of the Supreme Leader! Her knees buckled momentarily as he guided her to the marble floor. The general tucked his arm around the small of her back and took her hand into his as he extended his arm in a classic, respectful dance pose. She moved stiffly trying to follow his lead, concentrating so much on mechanics that she was barely aware of the music or its beat. He held her closer almost lifting her with his right arm as he slowly stepped and turned.

By the third song she had gotten in sync with the music and began keeping pace with the general. This wasn't so hard after all. Her tension began to fade, as her movements became more fluid. She even laughed a bit as he twirled her more quickly.

"You are learning well," he smiled. "You're a gifted student."

The fourth song was slow. She knew its lyrics proclaimed the loving nature of Kim Jong Il as he embraced the Korean people and protected them from all harm. It might have been a political song but, without its lyrics, the instrumental felt serene and comforting. She thought of Kun-Woo and wished she could dance with him. Wished he were here with her.

Soon Yi was picturing Kun-Woo's face when the general's hand slipped down and firmly pressed her bottom, forcing her into him. She stiffened and fought to catch her breath. All she could think was, this is a general and we're on Kim Jong Il's dance floor. Kim might even be watching her this very moment. She flushed with fear and humility, but dared not pull away. He dropped her right hand, putting his other arm around her and caressing her back. Their dance slowed to a swaying movement. She could barely breathe.

Kim disappeared halfway through the event. Everyone waited expectantly for him to return, but General Moon confided that the Dear Leader often left early to pursue his own entertainment and would rarely return.

They left the mansion just after midnight. General Moon staggered slightly, sputtering about how well he knew Kim, how the Commander in Chief often sought his advice. He held Soon Yi's arm and helped her into the car while the driver stood at stiff attention. His driver then rushed to the other side to open the general's door. He could have taken his time. The general stood staring at Soon Yi through the window for several seconds. A broad satisfied smile came over his face. He straightened up and ambled around the back of the car to the other door, then poured himself inside and scrunched close to Soon Yi.

"Did you enjoy the party?"

"Yes, General, it was quite magnificent. I didn't expect Leader Kim to actually attend." She shifted away from him slightly.

"I'm often invited to such parties. You will have opportunities to attend many more," he placed a hand on her knee, "especially now that you dance so well." He leaned toward the front seat and whispered something to the driver. The car pulled away from the curb.

Rain began to fall, growing more intense, splattering the car. She couldn't tell where they were going through the darkened city. But Soon Yi sensed they were not heading to her apartment. She looked for landmarks but, even if she could see the buildings, her knowledge of Pyongyang remained limited at best. Her body tensed as she tried to focus on the road ahead and the buildings passing by her on the left. She placed her hands on her knees, bowed toward them and said, "A long night. I am looking forward to getting home."

"Of course. Just one stop first. I want to show you something."

"I have a great deal of work to do. I really must get back to my studies."

"You mustn't worry about grades. You will be given honors."

"But my English, I need to work hard to catch up to the others."

"You will catch up. Believe me, you'll be fine." He smiled and lifted his hand to her cheek, turning her face to his. "You will be a star pupil. I am sure of it." His breath smelled of whisky and cigars.

Their car pulled into a parking garage. "Well, it seems we've arrived. I want you to see where I live. You may be a general yourself one day. It will be good for you to see how we live."

"Sir, I really must get back."

"Just a brief stop. It will do you good."

As he spoke her door was opened. The driver reached in and took her arm, guiding her from her seat. This time the general rounded the car quickly to join her. "It's just this way. I have a private entrance."

Once inside his tenth-floor apartment, General Moon pulled back the drapes. He and Soon Yi stood staring out over the rain-soaked city. He was proud of the view and, on a clear day, or a sparkling night when the electric lights were on, the view could be impressive. Tonight, it offered a smudgy view. The general poured two glasses of Scotch.

"I have some photos you might want to see. They're from your hometown. You might recognize a face or two."

He downed his drink and walked to the coffee table where he picked up a large manila envelope. "Ah, here they are." He pulled out a number of photographs and smiled as he handed them to her.

Her eyes focused, and she sucked in a large gulp of air. The first picture showed her two brothers crouching near a road.

The following pictures were close-ups that must have been taken with a telephoto lens. Then came a picture of the boys chasing a military truck. In the next shot one of the boys had clambered onto the back, his hand firmly on a bag of food. Another photo showed him heaving the bag onto the ground and then jumping back to the road. The final picture showed the boys holding each side of the sack and running.

"Naughty boys," the general chortled. "If they're caught, their whole family will be punished. It's a shame. They're such young boys."

Soon Yi sipped from her glass and winced at the strong taste. She set the glass on the windowsill and moved away from it.

"Do you know who they are?" she asked.

"Oh, we know a great a deal. It could go very hard on them."

"But, as you have said, they're very young. Surely they can be forgiven."

"You know the rules as well as I. We must be vigilant against those who would steal from the people. Three generations will have to be punished, unless ..."

He approached, putting his hands on her hips. "Perhaps I could be persuaded to intervene. I have ways to protect certain people. Would you like to persuade me?" He drew her close and kissed her coarsely on the lips. Her body went rigid. His breath now reeked of, Scotch, nicotine, and lust.

The next morning, she sat alone in the back of his car and cried the entire drive home. Her family was safe, for now, but Soon Yi was lost, empty, humiliated, and sick to her stomach.

31 A MODEST PROPOSAL

The BBC aired new videos of Christopher shopping in a busy North Korean store, footage of him being fitted for new clothes. A clerk knelt below him, gracefully placing shoes on his feet, taking great care as he laced each one. Chris riding an escalator, and trying on a new suit jacket. Clerks appeared to be fawning over him. Then, dressed in his new suit, exiting a Mercedes, dockside. His tour of the Pueblo captured from several angles and culminating in Chris enjoying lunch with both a North Korean admiral and a general. In several of the shots Soon Yi smiled warmly at Chris. She had changed into a soft purple gown and wore her hair down, flattering her face. No audio accompanied the pictures, but Chris did not appear to be under any duress.

Across the Potomac River from Washington DC, at the end of Key Bridge, Rosslyn, Virginia burst with high-rise office buildings, apartments, restaurants and shops. Its underground metro station was two stops from the Pentagon, three stops from the White House, and five stops from Ronald Reagan National Airport. The buildings were filled with defense contractors, aerospace firms, and companies whose real identities were buried in the deepest part of the US Intelligence budget.

Despite advancing age, Milton Conrad carried himself with a rigid bearing. He wore civilian clothes, but his close-cropped hair, athletic physique, and highly polished shoes clearly shouted: *military*. He had retired from the Marines as a full colonel eight years ago with an exemplary record, much of which remained classified.

Milton exited the metro car and bounded up the escalator with a sense of urgency. It was the third longest escalator in the world. Milton took it quickly, two steps at a time. Never a patient man, he couldn't abide people who stood stock-still on escalators impeding his progress. A couple of teenagers were standing half-way up, side-by-side, texting God-knows-what on their phones. He approached them quickly from behind, strongly tempted to grab each by their backpacks and hurl them out of his way. He had a mission though, and fought the impulse.

Once out of the station he walked four blocks, entered a tall gray building, and took an elevator to the eighth floor. The sign on the double glass door read *Lumina Insights*. A marble entrance funneled guests to a high curved walnut reception desk. The receptionist had a telephone headset over her very straight, very long, very black hair. Anyone seeing her from behind would assume her to be Asian; Milton knew otherwise, that she was Irish, and an avid fan of Goth couture in her free time.

"He's waiting for you," she shook her head toward the hallway on her right, "and he's not happy about something."

"Thanks, Tracey. I appreciate the heads up."

He went to the solid mahogany door at the end of the hall and knocked once, immediately letting himself in.

"Good to see you, Colonel." An athletic bald man unfolded himself from his chair and stood to his full six-foot, eight-inch height, towering over Milton.

"Good to see you, sir. It's been a long time."

"I'd invite you to sit, but this won't take long." He held out a folder with the words Top Secret stamped across the front. Almost every assignment Milton dealt with these days involved highly sensitive material. But since 9/11, practically anything could earn a "Top Secret" stamp. The tone with which this one was delivered convinced him it deserved its classification.

154

"This comes directly from the highest levels. Our North Korean situation needs to be addressed. It must be handled with a great deal of delicacy. No one must suspect our hand in it, and no one must suspect anything other than accidental or natural causes. You understand?"

"Perfectly, Sir. I know how to handle this and who can make it happen. It'll be discreet, but it may take a while."

"We don't have a while. Make it happen!"

"Yes, Sir."

"You leave for Seoul from Reagan at 1800 hours. You'll refuel in San Francisco. It's the usual aircraft. I believe you know the plane and the hangar. You'll have approximately four hours in country before wheels up again."

Milton placed the file in his briefcase and locked it. "Seems I've got some light packing to do." He turned and retraced his steps to the metro, making two crucial calls on his cell before reaching the station.

The flight took nearly twenty hours. Milton slept most of the time, and felt relatively fresh when his Gulfstream 500 touched down at Seoul's Incheon International Airport. Incheon was rated among the top airports in the world, with amenities that included a golf course, a spa, an ice skating rink, a casino, indoor gardens, private sleeping rooms, fine restaurants, and the Museum of Korean Culture. Milton wouldn't see any of it.

His jet taxied to a private hangar at the far end of the airport, and disappeared inside. The pilot made sure the hangar doors were closed before opening the jet's door. Milton descended the stairs and went immediately to a custom black Hyundai limousine parked at the far end of the hanger. A driver got out and opened the back door for him.

"Wait outside," Milton ordered. He ducked inside and greeted the occupant. "Good to see you, Walter. I've got some work for you."

"I'm not surprised. Actually, given the news, I thought you'd have been here weeks ago."

"I should've been. Whatever's up with Lt. McCarty, it has to end. It has to end soon, but it can't be a sniper or an explosion. It must be purely accidental or 'natural causes.' Are you sure your man can do that?"

"We've used him before. He's very good. Leaves no fingerprints. But getting close to McCarty won't be easy. He's their prize possession at the moment.

"But it can be done?"

"Yes, it can be done. Our man's a doctor in Pyongyang. We've code named him 'Hung Duck.' He treats their senior military officers. We think he's even in a position to have direct access to Kim Jong Il before too long."

32 JOEY'S APPLE TREE

Joey went to the apple orchard to collect treats for Commander and Daisy. Earlier, Uncle Ed had let him sit on Daisy, perched on a saddle so large that his feet flopped in the air above the stirrups. He clung tightly to the saddle horn while Ed held the reins and walked the horse from the front of the barn into the fenced paddock.

"Grip with your legs," he instructed. "You look good up there."

"I'm doing it, aren't I, Uncle Ed?"

"You sure are. Looks like you were born to be a cowboy."

Ed walked the horse around the paddock four times and then led Daisy and Joey back to the barn. He helped Joey down, removed the saddle, and showed the boy how to groom the animal. Joey was enthralled. He liked the feel of the horse flesh, and the smell of the barn. He shuffled through the straw on the floor and, for the first time in weeks, felt happy.

When they were done, Ed said, "I've got a present for you." He handed Joey a balsa wood glider and helped him insert the wing through the slot in the middle of the plane. Joey had fun launching it into the wind and was following it around the yard when he got the idea of finding treats for the horses.

Out in the orchard he wanted to find the best possible apples. But, in early spring, the trees held blossoms without an apple in sight. Joey thought it would be fun to climb a tree and found one with a branch low enough he could reach up and wrap his arms around it. Once his arms felt secure he hoisted his legs up and wrapped them around the branch so he dangled under it like a sloth. He squirmed and muscled his way up and over, lying on top of the branch.

Joey pushed up with his arms and brought his feet under him until he could nearly stand, then reached for the branch above him, steadying himself. That made standing easier as he studied the branches over him. He climbed from one to another in a zigzag fashion until the limbs got too crowded and he couldn't go any further. He had never climbed a tree before, just as he'd never ridden a horse before this week. Joey felt proud of himself.

He looked out at the rolling green hills of the Bucks County landscape. The sky shone clear blue with only a few puffs of white clouds drifting on a subtle breeze. Trees were sprouting buds, not yet fully covered in leaves, allowing him to see out into the distance. Off to his right his eyes followed the slope of a distant hill to make out the narrow road that led down one side and up the other. The red roof of a covered bridge was visible just below where the road began to meet the rising hill. He hoped Uncle Ed would take him and his mom exploring so they could see the bridge up close.

A strong gust of wind burst up, and his tree swayed with the whole orchard. Blossoms flew and swirled down to the ground. Joey nearly lost his balance. He grabbed the trunk to steady himself and looked down for the first time. The ground lay farther away than he expected. Climbing up had been one thing; getting down was something else entirely. There wasn't a clear path down he could see, nor could he remember exactly how he got to the branch he stood on. The wind picked up again. Joey pressed closer to the trunk, hugging it firmly with his arms. Fear took over, and he froze in place.

He stood stock still even after the wind died down. He thought he might be able to get into a sitting position on the branch, but was too afraid to try. He slowly moved his left foot and lowered it trying to reach the branch below. He let it down so that his knee went below the level where he stood. Not finding anything, he tried moving his leg slightly in one direction, then the next, feeling nothing but air. Joey gripped the trunk with more force and brought his foot back to his standing branch. He was too frightened to move.

Maureen stood in the kitchen talking to her parents on the phone, while Joan joined in from the living room on the extension. They were making arrangements for their parents to join them for a weekend.

"You could come on Thursday and stay at least through Sunday. Joey'd love to see you both. It's so peaceful here. You should see how much Joan has done since last year."

"Yes, please come," Joan said. "You two need some peace and quiet as well. Mo said you've had the press staking out your place."

"They're mostly gone now. But every time we think they've given up, another batch pops up. It's hard to leave the house."

"Then you definitely have to come! Get away from all that nonsense. Ed would love to see you as well. Maybe we'll even ask Colleen to join us so the whole family can be together for a change."

Her father laughed. "Just what Ed needs: in-laws and sisters-in-law. We'll drive him nuts."

"No," Joan protested, "Ed will think it's fun. He'll make a party out of it. You should see how good he is with Joey. He's teaching him to ride. The two of them are becoming inseparable."

"Joey must be in heaven. Put him on. We want to hear what he says about the horses."

"He's outside," Joan said. "Ed got him one of those balsa gliders. I think he's trying to see how far it can fly. Hold on, I'll have Ed bring him in."

Joan set the phone on the table and headed out the kitchen door, leaving it slightly ajar. She scanned for Ed and Joey, looking first toward the barn and then past the driveway to the open field. Joan called for Ed but got no reply. Assuming they must be in the barn, she set out quickly to find them. The wind accelerated, blowing the kitchen door shut behind her, causing her to run hugging her shoulders with her arms.

Ed was in the barn filling the feed pails when she came in. He smiled and said, "What's up?"

"Mom and Dad are on the phone. They want to talk to Joey."

"Joey's not here. Isn't he in the house?"

"No, I thought he was here with you."

"The last time I saw him he was flying his glider and following it to the back door of the house."

"Well, he's not inside. How long ago was that?"

"I don't know, ten minutes?"

"Crap! Help me find him. What were you thinking?"

He looked sheepish but thought she was being overly dramatic.

They walked quickly toward the back of the house and veered left toward the orchard. Joan moved further to the left to cover more ground while Ed took a straight path to the middle. Halfway there he saw the wooden glider upside down with its wing at a crooked angle. He spun around slowly, looking in all directions but, seeing nothing, continued to the orchard calling Joey's name.

Joey hugged the trunk with his head down, positioned to the side of the tree that blocked the wind. He heard Ed calling and looked up. His uncle walked briskly into the orchard headed from the front toward the back. Joey's tree stood near the outer edge. If Ed kept going, he would be running farther from Joey's perch. The child let out a yell. He tried to wave with his right arm, moved back a step, and lost his balance, falling backward. His shoulder hit a rough branch, then his face scraped on a limb as he collapsed further. He bounced to his right, struck his head, and fell hard on to the ground.

Ed heard Joey's fall. Joan saw it, and both ran to his side. Joey didn't move. His cheek was badly scratched and bleeding; his arm lay twisted in an unnatural position.

Joan got to him first. "Oh, my God! Joey. Joey!" No response.

Ed put his hand on Joey's chest and lowered his ear to the boy's lips. "He's breathing." He gently nudged Joey, but got no response. "I don't think we should move him." He took off his jacket and placed it over the boy. "I don't have my cell phone. Do you?"

Joan patted the back of her jeans. Then shook her head and held her arms out in desperate frustration.

"You stay with him; I'll get an ambulance." He ran to the house at full speed, cursing and praying that God would "*let Joey be all right. Please, God! Don't take Joey.*"

He flung open the back door, grabbed the phone off the hook, and had started dialing when he heard voices on the other end. Maureen said, "Hey, we're in here. Mom and Dad want to talk to Joey."

"Oh, Christ. Hang up! Everybody hang up! Joey's hurt; I need to call an ambulance." Stunned silence. Ed ran into the family room. "Please hang up. He fell from a tree. Joan's with him in the orchard."

Maureen slammed the phone down and bounded past him. The ambulance arrived in nine minutes. Joey remained unconscious but still breathing.

"He took quite a fall, pretty bad concussion." The paramedic stated the obvious. He carefully felt along the back of Joey's neck and along his arms and legs. "His arm's broken. Might have broken some ribs too. We won't know till we get him to the hospital. Which one of you is his mother?"

Maureen held her hand up weakly. She knelt on the grass, sobbing and praying.

"You can ride with him, ma'am. Once we get him inside, you're welcome to sit in back."

Ed and Joan followed the ambulance. Joan called her parents from the car and explained what had happened, promised she'd call again as soon as she had news, and said, "We really need you to come out now. Maureen is at the breaking point." They agreed to come as soon as they could arrange a flight.

Joey regained consciousness shortly after getting to the hospital, frightened and in pain. His head throbbed and he felt as if everything phased out of sync. He couldn't understand why he was in a hospital.

His arm was in a splint and needed to be reset. Doctors were concerned about his shoulder, too, and were just waiting for the x-ray results. When that was addressed, Joey would need a CT scan for his brain.

Maureen held up well during the first hour. Her adrenaline kicked in, and she was quite capable of asking intelligent questions and understanding the implications of the answers.

When they wheeled Joey out for his CT scan, she asked the nurse if they had a chapel and was directed to a room on the first floor. The sign read "Interfaith Chapel and Meditation Sanctuary." She sat alone in the room, praying for her son, savoring the quiet, forcing herself to calm down. And then she began to weep. For the first time, she blamed Christopher. How could he let this happen? Why wasn't he here with her? Why did she have to go through this alone? She knew she shouldn't feel that way but *Damn him!* She thought of the pictures of Chris and Soon Yi.

33 A GARDEN OF THEIR OWN

The Americans were moved to new quarters, with the pilot kept carefully out of the public eye. His only purpose was to provide leverage against Chris. They were moved to a low, one-story cinderblock building that sat inside and at the edge of a military base. Chris had a tiny room, a flimsy mattress, a wooden chair, a small chest with two drawers, and a sink that dripped slowly, incessantly. A ragged, plastic curtain shielded an old metal toilet, with no seat, holding a small puddle of putrid, rusty water. He had a tiny window and a steel door to the outside. Calvin's room was identical but with no access to the outside world. He had no window, and his hallway door remained locked, opened only by soldiers who brought food and interrogated him twice a day.

Four days later, a crew of workers arrived out front. They constructed a tall concrete wall jetting out from each side of the building to form a large courtyard approximately twenty feet wide and thirty feet deep. Shortly after construction began, a team of laborers worked turning earth and creating flowerbeds. Whole plants were hauled in, many in full bloom, and then tomato plants and cabbages were planted, along with peas. Soldiers carried an ornamental bench in and placed it just outside the door to Chris's room. At the end of the week, a large carved wooden door was mounted in the far center of the new courtyard wall. The front of the building received a fresh coat of paint with offsetting trim. From all appearances, Chris now had a lovely country cottage with a garden.

Once this was complete, Soon Yi arrived, dressed in a pretty gown, with two comrades in tow. She unlocked his door, signaling for Chris to step into the courtyard.

"You have a garden now, so you may grow food. Tend to it well, and you may share food with your friend. If you fail, Calvin may starve."

Chris looked at her skeptically. "We have a garden?"

"If you take care of it, and are seen working on it with happiness." She gestured toward the entrance gate. Photographers were gathered just inside, filming every movement. "Now, when I step away, I want you to admire your garden and bend down to examine your flowers and your vegetables. Perhaps you can sift some earth through your fingers like a happy farmer in his new home."

Chris glared at her and then at the cameras. He turned briskly, heading back toward his room.

"Or we can tear it all out and you will lose your only chance for extra food. If you don't want to grow food, we will understand. I will tell the guards that Calvin must not need much to eat at all."

He stopped dead still with his back to her, clenched his fists, straightened his back, and slowly turned. Chris looked at her for several seconds, holding her eyes with his.

"Is there anything honest or decent about anyone in this damned country?"

She seemed to deflate a bit, but then pointed at the garden. "You should enjoy your little farm, now."

Chris shuffled his feet as he approached the flowers. *Hold steady. This is better than my hospital, better than my cell.* But an overwhelming feeling hit him: *I'm never going home.* He knelt, almost collapsing, in front of the flowerbeds and sifted the earth through his fingers. With his back to the cameras he shouted: "Is that enough for you? Are you done now?"

"Not quite yet. Please, there is a watering can next to your bench. It would be good to see you watering your crops."

Chris stood, keeping his back to the cameras, walked over, grabbed the watering can, and started back toward the garden.

"We need to see you are happy," she harped.

He looked up, forced a smile and began to water the plants.

"That's good. Now, one more thing." She handed him a magazine. "Sit on your bench in the sunshine and read your magazine."

He grabbed the magazine out of her hand. It appeared to be a propaganda piece filled with pictures of happy, industrious North Koreans living the good life. Chris sat on the bench, crossed his knees and began to stare at the pictures. If she let him keep it, the pages would be cherished, as toilet paper.

"Oh wait, I nearly forgot." She approached Chris and gave him a large apple. "You should eat as you read." She turned, smiling at the cameras, before backing up out of the shot. He glared at her as he bit into the apple, and then paused as he realized how long it had been since he had tasted fresh fruit. He savored every bite; the juice filling his mouth felt like sunshine, even the core and seeds were devoured. He saved the stem to chew on later.

The next release from North Korea would be an idyllic scene of Officer McCarty enjoying his garden and basking in sunlight while he relaxed over a magazine. A pretty young woman handed him an apple. Long before becoming North Korea's leader, Kim had spent years as Director of Propaganda, turning out films that were every bit as cloying and misleading as the picture of Chris in his garden.

When the filming ended, with Chris locked back in his room, he suddenly realized he'd lost an opportunity to send a message to Maureen. He should have signaled something, given her some sign of hope, done the LYMT thing. He became furious with himself.

Calvin pounded on his wall. "What's going on out there? Are you still here, Chris?" The walls were just thin enough that they could hear each other if they talked loudly.

"We have a garden."

"What the f...? Sounded like you said garden."

"Yep. All that noise for the last few days was walls going up and a garden going in. They're using it to fool the world into thinking I like it here. That I have my own little cottage and my own country garden."

During the first few days in their new surroundings, they had been able to communicate by standing close to their common wall, speaking loud enough to hear one another but, hopefully, not so loud that guards could hear them. Chris brought Calvin up to date with what had transpired since the day he awoke in the hospital. Calvin told him everything he'd been through, which had not been nearly so pleasant. No dancing children, no opera, and certainly no state dinner. He had been beaten frequently. They asked a lot of questions about US Naval operations, but also a lot about Christopher McCarty. Now he knew why. They both agreed that none of the other sailors had survived the crash.

"How's your leg?" Chris asked.

"A little better. I can put some weight on it now."

They compared notes. Chris clearly had gotten better treatment. He had to look good on film, so his food had been more plentiful, still meager by most standards but better than Calvin's. He had received better medical treatment and better clothes.

Chris tapped on the wall about two feet off the floor. "Can you tell where I'm tapping?"

"Yeah." Calvin tapped back on the opposite side.

"Is there anything against the wall where you are?"

"No. Why?"

"I have a small dresser here. I just moved it out of the way. If I make a small hole behind it can you cover it with anything on your side?"

"You have a dresser?"

"It's very small, with a broken leg, and one drawer that won't shut, and nothing to put in it. What do you have that can cover a hole?"

"All I have is a little wooden chair and a smelly old mat."

"Damn. If your chair's like mine, they can see right through it."

"How big a hole you going to make?"

"I don't know. Small. Just so we can pass things back and forth."

"You got stuff to pass?"

"Not now. But I will have. They give me more food than you. I can share some of what I get and, later on, food from the garden."

"You don't need to share nothin' with me. If we get caught . . ."

"Expect great things of us, Cal. We're going to break out of here someday, and when we do you need to be strong. There must be something you can use to cover an opening in the wall."

"I can put the chair against it and then hang the rag over it they gave me for a towel. That'll cover it. But if they move the rag or the chair we're screwed."

"We're already screwed."

Chris reached into his crotch and took out a rough piece of concrete he had been able to retrieve in the garden. He had come across it while sifting the dirt, and pushed it down his pants while his back had turned to the cameras. He started to corkscrew it into the wall but then stopped.

"Tap the wall where you think the rag will cover it best."

Calvin tapped, and Chris moved the concrete a few inches. He applied pressure while turning it. The wall gave way more easily than he expected and soon a hole nearly the size of a baseball was dug out of it. He scraped the sides of it from his end, and Calvin smoothed his edges from his side. Chris bent down and peered through the hole. Calvin did the same so they were eye to eye with their heads sideways, parallel to the floor.

"Good to see you, Calvin. I need you strong so you can fly us out of here one day."

"You're look'n pretty good, Christopher. I'll be ready to fly when you are."

"Here's what I'll do. I'll always tap twice before passing anything through. If for any reason you're not alone in there, or don't think I should do it, just sit tight. If the coast is clear, tap back twice."

"Sounds like a plan. We'd better cover this back up."

34 DOCTOR'S HOUSE CALL

Their routine remained the same each day. Two soldiers would arrive at 0600 with a small breakfast. For Chris, cornmeal and tea with an occasional shriveled piece of fruit. Calvin received only half as much cornmeal, and no fruit. Chris took pride in sharing so their caloric intake was approximately equal.

At 0700 sharp, soldiers would arrive to ask the same questions over and over. Did Chris understand his life had permanently changed? Did he comprehend that his country had abandoned him? They interrogated him several hours a day about US naval capabilities and surveillance techniques. And then one day: did he know his wife and son had not been seen for several weeks?

Chris was never beaten, and he withstood their questions day after day using a mind game. He pretended they were teddy bears, acting in a play, reading lines that had been written for them. They weren't real, so nothing they said was real. He knew, however, that Calvin had been beaten often, though he managed to impart facts that would only confuse his captors. This new information about Maureen and Joey being missing concerned him, probably just an interrogation tactic, but he didn't like it. An undercurrent of anger and frustration lay just below the surface. His mind filled with the image of her being led from the house in her nightgown, in handcuffs.

Days grew longer and much hotter. Humidity soared with the temperature. Mosquitoes and cockroaches were frequent visitors, along with hordes of black flies. Both men perspired profusely and stayed mostly shirtless except for the early morning and evening hours when the mosquitoes hung like clouds in their rooms. They splashed themselves with sparse warm rusty water from their sinks but it offered little comfort.

Christopher ran his fingers along his rib cage, feeling each bone. If he continued losing weight at this pace he wouldn't survive the winter. Calvin had even less of a chance. He watched a large black cockroach as it ambled across the floor toward him, stopping just beside his toes, its antennas quivering. He reached down, plucking the shiny insect between his thumb and forefinger, raising it in the air. Its legs flailing like a panicked swimmer searching for safety. He closed his eyes tightly, brought it to his mouth and crunched it with his teeth. Chris swallowed hard, feeling the juice slide down his throat, then stuck out his tongue, and winced, quickly shaking his head, before swallowing again.

Eventually, they both took to catching and eating cockroaches to supplement their meals, referring to them as peanuts.

Chris could work his garden an hour every other day under careful supervision. He watered the vegetables, impressed to see the tomatoes and cabbages, coming along nicely. When the first small tomato turned red he picked it and proudly knocked twice on the wall for Calvin. With the return knock, he pushed the dresser aside and slid his gift gently through the hole. Calvin let out a sustained whistle.

"Manna from heaven, Christopher. Manna from heaven!"

"Better than peanuts, right?"

There was precious little to share after that. Crews would film him working the garden, but soldiers eagerly harvested what they could, often long before it was fully grown. Chris learned to hide baby beans or carrots in his underwear while digging in the earth for photographers.

At the end of the sixth week Soon Yi appeared with a doctor. "You see what good care we take of you. This is

Doctor Wan. He is the chief medical officer who cares for our most senior military officers. He has asked personally to see you and to be sure you are in good health. I will leave you and the doctor alone for now."

The doctor bowed and greeted Chris in broken English. He conducted a cursory evaluation taking his pulse and blood pressure. He examined Chris's eyes and ears, listened to his heart, checked his breathing front and back, thumped his chest with two stiff fingers and then opened his medical bag. He withdrew a small vial of clear liquid and a hypodermic needle, which he dipped into the rubber stop on the top of the glass, then pushed in and slowly withdrew the plunger filling the needle. He held it upside down at eye level and gently depressed the plunger just enough to let a few drops of liquid escape.

"To protect from flu," he said.

"For both Americans? Will you be treating my friend?"

The doctor understood some English. "You have friend?"

"Next door," Chris pointed to the wall. "Will you examine my friend?"

The doctor lowered the needle and called Soon Yi into the room. They spoke briefly in Korean. Soon Yi seemed to be agreeing that another American was present. The doctor looked flustered, he shoved the needle back into his bag, bowed to Soon Yi and hurried out.

Soon Yi looked at Chris. "He is only sent for you. You are never to talk about Calvin to anyone. Ever!" She slammed the door and hurried after the doctor.

Two days later Milton Conrad's private cell phone rang at two o'clock in the morning. Very few people had access to that number. Milton sat up in bed.

"Milt it's me, Walter. We have word from Hung Duck."

"Is it done?"

"No, it's not done! He was in the same room with McCarty, ready to give him a nice slow-acting bit of disease that would have shown up in about a week and left him dead ten days after that."

"So, what's the problem?"

"The problem is there's another American in captivity with him! Hung Duck doesn't know if you want them both dead or whether you want anyone dead at this point."

"Another American? Who?"

"He just said Lt. McCarty told him he was a friend. His guard mentioned something about a pilot."

"Holy shit. They've got another officer they're not talking about?"

"That's the report. What do you want me to do?"

"Can you get him back in there? We need Hung Duck to find out who this is. Holy crap. How could we not know about this?"

"I'll try getting him back to see both of them. But I think he's spooked now. He doesn't think he handled himself very well. He sounded pretty tentative."

"Look, he has to get some answers; tell him not to administer anything yet. I need to take this upstairs for review."

"Roger that. Let me know what they decide."

"Will do."

Milton hung up the phone, muttered, "How the hell?" and dialed a number in the White House.

35 THE PLAN IS HATCHED

Since her experience with General Moon the night of Kim's gambling party, Soon Yi's life seemed completely out of her control. She had saved her family, but for how long? She witnessed the most powerful and the most decadent side of Korea's power elite, but she wasn't seeing Kun-Woo. She didn't think she could ever face him again. She learned English, but grew less and less enamored of representing Korea to the outside world. She clung to the belief that if she persevered and excelled in her studies she could somehow reclaim herself.

Her most immediate fear was pregnancy. Women are not allowed to have children out of wedlock, especially military women. She had seen it several times already. A young woman would be the constant escort of a fat colonel until she became pregnant, and then she simply disappeared. It became a frequent fate for the women who pinned their hopes on the rising stars of Korea's military. She knew her family's future hinged on her remaining without a child. But she didn't know how to prevent it and didn't know a single person she could talk to about it. Pregnancy remained an inevitable death sentence hanging over her head. She was repulsed when the General forced himself into her mouth, but saw it as her only chance to avoid the inevitable, and so she mastered the art of pleasuring him orally.

Soon Yi became a trusted member of the inner circle. She attended film screenings at Kim's mansions, toured the most secret military installations with the general, saw where Kim ran his counterfeit operations, where he kept his exotic animals, his warehouses of luxury cars, and was even allowed to ride on one of his private rail cars. Kim didn't keep jets. He was deathly afraid of flying, so his six trains were armored, and decked out in the most luxurious fashion imaginable.

He inherited a fear to flying from his father, Kim Il-Sung, who used trains extensively during the Korean War and constructed 19 palaces in locations only accessible by private rail. Kim traveled in a three-train caravan. The first to test the track, the second—trailing by 20 minutes—usually carrying Kim and his guests, and the third with his staff and advanced communications equipment.

General Moon was part of the senior planning team that advised Kim Jong Il. He had come up with the plot that eventually brought Christopher and Calvin to North Korea. As Soon Yi's proficiency in English grew, he realized she would be the perfect person to serve as interpreter for whomever they caught in their net.

Soon Yi persuaded Moon to send more food to her family. Her father now had a job at another plant where he received a token wage to use at government stores. Her brothers were told, in no uncertain terms, they were never to steal so much as a kernel of corn if they valued their parents' lives and their own. They were also shown how photogenic they were.

Kim's original plan had been to simply shoot down an American surveillance plane or helicopter. It had been done before when the United States found itself embroiled in Vietnam. Now that America was bogged down in two wars, Iraq and Afghanistan, it seemed an ideal time to probe America's resolve. China might appreciate the gesture. They might even offer more assistance to calm the waters. America would have to rethink why it kept twenty-eight thousand troops in South Korea, especially if they might provoke a third war America couldn't bear to fight.

A senior-level meeting convened to work out the details and one of the naval officers asked if any attempt should be made to rescue crewmen when the plane was downed. Some suggested it would be a good idea to capture survivors and parade them as hostages until concessions could be wrung from America and, perhaps, the United Nations.

Kim appeared uncertain, so General Moon offered an alternate plan. "We might persuade them to defect. It would be a tribute to you, Dear Leader, if the world believed they chose you over their own country."

The idea was greeted with polite laughter as if it had been intended as a joke. Moon felt pressed to defend his idea and offered an off-the-cuff alternative. "We can make it look like they've defected." The room quieted with everyone looking at the general, challenging him to go on.

"We simply treat them as honored guests, entertain them, and show our hospitality. We can film every event of laughing happy Americans drinking, having a good time in Pyongyang, and then release film to the world saying they have chosen to defect."

A couple of officers smirked but quickly stopped. All eyes were on Kim who clearly enjoyed the idea.

"Can we bring down a plane in a way that insures survivors?" Kim asked.

Officers looked at one another, not wanting to give assurances they couldn't back up. A naval weapons officer spoke up.

"We can easily track their flights. Helicopters make the best targets. They're slow, easy to verify, and often fly at low altitudes over water. We can position several small fishing boats along their most frequent routes. Those won't attract much attention, and we could use a smaller shoulder-fired missile to cripple the chopper without blowing it up. If it could be done during a storm we might even avoid detection. We rescue the crew, the chopper sinks to the bottom of the sea, and the next thing the world knows is these men love Korea."

Kim broke into laughter. He banged the table, clapped his hands, and stood triumphantly. "It is brilliant. Here is what we will do ..." and he went on to basically repeat the naval commander's and General Moon's suggestions word for word. The room erupted in enthusiastic applause.

It took nearly seven months before everything was in place and the right conditions existed for Calvin to fly within striking distance of a shoulder-fired missile.

36 MEETING AT THE INN

Three months after his fall from the apple tree, Joey had fully recovered. He'd spent one week in the hospital, three more weeks at Uncle Ed and Aunt Joan's farm, and then home to Virginia with his arm in a cast for two additional weeks.

Maureen's recovery evolved more slowly, a work in progress. Her parents had come to New Hope and stayed until Joey felt strong enough for Maureen to take him home. Christopher's mother, Anne, had come for two days right after the accident and stayed at The Inn at Phillips Mill just a mile and a half north of New Hope. Joan had recommended the inn as a special hideaway.

Joan told her, "It's nice and quiet. They don't have television or Internet, just a peaceful oasis. The inn is charming, and serves what may be the best French country cuisine in America. It was built in 1756. So, when George Washington crossed the Delaware six miles down the road, the inn was already 20 years old."

Maureen met her mother-in-law shortly after she checked in. They hugged. Anne took both of Maureen's hands into hers, rocked back a step, and looked into her eyes.

"How're you holding up? You've been through so much. We all have. Is Joey okay?"

"Joey's getting better, and I'm okay. We're truly grateful you're here."

Maureen said that Joey still hurt, but his prognosis was good. The real scare was mostly behind them now.

"We have dinner reservations at seven. I thought we could walk for a bit first and catch up. And I thought this might come in handy." She reached into her shoulder bag and handed Anne a bottle of Sauvignon blanc.

"Joan might not have mentioned it, but this is a BYOB Inn—always has been."

They walked the gardens, admired the flowers, and remarked at how well the cats were getting along with the chickens strutting about. Both women felt fragile. Christopher's absence had left a large tender hole in their lives. There was no understanding it. Why wasn't anyone doing anything to bring him home? Maureen explained the hand signals she had seen in the videos. Anne acknowledged she thought he had signaled something with his hands. Then she burst out laughing.

"Wasn't that the worst Forest Gump impersonation you've ever heard?"

Maureen smiled. "He's a unique individual. You raised quite a boy."

Anne put her arm around her. "We'll see him again, Mo. I just know we'll get him back someday. In the meantime: cherish Joey. He needs all you can give him at this point."

"I need all he can give me. He's looking forward to seeing you."

Anne told stories about Christopher's childhood, how he always needed to know what made things work. He was a natural athlete, excelled at sports without making a big deal of it. He'd been an altar boy at church, a friendly outgoing happy kid, until his father died.

"I've never seen anyone more determined or focused than Chris after that. He's the very last person who would ever betray this country. Why can't they see that? Anyway, I have something to talk to you about at dinner. Something I think will help."

Dinner at the inn was by candlelight near the glow of an open fireplace. Service dragged, slow and uneven, but the food lived up to its reputation. Anne explained that her husband had left a fairly large trust for her and for each of their sons. Anne was the trustee until Christopher turned thirty-five, at which time all assets would transfer directly to him. A trust of that type is usually meant to protect money from an unworthy spouse or from "creditors and predators" who might seek to deplete it. Anne had the power to control disbursements for certain specific purposes. In fact, the down payment for his home with Maureen had come from the trust. Anne assured Mo the trust would make mortgage payments until Chris came home. She also wanted Maureen to know she had established a college fund for Joey.

"I don't want you worrying about finances. You just concentrate on caring for Joey. What are you doing for income?"

"I lost my job. Christopher's military pay is still being deposited into our account at the Navy Credit Union, but I've no idea how long that will last."

"What do you need for living expenses?"

"Oh, no. Seriously, I have some savings, and my parents are helping out. The mortgage is a huge relief. You've no idea. And I promise I'll pay you back."

"It's not my money; it's your husband's. I'm quite certain Christopher will want you and Joey to have a roof over your heads. So please, don't stress over finances. Get yourself well, and get Joey well."

She lifted her wine glass, "To Christopher and his safe return.

"Amen." Maureen looked around the quaint restaurant with happy couples silhouetted in flickering candlelight. She smelled the fragrant flowers from her table vase and thought, *Chris should be here.* She suspected Anne had the same thought about her Tom.

37 MAUREEN'S NEW PROJECT

Summer had been tough. But by October reporters were off pursuing other stories, and Joey was back in preschool. Maureen tried to maintain some balance. Bouts of depression washed over her every week. Sometimes her son could vanquish them just by being his bouncy self or with tender hugs. Other times she would feel so fragile she thought she might break at any minute.

It was during a call with sister, Colleen, that Mo found the beginnings of her recovery. Colleen had taken lots of ribbing from Maureen over the years for her geeky pursuits. She loved computers and understood them intuitively. Her first job after college was creating websites, but she quickly branched out into advanced programming. By the time she turned twenty-six, Colleen ran her own software development company.

Colleen called to check in and to see if there was anything she could do to help her younger sister.

"What you need is something to occupy your time, something you're passionate about."

"Like traveling back in time and preventing this nightmare from ever happening?"

"No, seriously, you used to care a lot about education. Isn't there something related to that you could do?"

"I don't think schools will line up to hear my ideas. They probably wouldn't even let me in the building."

"Well, if you could do something to make teaching more effective, what would it be?"

"I don't know. I've always wanted something to get kids more engaged. There is an idea I have, but I doubt it'll ever happen."

"Yeah? What is it?"

"It's kind of a role-playing Facebook approach to teaching…"

"Meaning?"

"Do you really want to hear this?"

"Very much. Go on."

"Well, let's say you're teaching history and covering the Civil War. Each of your students becomes a character from that time. You'd have a class populated by General Lee, and General Grant. Someone would be Lincoln; someone would be a female spy for the Confederates. Each student would use something like a social network page online where they build a profile about their character. "

"And?"

"Then you, as the teacher, drive a timeline, and the students have to respond in their character. You might announce the Battle of Gettysburg and everyone would have to write, in character, how they heard the news, what they were doing when they heard it, how it would affect their future decisions, and their family.

"Anyway, my thought is the students would be living history in a way, not just hearing it or reading it. So it becomes a part of them and they retain it more deeply."

"Mo, that's quite an idea. But I suspect someone's already created it."

"Nope. I don't think so. I've checked, and can't find anything like it."

"Well, it's promising. You know, I could help you build this."

"You could? Really?"

"I could. It shouldn't be too hard. Let me think it through."

For the first time, Maureen felt a spark of life, a sense of purpose. Maybe she could do this. Maybe one day Joey would be in a classroom learning lessons from a program she'd developed. Up until now her sleepless nights had been filled with thoughts of Chris and all their problems. Now she spent nights lying awake planning the look and feel of her new program. She often called Colleen at the break of day excited to know if certain ideas were possible, wanting to know how to incorporate new features.

38 A TALK WITH SOON YI

News feeds from North Korea had settled down. Lieutenant McCarty wasn't in the consciousness of most Americans any more. In North Korea, his little garden had yielded the last of its bounty, and the plants were withering into their winter retreat. Chris could still go outside for brief periods some days. He had been photographed throughout the summer enjoying his idyllic garden. Twice he had been dressed in new clothes and taken to view military parades. Before each outing, he was drugged so that he had the most pleasant feelings. Chris could be seen smiling at troops and missiles as they passed by.

From what he could tell, his little walled garden sat in the far edge of an isolated military installation where guards in towers oversaw every movement, soldiers with dogs patrolled the perimeters of the camp, and cameras constantly swept the compound. Escape seemed impossible.

Chris sat on the bench by his door on a late afternoon watching the sky darken and wondering how bad winter would be. Months of observation had yielded no credible way of escape. He heard the gate unlock from the outside and looked up. Soon Yi entered alone, dressed in her uniform. He stared at her with a sense of dread, convinced she had come delivering bad news.

She approached quietly, almost timidly, and sat beside him. After a long silence, she said, "Tell me about America."

"You people don't give up, do you? I've been interrogated for months, and I've said all I have to say."

"I don't mean that. Not any secrets. Tell me about life in your country. Just everyday life, nothing secret."

"Well, for one thing, we have electricity, everywhere, all the time."

She felt rebuked. He gathered steam.

"We have food in America. All the food we want, too much food. Our farmers feed half the world. We ship food here to North Korea, but your average person probably never sees it.

"We have freedom in America. We choose our own leaders. If we don't like them we tell them so, or we vote them out."

"Then why do you want war with Korea? Why do you crowd our borders if your country has so much to offer?"

"Nobody in America wants war with Korea. Most people never give your country a single thought. Hell, they couldn't find North Korea on a map. We only have troops in South Korea to protect her people there from you."

She stiffened. "Your military is always poised to attack us. You threaten us with nuclear weapons like you used on Japan. You have the second largest military in the world, and only the courage of our leaders has kept you away."

He looked at her and shook his head. "Very few Americans are in the military. Maybe one percent of our population is in uniform. The rest of the country is busy raising families, running stores, or businesses, selling insurance or cars, playing football, watching movies. We couldn't care less what Korea does unless you threaten your neighbors.

"Everyone has a car. Most families have two or three. I can get in a car and drive wherever I want. I can leave the country if I want to. No one tells me where I can or can't go. I can watch television from all around the world, and can connect to anyone I want through the Internet. I can work whatever job I want. I can own my own home and live wherever I please.

"Education is free. My son will be starting school in a couple of years. He'll have a good education in a building

184

that's heated in the winter and air-conditioned in the summer. He'll have books and videos and computers to help him learn.

"You know what he won't have? He won't have his father. That's *your* fault! I'm part of your big joke, but he's just a little a boy growing up without a dad. I suppose that makes you happy."

She sat silently then put a hand on his arm. "It isn't me. I have no control over this. They control me more than they control you. I truly hope you see your son again someday."

Soon Yi stood and walked slowly back to the gate. Someone on the other side unlocked it as she approached. He watched her go. Soon Yi didn't look back, and Chris had a sense he might never see her again.

39 ONE DAY AT A TIME

Nights grew painfully cold by mid-November. Sharp winds rushed down from the mountains into their compound. Frigid rain turned to sleet and finally to blinding wet snow swirling endlessly. Bitter cold bit deeply into their bones.

In their separate rooms, they mirrored each other. Calvin and Christopher each huddled on their stiff mats in the fetal position, gripping the one thin blanket they each had, shivering and praying for sleep. Wind forced its way easily through their walls, skating across them like frigid laughter, washing over their bare gaunt skin. Teeth chattered. Muscles stiffened and twitched.

Chris thought: *At least if I die they won't be able to use me anymore.* And then he thought: *My family won't even know I'm gone. Please, God, don't let them bury me in North Korea.* A tear slid down his cheek. He didn't care.

He was sleeping fitfully when the guards arrived. A soldier kicked him roughly with his boot. Chris flinched and curled more tightly into himself. The guard lifted the thin blanket from Chris, rolled it tightly and whipped him across the face with it. The American yelped and scrambled to his feet. Another guard carried a small metal grill, placing it on the floor close to Chris. He lit charcoal that provided fuel for the tiny stove. It sparked, nurturing a small blue flame. A bundle of twigs was brought in and dropped on the floor. Chris was told through sign language that it was to help him stay warm.

Chris sat up and looked at the guards. He pointed to Calvin's room. "And for him?" he asked. Chris pointed at the grill and then again to Calvin's room. He repeated the gestures more emphatically. The first guard seemed to understand. He nodded "yes"; then both turned and left him to his cold stale breakfast. He heard them in with Calvin and waited for them to leave.

Chris went to the dresser and silently moved it out of the way. He knocked twice. Two knocks replied. Chris bent close to the hole. "Calvin, did they bring you a heater?"

Calvin began coughing and sneezing. It took a full minute for him to compose himself. "Yeah, it's not much, but it'll help."

"It's very kind of them. Guess they aren't ready for us to die just yet."

Chris slid the dresser back and returned to his mat, bending his knees and hunching over the small grill. He warmed his hands, nearly losing his balance. His leg muscles had grown weak and stiff. A bowl of corn mush had been left next to his mat. He picked it up and held the bowl over flames to heat it. When it was barely warm he lifted the bowl to his mouth and let the food slide into him; next he used his hand to scrape the remaining bits onto his fingers and into his mouth; then he licked the bowl and his fingers for any last bit of residue.

He went to his small toilet and saw that the small dribble of water in the bowl had frozen. Chris urinated, watching steam rise from the ice. He realized they wouldn't survive the winter. He felt his rib cage again, fingering bones through thin dry skin. Even the little 'peanuts' he'd learned to eat had stopped scuttling into his room. He knew Calvin's situation must be even worse.

He retrieved the two rice biscuits that had been left with his breakfast, knocked twice on the wall again, and waited. Calvin knocked back. Chris bent down, looked through the small hole, and saw Calvin's eyes staring back at him.

"It's all I have," he said, sliding both crackers through.

"Keep one for yourself."

187

"No, I'm good. I need you to be strong."

"This is useless, Chris. There's nothing to be strong for. We both know we're going to die here."

"We're not dead yet. I refuse to be buried here. We can still control our world. If we make it to spring, we can find a way out."

"Right. A six-foot-two, blond American, who just happens to be the hero of North Korean television, and an old African American will just waltz out of here, and no one will notice."

"One day at a time, Calvin. One day at a time."

40 AUNTIE'S VISIT

Soon Yi opened her door and blinked several times before really focusing. Her mouth opened slightly when she recognized her aunt's face. She hadn't seen Auntie, or any member of her family, for nearly two years. Her usual response would be to bow slightly and hug her mother's only sister. Instead she took a step back, her eyes frozen on the downcast face in front of her, fearing the worst.

She paused, stretched her right arm out to reach her aunt's shoulder, and guided her inside. "Welcome, Auntie. Apologies, I didn't expect to see you in Pyongyang. Please come in. I have tea."

Soon Yi turned on her hot plate, relieved the electricity hadn't gone out yet. She poured water into her teapot and set it on the burner, while keeping her back to her aunt and steeling herself for what she suspected would be unpleasant news from home.

When she turned, her aunt sat on the stiff wooden chair, hunched forward with her head bowed and her hands resting on her knees, looking much thinner than she had two years before. Her frailty was likely compounded by both sickness and malnutrition. Her chest heaved a bit. Her niece couldn't tell if she was sobbing or stifling a cough.

Soon Yi placed a warm cup in her aunt's hands and launched into a rapid-fire description of her life in the capital, how well she was doing, how trusted she had become among the military leadership. She feared any bit of silence would be filled with something troubling from her aunt.

189

The older woman lifted her head, straightened her back, stood slowly, and raised a hand to silence Soon Yi.

"They are gone," she said weakly. "All gone. Your parents died hungry and cold. Your brothers found them huddled together. It may have been complete lack of food, or maybe they ate some root or plant that poisoned them."

"But my brothers ..."

"Days after your parents died, another family took their home, beat your brothers, and threw them out. They sought refuge at the train station; soldiers caught them stealing and shot them for sport. I am deeply sorry, deeply sad."

Soon Yi sank to her knees, balled her hands into tight fists, and wailed in anguish and desperation. Her aunt placed both hands on Soon Yi's shoulders, knelt beside her, and held her while she sobbed.

"We have only each other now."

Soon Yi felt completely empty, as if her tears had drained the last bit of meaning from her life. Blackness crowded into her. Then, when it had nearly obliterated all her light, a small spark of anger began to glow deep inside her like a dying ember suddenly bursting into flame. A clear plan formed in her mind as if branded there by a hot iron. She would ruin General Moon, and Lt. McCarty would be the instrument of his destruction. She crossed her arms in front of her, resting each hand on an opposite shoulder, rose to a full standing position, stared down at her aunt, and said, "We can't all be survivors." And then she smiled slowly, but not with her eyes.

"Thank you for coming, Auntie, for telling me. Please have more tea. I hope you will stay with me a few days. Please stay? I have to go someplace."

She already had her coat on because the apartment was constantly cold. It had been worn inside nearly every day since October. She grabbed the military scarf from its hook, wrapped it tightly around her, and opened the door.

"Please be here when I return, Auntie. I won't be long."

The dark hallway always carried a pungent odor, a mixture of fish, stale food, cigarette smoke, and mold. She took the

190

stairs two at a time, down four flights, banged the door open and rushed into the frigid night air. Her only thought was to find Kun-Woo. He would understand.

She found him at his station and explained a plan that would allow them to be together. It involved escaping North Korea, and would be contingent on him helping with another escape. For the next three weeks, she peppered him for information, instructed him on his assignments, taught him rudimentary English, and wrote a series of letters in English.

41 TRIMMING THE CHRISTMAS TREE

Christmas approached, just nine days away. Maureen took Joey to see Santa Claus at the mall. She steeled herself, knowing he would ask Santa to bring his father home, and fearing what Santa might say. Instead Joey asked for a pony, and a Lego Star Wars spaceship. Maureen stood off to the side. Her hand rose involuntarily, covering her lips with her fingers. Her eyes moistened. Now she feared Joey was losing memory of his father. "I'll Be Home for Christmas" played on the store's speakers. She bit her lip and hoisted Joey up to her shoulder. He was heavier now, harder to hold.

On Saturday, they selected a tree and decorated it while *Charlie Brown Christmas* played on TV. In between hanging bulbs and stringing ribbon, they sipped apple cider and ate gingerbread men they'd baked together that morning. The scent of the tree filled the room. She ached to have her husband with her, to share in the decorations, to share in Christmas with their son.

"Your father would love this tree."

Joey didn't answer. He took a candy cane and hung it on the highest branch he could reach. He admired it for a moment, stood on tiptoes to push it a bit higher, and then turned to get another.

"He'd be so proud of you, Joey. He misses us very much."

Joey took a sip from his cup and sat on the edge of the coffee table.

"I should've asked for a puppy. A pony's too big to fit down the chimney. Do you think Santa'll know that and bring me a puppy instead?"

Maureen stood at the hutch arranging her little Christmas village with the same models her mother-in-law always used. She had spread cotton as snow beneath them, and was adding a model train station when Joey spoke. She went and sat next him on the table.

"You know your dad wants to be here."

Joey looked down, kicking his feet slowly back and forth. He looked up at the tree.

"It needs icicles."

"Joey, don't you want to talk about your father?"

"No. He left us!"

She put her arm around him drawing him near, but he resisted and squirmed away.

"Joey, your dad didn't leave us; he was taken away. He wants so much to be here with us. He loves you, buddy. Very much."

Joey picked up a bright red ornament and smashed it on the floor. He shot to his feet, looked at her fiercely, and yelled, "Daddy hates us! He hates us and he left us and he's never coming home!"

He ran down the hall and slammed the door to his room. Maureen lowered her head and sat completely still, defeated and sad. Sadness turned to anger. She snapped a candy cane in half, and thought: '*Why isn't he here? How could he do this to me?*' And then she felt ashamed. She never intended to waiver in support of him. No one else might believe in him, but she always would.

42 AN EXIT STRATEGY

Calvin lay tightly curled, with his arms crossed and his hands cupped under his armpits for warmth. His body shivered almost to the point of convulsions, but he was content.

In his mind, he was seventeen again, lying on the frayed green sofa in his mother's living room where he could smell bacon and pancakes she cooked for breakfast. He heard her humming as she worked, praising Jesus and breaking out into that old spiritual she sang so often it became her anthem. He knew she praised God because he was still alive and had survived the shooting.

In his dream, Calvin recalled every detail of the day he nearly died. His cousin, Anthony, and he were out on the street throwing an old football so under-inflated his fingers pressed dimples when he gripped it to throw. It was a Sunday evening, October 27, 1985. The Detroit Lions had just defeated the Miami Dolphins. Eric Hipple had outplayed Dan Marino, throwing three touchdowns to Marino's two. Now Calvin stood in the middle of Dexter Street, pretending to be Hipple, faking to his right, dropping back, and arching a fluttering spiral to his cousin, now the embodiment of Leonard Thompson. Anthony caught the ball, zigzagged to avoid imaginary defenders, and spiked the ball when he reached the ally.

Calvin ran after him, and they jumped and high-fived in the end zone right outside Donnie Johnson's duplex. The ball wobbled into the alley. Calvin went to retrieve it just as

Donnie's green Pontiac Bonneville screeched in behind him. Calvin grabbed the ball, stepping back against the wall of the duplex, pressed against the brick across from the passenger side when Donnie opened the driver's side door. He put one foot onto the pavement and still had his right hand on the steering wheel when a burst of shots rang out. Donnie never made another move. Blood spurted from his throat and poured down the side of his door. Calvin fell to the ground, his hands over his head, his eyes clamped shut. He heard a car squeal away but made no effort to move or look up.

When he finally lifted his head, he heard shrieking from Donnie's front porch. Alicia, holding their two-year-old son, wailed for help. Calvin got up and moved cautiously to the back of the car toward the street. That's when he saw Anthony lying with his eyes open, blood pooling from the center of his chest, and urine pooling from between his legs.

Two weeks later, Calvin's mother still made him a full breakfast every morning, still singing, still praising the Lord. That's where Calvin was in his mind: sleeping on his sofa while his mother loved on him.

His mother loved him so much she took him down to the Naval Recruiter's office that Friday, a month before his eighteenth birthday, and made sure he'd get out of Detroit. Three times a day, every day, she prayed that Jesus and the United States Navy would save her only son.

The images of home started to fade. Calvin wanted to hold them, longed for them to continue, but the reality of North Korea washed over him. He gritted his teeth and cursed. He had a wife and two teenage sons at home in San Diego. He had a mother who cherished him and an exemplary military career. He raged at his captors for taking all that from him.

Calvin decided to tell the North Koreans everything they wanted to know. After all, he was probably dead anyway. When the guards arrived, he told them he couldn't stand it any longer. He promised to tell them the largest secrets of the United States military, but first they would have to bring him more food, more blankets, and a warm change of clothes. Their first reaction was to threaten him with another beating.

They were suspicious but, this being the first indication of cooperation they'd ever received, they agreed. The soldiers returned with a large tray of bland food along with two blankets, and clothes that nearly fit him.

Calvin stretched out on his mat, more refreshed, and warmer than he had been in a long time. The guards grew impatient and started yelling that they would take everything away including his small heater. One guard drew a club from his belt. Calvin raised his hand.

"What I'm gonna tell you is the single largest secret in the entire US military. Only the president and our highest officers know anything about this. I know about it because I've been there. I was stationed in that very place nine years ago." The guards knelt next to him to catch every word.

"Some people think they've figured it out, but they don't know anything for sure. Our government kept it secret for nearly sixty years." He beckoned the soldiers closer and brought his voice down to a whisper while he stared up at the ceiling.

"They may be able to hear what I'm saying. If they do we're all in great danger." The soldiers looked at the ceiling and then at one another. They wanted to understand everything he said, but had only a rudimentary grasp of English.

"We have weapons you can't see. They're invisible. We have technology you can't even dream of. We didn't develop them on our own. We had help. Why do you think we developed nuclear weapons sixty years before you? Why do you think we're the richest nation on earth? Like I said: *We had help.*

"It started in 1947. Your intelligence service will be able to find clues of it. It happened in the middle of summer, a hot July day in a hot part of America, in a state we call New Mexico. That's when our special help arrived.

"We have a secret base not far from there. It doesn't even have a name. We just call it Area 51. Our most advanced weapons are developed there."

One of the guards put a hand on Calvin's shoulder. "Wait. You tell Colonel. Colonel comes tomorrow. You tell everything to him. But what you tell must be truth. Only truth."

"Yes, of course, only truth. I'll tell your colonel everything tomorrow."

The guards hurried out, eager to announce that the black American had finally cracked.

Calvin waited a couple of minutes before rapping twice on the wall. Chris knocked back immediately. He'd heard the movement and voices from Calvin's room and wanted to know what had happened. He moved the dresser away from their hole and peered through it. Calvin peered back, smiling broadly, something Chris hadn't seen him do since boarding the helicopter.

"What's going on, Cal?"

Calvin's voice sounded almost giddy. "I'm totally screwed. I think I just signed my death warrant." Still smiling. He was matter-of-fact, almost upbeat. "I played with the guards, and they're bringing their Colonel tomorrow to hear everything I have to say."

"Everything you have to say about what?"

"Oh, I started telling them our big secret is Roswell and Area 51. By the time their superiors find out what I'm talk'n about, the guards will likely be demoted and I'll become the newest version of a North Korean piñata. I had them bring me a big breakfast and warm clothes. It seemed like a good idea at the time. They're gonna be really pissed. They're gonna kill me."

He nearly sang, "I think they're gonna kill me," then coughed uncontrollably.

Chris waited for the coughs to subside. "Maybe not. Maybe they won't catch on for a while. We might be able to play this out. What exactly did you say to them?"

Chris listened carefully, and then had Calvin repeat everything to be sure he understood what the guards had heard.

"Okay. So, you didn't exactly tell them aliens are helping us. We can build something credible around this that'll keep them occupied for a while."

They spent most of the day crafting a story that the guards would believe enough to buy them time. Calvin rehearsed his part, and Chris came up with a way to affirm it so that the guards would think they were tricking him into verifying Calvin's story.

Their talk had just ended, and Chris had slid the dresser back over the hole, when footsteps approached his outer door. The key turned quickly, and the door was thrust forcefully open. A soldier with an AK-47 pushed into the room, standing at attention just inside the door. Soon Yi entered behind him. Chris stood with his thin blanket over his shoulders expecting the worst.

She approached slowly, watched him for a moment as he shivered, and finally said, "I know you have no reason to trust me, but I have come to get you out of here, both of you."

"You're right. I don't trust you. Is this where Calvin and I get shot in the back for escaping?"

"No. It's where I do what's right. I know what it's like to lose a family. It's time you saw your wife and child again. I have papers for your transfer. This soldier is my dearest friend, Kun-Woo. He will help you escape. The prison guards will think you're being moved to another camp. Kun-Woo will shelter you. You can trust him."

Chris stared at Soon Yi and then at Kun-Woo. "He doesn't look all that trustworthy. How can he get us out without getting caught?"

"He has a plan. He has contacts. Kun-Woo will protect you."

"This should be good. Exactly how will he get us out of Korea?"

"I can't tell you that. If you're captured, you must not be able to tell who is helping you. It would mean death to anyone involved, death to their entire families."

"And when do we leave?"

"You leave now." She took a pair of handcuffs from her belt. "These you wear only until we're free of the camp."

Chris hesitated, looked intently into her eyes, and then slowly turned and brought his wrists up together behind him.

"Me and Calvin together, right?"

"Yes, you go together." She turned him around and cuffed his hands in front of him.

She said something in Korean to Kun-Woo. He stepped into the hallway and signaled to two other soldiers who entered Calvin's room and escorted him to Christopher and Soon Yi.

Chris gasped, startled at how thin and fragile Calvin looked. Except for what little he could see through their hole in their wall, he hadn't seen Calvin in months. Now he looked gaunt, his eyes were more yellow than white; a pronounced limp and scruffy beard, mostly white, gave the impression he'd aged ten years or more. Calvin looked apprehensive. He saw handcuffs on Chris and felt sure this was a prelude to their execution.

"I'm sorry Chris, I didn't mean to cause this. I just wanted to mess with the guards. Didn't think they'd really take it like this. Chris, it's on me, man."

He started to appeal to Soon Yi, but she held her hand up and ordered him to be quiet.

Chris held his cuffed hands up as well and told Calvin to hush. "It's okay, man, come here." He whispered what Soon Yi had promised and asked him to go along with getting cuffed.

Calvin started to say, "And you believe this bitch?" but Chris cut him off again.

"You got a better plan ... any plan?"

Calvin turned, cautiously extending his arms behind him to be handcuffed by Kun-Woo. Soon Yi barked an order to the other guards who closed ranks behind Chris and Calvin. Together they escorted them through the courtyard, through the ornate gate, out into the military base, and across a narrow path to an aging, green, army van. One of the soldiers roughly pushed the two Americans into the back. He seemed proud of inflicting discomfort on imperialistic foreigners, enemies of the state. A platoon of soldiers goose-stepped in formation facing them from about fifty yards out, each eyeing the tall Americans with suspicion.

Kun-Woo and Soon Yi got in the front seats, and Kun-Woo turned the key. The engine revved and then died. He tried again, and again the engine sputtered to a stop. Calvin leaned forward to Soon Yi and said, "Tell him to pump the accelerator three times, take his foot off, and then turn the key." She translated for Kun-Woo who complied. The engine finally started and settled into a rough idle that smoothed out as he pushed down gently on the pedal.

Soon Yi saluted the two escorts, the van was put into gear, and they lurched forward. In three hundred yards, they were at the front gate. A barrier extended across the road, so vehicles had to stop for inspection. Soon Yi presented papers to the soldiers, who looked impressed and snapped to attention as they spoke with her. The gate quickly opened, and they drove through trailing a cloud of dark smoke behind them.

Soon Yi allowed herself a half smile. General Moon's orders, though forged, carried a good deal of weight. After removing their handcuffs, she reached under her seat and pulled up a military backpack.

"I thought you might want to take a gift back to America," she said, her smile broadening. "Perhaps this will help you."

Chris took the backpack. It felt heavier than he expected. "What is it?"

"See for yourself." She was obviously proud of its contents.

Chris reached into the backpack and pulled out a heavy metal object. It took him almost a full minute in the evening light to realize what it was. He held it up looking at both sides and slowly realizing why it seemed familiar. *Holy shit!* He thought, *this is a plate for printing $100 bills—US currency.*

"Is this real? How'd you get this?"

"Yes, very real. Chairman Kim uses it to make his counterfeit American money. He delights in it, uses dollars to buy his luxuries from the West. Your government might be more willing to believe you weren't cooperating with Kim when you bring them this."

"But how …?"

"I have friends in low places."

"No, seriously!"

"It is most happily released on written orders signed by General Moon himself."

"Who is General Moon?"

"Someone who destroyed my family and is about to lose everything he ever cared about. He just doesn't know it yet."

Chris handed the plate to Calvin. "Can you believe this?"

Calvin handled it, turned it over twice, and whistled. He looked at Chris and nodded toward Soon Yi. "She's good!"

They drove another thirty minutes up a steep, curving mountain road, heading north. Snow swirled, falling on ground already patched with ice. Few roads in North Korea had ever been paved, and this one was no exception.

Just after cresting a high mountain pass, Kun-Woo turned left between a stand of trees and a large jutting boulder, traversing a path that was barely visible. A short distance up he made another left into a clearing, pulling aside a large Russian-made jeep.

"We change vehicles here," Soon Yi explained. "They will be looking for the van."

The frigid air assaulted them as they moved to the jeep, blowing into their hands for warmth. Soon Yi told Chris and Calvin they would have to take turns with one on the floor in the back and the other hidden under blankets on the back seat. Two large empty aluminum boxes would be placed over them with stencils designating them as military waste. If patrols stopped the jeep, no one would demand bribes from 'military waste.' They were ready to settle in when Soon Yi said she wouldn't be going with them.

"I say goodbye here," she said. "I am sorry for what my country did to you. I hope you will forgive me one day … one day when you are free and with your families."

Chris felt like hugging this woman who had been his tormentor for so long. But she only bowed politely, so he returned the courtesy, nothing more. He watched her return to the van and wondered what could have led her from enemy to savior.

Kun-Woo motioned for them to get in the jeep. With both of them in the back seat, he reached down and produced two bowls, which he handed to them. "Kimchi." He smiled motioning them to eat. It consisted of cold cabbage fermented in ginger and garlic, tangy and salty. They ate it quickly, and Kun-Woo collected their bowls.

They got situated and followed Soon Yi's van back to the main mountain road. Once there, Kun-Woo turned left and Soon Yi turned right, the two vehicles descending opposite sides of the mountain.

She gripped the wheel tightly, focusing on navigating the icy road that, even at slow speeds, caused her to bump and slide close to the sharp drop off on her left. She finally made it down and drove past the military base, heading in the opposite direction from Kun-Woo. If her van were spotted, it would lead them in the wrong direction. No sign of alarm had been raised from the base yet.

After several miles, she started another steep climb. Once her van slowed too much and slipped backward. She pumped her brakes, sending the back of the van into a skid with her wheels locked. She let the van carefully slide back to where she could gain traction and began heading up again. It took a long time, but she finally reached the summit.

Soon Yi pulled her van to a stop just over the peak of the mountain. She gazed out across a dark valley and reflected on her plan. It might work, or it might lead to two dead Americans. She sincerely hoped for the former.

She turned on the dome light, reached into her briefcase, and took out two wrinkled photographs. The first was a picture General Moon had shown her of her brothers stealing from a truck. The second showed Soon Yi on her bicycle, her mother and father standing smiling behind her. She thought about her father sitting in their apartment staring out at the sea. She heard her mother's voice: *Make me proud, little bee. Make me proud.*

Soon Yi kissed the photographs, placed them against her chest inside her coat, switched off the dome light, and pressed the accelerator. The van picked up speed. She pressed harder. Tears partially blocked her vision, but she focused on the beam of her headlights. A sharp turn lay ahead. Soon Yi aimed for a large boulder just before the turn and drove into it with tremendous force. The van collapsed, crushing her. It bounced off the rock, and rolled over, flipping down a long steep embankment tumbling and breaking apart. This part of her plan was done.

43 TRAVEL BY RAIL

Kun-Woo drove unpaved, bumpy roads throughout the night, heading north and then east to the edge of Hamhung City. He had been on paved road for only the past ten minutes, driving parallel to railroad tracks. Just before dawn, he turned right onto an access road that took them over the tracks. A gray wooden shack stood in the snow just off the rails to their left. He stopped the jeep and studied the area in all directions before reaching back and pushing one of the aluminum crates out of the way.

"We here," he said.

Calvin lifted his head and stared out into the dark gray dawn. He reached down and tapped Chris, who stiffly shifted his weight and forced himself up between the boxes.

They were peering out opposite sides of the vehicle. Aside from the shack, there wasn't anything but railroad tracks as far as they could see.

"There's nothing here," Calvin said.

"Less than nothing," Chris replied. He began to fear again that the whole escape had been a trick and that they were about to die. Visions of mob movies where unsuspecting gangsters were taken for a ride in the woods, never to return, weighed on him. He looked apprehensively at Kun-Woo, who opened his door and beckoned for them to do the same. They got out stiff from the ride, stiff from the cold, and now stiff with growing apprehension.

Kun-Woo led them quickly to the shack, unlocked a large iron padlock on the door, and ducked inside. He fumbled for a moment, then struck a match, lighting an old lantern. Chris and Calvin each had to turn sideways and bend down to fit through the door. Inside they stood shoulder-to-shoulder, pressed against Kun-Woo's chest. The shack smelled of coal and heavy oil. Kun-Woo squirmed down to open a rusty toolbox and retrieve a note which he handed to Chris.

So glad you found your way here. My trusted friend has guided you well. Please stay the day inside. Early tomorrow a train will stop to take on coal. When it does, my friend will lead you to a railcar where you will hide. It will take you past five stops. After the fifth stop you must watch for a lighthouse in the distance on your right. The train slows almost to a stop there. Even in the dark you will see a white abandoned factory very close to the tracks with its roof caved in. You must jump just before it and take refuge there. My friend will come again for you. I wish you safe travel home. Soon Yi.

Christopher noticed she hadn't mentioned Kun-Woo by name; she was protecting him. It made him wonder why she'd taken the risk of signing her own name. He handed the note to Calvin, who lifted the lantern to read it. Kun-Woo motioned him to hurry so they could extinguish the light. He pushed his way past them, returned to the jeep, and retrieved the blankets and a water canteen. There wasn't room to lie down, so Chris and Calvin sat with their backs to opposing walls, wrapped the blankets tightly around themselves, and were plunged into darkness as Kun-Woo closed the door, locking them in. They heard him working outside and realized he was brushing snow to hide their footprints. They listened as his jeep drove away.

Calvin convulsed in an extended series of coughs. His voice sounded raspy and dry. Chris reached out hugging him, patting his back to ease the coughing.

"Will you be all right? We need to be quiet. There's no way of telling if someone comes by."

Calvin half grunted, working hard to stifle his coughs. "You still got that backpack?"

Chris slapped the pack. "Still here, counterfeit plate and all."

"Maybe she's legit. I won't believe it until we're on American soil."

"Where do you think we're headed, Cal?"

"I watched the stars most of the night. We headed north for a couple of hours, then turned east. I thought we'd end up in China, but with the turn east we're closer to the Sea of Japan. The tracks outside run north and south. If we take a train straight north, I think we end up in Russia. If I remember right, we'd end up in Vladivostok. It's a major port just over the border. That lady's pretty whacked. Do you think she'd sell us to the Russians or the Chinese?"

"I can't see why she'd do that, and she wouldn't need to give us the plate if she did. Something's been changing with her. It's like it built up to the point that she couldn't stand it anymore. She's been asking me about life in America. Nothing strategic, just our way of life. It's almost like she's been feeling ashamed."

"Damn right she's ashamed. This whole miserable country should be ashamed!" Calvin began to shiver and wheeze. Chris reached out and cradled him in his arms. They fought against the cold for hours before finally yielding to fitful sleep.

The loud thunder of a locomotive woke them with a start. It sounded as if the engine would smash through their thin wooden walls. The rumbling eased, followed by a loud screeching, grinding noise as the train slowed to a stop.

Footsteps crunched the snow outside and metal clicked as the padlock released. Kun-Woo opened the door and beckoned them to come out. Calvin crouched on his hands and knees. He crawled out just far enough to search the landscape in every direction, shielding his eyes from the blinding daylight. No one else was in sight. He pulled himself up to a standing position using the side of the door for support. His muscles ached, rigid from his confinement, and from the cold. He looked back at Chris.

"Looks clear," in a rough whisper.

Chris eased himself to a standing position and peered out at the train. It had twelve or fifteen cars, most carrying coal with a few enclosed boxcars. He and Calvin wrapped their blankets tightly around their shoulders and surveyed the situation. Four empty coal cars on an adjoining track about 200 yards away were being pushed slowly to join the others.

Kun-Woo signaled for them to stay low, as he crouched and moved toward a middle coal car. It was identical to the others except for a large metal North Korean star affixed toward the back of it on either side. He waved them forward, and they followed to the back of the car, where a small platform stood almost completely hidden by the back half of the stars. An angled steel plate jutted down from the top rear of the car, mostly covering their hiding place. Kun-Woo motioned for them to climb on. Chris scrambled onto the platform, but Calvin collapsed into a ball on the snow. Chris and Kun-Woo helped him up, and Chris realized how light Calvin felt. Once aboard, they found a duffle bag with army jackets, gloves, hats, pants, and scarves. A sack containing dried fish, potatoes, and corncobs was at the bottom along with a large thermos of coffee. Kun-Woo made the number five with his fingers, watched to make sure they understood, and then hurried to the front of the train.

It was the first coffee they'd had in nearly a year. It tasted bitter but they savored it. Their food went quickly. But the train didn't move for thirty minutes. When the locomotive did start, its motion was almost imperceptible. The clear sky offered no threat of snow. Calvin began to focus on the sun for direction. They were headed due north.

"Count the stops," Calvin said. "We need to stay awake."

The first two stops were uneventful, lasting just fifteen minutes with activity only at the front of the train. The third was different. Temperatures had risen into the low forties and bright sunlight glistened off the sparse snow. As the train slowed to a stop Chris felt confident enough to poke his head out beyond the shelter of their metal star. He looked at the tracks behind to see how many railcars were there, wanting to know if anyone in the rear could spot them when it came time to jump. He was relieved to see only coal cars and no caboose. Turning toward the front he suddenly realized two soldiers were walking the tracks heading from front to back deep in conversation. He darted his head back and motioned for Calvin to be still. Chris pressed himself tightly against the cold steel of the railcar.

The guards had been approaching at a slow pace when one of them started shouting. They picked up their pace and began running toward the back. From the sound of their footsteps the soldiers were only one car away. Chris picked up the thermos as though it were a club. He held it shoulder high, prepared to swing it into the face of the first soldier to mount their hideaway.

To his surprise, they ran past his position, picking up speed and shouting. They seemed to be two cars behind him when they stopped abruptly and began firing their weapons. There was a brief silence before the soldiers again began walking to the back of the train. Chris and Calvin exchanged puzzled looks. Calvin shrugged. Minutes later the guards could be heard talking and moving back toward the front.

The platform that sheltered Calvin and Chris was nearly invisible from the side or the front. Someone coming close to the car from behind had a far better chance of spotting it. The soldiers were moving slowly. Chris felt his heartbeat accelerate. He held his breath so that that steam wouldn't rise into the chilly air, and waited. The soldiers trudged past. Chris caught a brief glance of them as they approached carrying the body of a woman. She had been shot in the chest, probably for trying to board the train, more likely for stealing coal for heat.

It took nearly thirty minutes before the train moved again. The sun had risen higher in the sky. Calvin determined it must be mid-afternoon. He had been holding in his coughs, but now he began to hack and wheeze uncontrollably. He shivered so badly Chris was afraid Calvin might lose his

208

footing and fall. He held him tightly, positioning his back against the wall of the car as Chris remained between him and the end of the platform. He guided Calvin into a sitting position and wrapped both blankets around him, wishing the coffee wasn't all gone.

The train curved further northeast until it was hugging the shoreline of the Sea of Japan to their right, now heading due north. Calvin felt certain they were headed to the Russian border and Vladivostok. The fourth stop was uneventful; the fifth remarkable only for time it took. Nearly an hour sitting, while the locomotive decoupled. Chris feared the train had broken down and that they would never make it to their drop-off point. They shivered and waited, while the day grew longer. Eventually, a smaller, older engine chugged back into place. It strained and groaned until, bit-by-bit, the cars began to move.

Chris kept watch on the right-hand side, searching the coastline for a lighthouse. Late afternoon began settling into evening. Chris worried it might be just dark enough to obscure the lighthouse but not yet dark enough for its light to be lit. When it did come into view, its lantern still dark, about three miles off on the horizon, it was barely perceptible against the growing dusk. Tracks curved sharply to the left and the train slowed almost to a stop. Chris signaled for Calvin to get ready. He spotted the abandoned white warehouse with its roof collapsed and pulled Calvin closer to his side of the platform.

"This is it. Are you all right to jump?"

"I guess I have to be. Let's do it."

Calvin bundled his blanket tightly in front of him, took a deep breath, and jumped. The train moved slowly, but he had to leap far enough to be sure he cleared the tracks. Graveled ground beyond the tracks rose to a high mound, covered with intermittent patches of ice. If he wasn't careful, and didn't achieve enough momentum, Calvin would hit the mound, bounce back, and roll under the train.

When he landed, his leg drove a sharp stabbing pain up into his hip. He yelped, curled onto his back with both hands pulling his knee up close to his chest. Loose gravel slid from under him, and he felt himself beginning to slide toward the tracks. Calvin dug in with the heel of his good foot, turned sideways, and reached his arm up to grab the top of the mound. He was able to wiggle up and roll over the other side. He hurt everywhere, but was clear of the tracks. Chris wrapped his blanket around the backpack and tossed it high enough and far enough to ensure it wouldn't roll down the embankment. He leapt and landed gracefully, his arms outstretched and then coming down in front of him, as he tucked and rolled forward. Calvin lay on his back thirty yards behind him. Chris backtracked, staying low to avoid being seen from the train or from vantage points nearby.

"You okay?" he whispered.

"Been better, been worse. Help me up."

They crouched low, using the mound for cover, and then lay flat waiting for the train to disappear. Chris crawled back to retrieve the blanket and knapsack, while Calvin rubbed his leg and felt the deepest part of his pain slowly subside.

They started to get up to advance on the building when they heard voices. Chris reached out, grabbed Calvin's jacket, carefully pulled him down, and then lay over him. He could feel both their hearts beating. Whoever spoke was getting closer, louder. Another voice rose higher and broke into laughter. By the sound, they were almost on top of the two Americans. Both held their breath. And then, silence. Chris realized his eyes were clenched shut. He opened them and slowly lifted his head. Something moved from left to right on the other side of the track. He focused and realized two villagers on bicycles were passing on the thin path across the rails from him. He tucked his head down and whispered to Calvin, "We're okay, but we're not alone here."

The warehouse stood fifty yards ahead. They approached cautiously, keeping low, stopping halfway to listen for any signs of activity. After several minutes of silence, they crept closer. There was a side door with dark green paint peeling from age and a broken padlock hanging from the latch above a rusty doorknob. Chris motioned for Calvin to wait while he went to explore the door. Once there, he slid almost into a sitting position with his back edging down the wall and resting on it for support. He reached out with his left hand and swung the door slowly outward. Nothing happened. He waited a few seconds, said a silent prayer, and ducked inside. A sudden rustling caused him to tense until he realized it was a small flock of birds in the building taking flight, nothing more. He crept back through the door and signaled Calvin to join him.

The warehouse contained a large central room with several smaller rooms around the perimeter. The roof had totally collapsed along the wall closest to the railroad tracks, but stood fairly well intact at the back of the building. Signs that other people might occupy the building quickly came to light. Cigarette butts, and thin dry apple cores were in the first small room. Human feces, somewhat recent, were in the corner of another. They silently searched for occupants and for anything useful. No one else was there, but nearly everything of value had been ripped out and stolen. They gathered an old tarp, a screwdriver missing half its handle, and a two-foot length of rope burned on one end, and collected a mound of dry sawdust and some splintered wooden wall studs to build a small fire. The last room they entered contained a surprise. A note was pinned to a wall with their names on the envelope.

If you find this, please know I am with you. My dear friend will meet you soon. You will go near my hometown where the houses and factories flow down to the sea. Since you came from the sea you should return the same. You are at the highest danger point. By now the alarm has been sounded. I hope they are looking elsewhere but you must be very careful. Trust my friend. He will protect you.
Soon Yi

Again, he wondered why she'd risked signing her name. He showed it to Calvin and then tore it into tiny pieces. The back

211

room seemed best suited for their fire, having no windows and no exterior doors, but with wide enough gaps in the roof to provide ventilation. They piled the sawdust into the middle of the room, sprinkled in pieces of Soon Yi's note, and then positioned the splintered wood in teepee fashion above them. Chris took nails they had pried from the wall and bent close over the sawdust. He used the screwdriver to strike the nails, sending off sparks from the concrete floor. It took several minutes, but the sparks finally ignited the dry sawdust, and a bright yellow flame sprouted from the pile. Calvin had been standing watch by the door. He approached the fire, and they both crouched down to warm their hands.

Chris spread the tarp on the floor next to the fire and told Calvin to lie down. He covered him with both blankets.

"I'll take the first watch. Get as much sleep as you can. Hopefully we won't be here long."

Calvin started to protest, but Chris just turned and walked into the large central room. He closed the flimsy door to keep as much heat in the smaller room as possible.

44 ECLIPSE OF THE MOON

General Moon had grown suspicious of Soon Yi. She had been more distant than usual during the past few weeks. He assumed she despised him, but he didn't care. He still controlled her; he could still use her whenever he wanted, for as long as he wanted. He hadn't been very attentive to her family in Chongjin other than to order a local captain to provide them food as necessary. As long as he had her family for leverage Soon Yi would do whatever he wanted. He never realized how quickly food had disappeared from her family's district.

He sent his car for her, but the driver returned alone reporting she wasn't at her apartment, hadn't attended classes at the university, and hadn't been seen by neighbors for over four days. The general went to see for himself. Her apartment looked clean and orderly, nothing out of place, and nothing to give an indication she planned to be away. All her clothes were in her closet. He lifted one of her scarfs to his nose and inhaled deeply. Yes. He needed to see her again. Her toothbrush and toiletries were all in the bathroom; every sign indicated she planned to be home.

The general instructed the driver to take him to his office at the Defense Ministry. On the way, he had his driver order a search for her. Not an emergency search, nothing to indicate any trouble, just a search to bring her to his office.

Moon had been going through paperwork for less than ten minutes when his orderly barged into the office, anxiously sputtering something about treason. The general stood as a group of armed soldiers forced their way in with weapons drawn.

"Who the hell are you? What's this all about?" he demanded.

"General, we have orders to arrest you for treason against the Democratic People's Republic of Korea and for treason against Premier Kim Sung Il. You are coming with us."

"Treason? I'm the most loyal …"

The lead soldier crossed behind the desk and slapped him hard across the face. The general staggered back and sputtered. He tried to protest but was spun around and tightly handcuffed, the metal sending sharp pain through his wrists.

Over the next three days General Moon endured torture, as did every member of his family. He was shown written orders he had signed. One authorized release of the counterfeit plate to him; another set ordered the American prisoners released for transit to another facility. The questions were always the same:

"What have you done with the counterfeit plate? Where is it?"

"Why did you help the Americans escape? Where are they?"

He tried to explain that it must have been Soon Yi, but they scoffed at the idea she, or any woman, could have accomplished any of it without his help.

On the fourth day, officers led him into a large courtyard where his son and daughter were tied standing on a platform, ropes around their wrists and necks.

The same questions were asked once more. Again, the general swore he knew nothing about any of those charges. He pleaded for mercy. Questions were asked again that he couldn't answer. A command was shouted; the general's daughter shrieked and fell through an opening on her platform. Her neck broke with an audible crack; her head tilted sideways, her eyes bulging, her body swinging. General Moon's mouth opened wide, but no sound emitted; his knees trembled, and he turned a pleading, shocked look to his captors.

The questions were asked again. The general cried and begged for understanding. He didn't know anything. Please, they had to believe him: he loved Kim Jong Il, he loved Korea, it wasn't him. Another order, another loud sound of wood falling away, a snapped neck, and his son was gone. The general lowered his head, refusing to watch, desperate to escape reality.

A chair was brought to the center of the courtyard. The general was ordered to sit facing the dangling bodies of his dead children. He sat sweating and crying for several minutes until a door opened and his wife was brought out in chains. They pushed her rudely up against a brick wall at the back of the courtyard. Mrs. Moon's blindfold was removed. Her eyes blinked, adjusting to the bright light, until she saw her children hanging limp and contorted in front of her. Her chest heaved, her throat began to convulse, and she vomited before passing out.

Soldiers revived her and placed her back on her feet. She shook badly.

Mrs. Moon sputtered and cried. She glared at her husband and cursed. Another order sounded and bullets flew from six rifles, tearing into her, shattering her chest and skull. General Moon fell to his knees sobbing uncontrollably, shivering with fear. He was picked up and marched to the same wall, positioned immediately behind the battered body of his wife, standing in her blood.

"Nothing to say, General?"

"Please, no! No! I didn't have anything to do with this. It wasn't me. It's Soon Yi. SOON YI. Please you must …

General Moon paused, his lip quivering, staring down at what had been his wife. He looked up at what had been his children, sucked in an enormous breath to fill his chest, straightened to attention, and stared straight ahead while sweat poured down his face, and urine dribbled down his shaking legs.

The order was given, and bullets found their mark.

45 PATH TO THE SEA

Chris estimated it must be nearly midnight in the dark warehouse. He fought sleep, walking back and forth, blowing on his hands, then placing them under his armpits for warmth, checking various windows for any sign of activity. He doubted he could stay awake much longer, but wanted Calvin to get as much rest as possible. He'd made several quiet visits back to Calvin's room, adding pieces of wood, scraps of paper, and even two small bits of coal he had found to stoke the fire. Each time he stayed only long enough to warm his frigid fingers before returning to sentry duty.

He sat in the large central room leaning against a wall fighting to keep his eyes open, but fading fast. His head lolled forward, and he began to dream of Maureen standing in his bedroom on New Year's Eve. He tried to draw her near but she extended her arms to gently push him away. "Not tonight, but soon." He awoke to see Kun-Woo standing over him. Chris tried to stand, but slipped and had to regain his balance. Kun-Woo reached down, lifting Chris under his arms.

"We go soon."

Chris nodded and led Kun-Woo back to the room where Calvin lay resting, happy to see the old pilot sleeping soundly. He knew things were touch and go for Calvin at this point.

Kun-Woo reached around to take off his backpack. He dug inside and retrieved a large brownish apple for the American. It looked awful but tasted wonderful as far as Chris was concerned. While he ate, Kun-Woo took an old map from the backpack and unfolded it. He placed it on the floor and used his flashlight to illuminate it, pointing to a spot indicating to Chris where they were to begin. His finger slid slowly north and then east into the Sea of Japan.

"Boat," he said. "Fish boat."

Chris nodded. "When?"

Kun-Woo didn't understand.

"When we go?" he asked tapping his left wrist to indicate a watch.

"We go now."

Chris bent to warm himself as much as he could by the waning fire. He was eager to move but wanted to buy Calvin a few more seconds of sleep. He finally stretched out his arm to gently nudge Calvin's shoulder. Calvin flinched but continued to sleep. Chris paused before nudging him again. This time Calvin rolled over and opened his eyes.

"Time for me to take the watch?"

"Nope. Time to go." He turned his head and rolled his eyes to the right. Calvin followed the gesture to see Kun-Woo standing above him.

"Looks like we're going by boat. Our friend brought a map. We're close to the city of Chongjin, and you're right: it's close to Russia." Kun-Woo offered a gnarled apple to Calvin, who devoured it in seconds. A thermos of coffee came out of the knapsack which they shared while Kun-Woo reached in and brought out a bottle of vodka.

"For fish boat."

Calvin looked at Chris and smiled. "I'm starting to like this guy."

Kun-Woo urged them to hurry as they gathered up what they could and headed out. It was still pitch black, at least three hours before dawn. They set out away from the railroad tracks in the direction of the sea. Chris knew the old lighthouse he'd watched for from the train must be ahead and to his left, but realized the lamp had never come on. The scent of the ocean mingled with fumes from nearby factories.

Chris let Calvin follow Kun-Woo so that his friend would always be in front of him. Calvin's limp improved slightly as they walked, but the rough terrain and darkness made going slow.

They reached an outcropping of rocks on high ground with the sea in front of them and a valley dipping down to their left. They could hear waves breaking on the rocks below. Kun-Woo pointed toward the valley and said, "Chongjin."

They stared in the direction he pointed. In the darkness, it was hard to see anything, but they could hear faint noises from that direction.

"It's the city," Calvin said. "About three miles in that direction."

Chris nodded, and realized Calvin's breathing had become more labored.

Kun-Woo gestured that they'd need to be more cautious now. He led them along a narrow path that brought them closer to the edge where the cliff disappeared into the sea below. Gusts of wind picked up as if challenging their escape. They carefully worked their way along the ledge heading progressively downward. At one point the path turned away from the sea to the edge of an open field, allowing them to move more quickly, but still cautiously since their descent took them closer to the town. The path leveled out forty feet above the water. Kun-Woo turned seaward for several yards and then stopped suddenly.

A metal fence, seven feet high, stretched the length of the hillside, blocking the entrance to the sea. Kun-Woo shook his head. This must have been new. He certainly wasn't expecting it. He turned left, then to his right, and back to his left again. There seemed no obvious solution.

Footsteps crunched the snow behind them. A sharp voice shouted an angry order. They turned to see a soldier with his AK-47 pointed at them. He shined a flashlight on their faces, alternating from one to the other, excitedly shouting commands. Kun-Woo put his hands on his head. Chris followed his lead and did the same. Calvin went into a coughing fit, hacking and wheezing to the point that he knelt on one knee with his head bowed, almost convulsing. The soldier approached, lowering his weapon to Calvin's head.

Suddenly the pilot reached up, grabbed the barrel, pushed hard, forcing the weapon violently into the soldier's chest. It was the soldier's turn to double over and take a knee. Calvin pulled back on the AK-47, yanked it free, and then swung it like a baseball bat at the soldier's head. They heard a loud cracking pop before the guard swayed and fell lifeless.

Calvin stood over him making sure he was dead. Then he looked up at Chris and with a sheepish smile said, "Little bastard pissed me off."

"You're the man, Calvin! I owe you big time."

"Yeah, I just hope I'm around to collect."

They turned their attention back to the fence. Chris pulled up a long reed from the ground and touched it to the fence. It crackled and curled in on itself, emitting a small wisp of smoke.

"Shit. It's electrified, and it's high voltage."

Calvin looked at the wire fence, then down at the dead soldier at his feet and shrugged. "This might help." He bent down grasped the soldier by the straps of his backpack and began pulling him toward the fence. Chris realized his plan and helped by grabbing dead man's shoulders. They elevated him nearly to a standing position in front of the fence and then pushed him onto the first three wires, which hissed and sparked. The smell of burnt skin and hair was immediate. Calvin reached down, picked up the AK-47, and placed the wooden butt on the ground in front of the fence, letting the metal barrel fall onto the fourth wire. No sparks.

"It's shorted out. You still got that rope?" he asked Chris.

Chris pulled it from his pack and tossed it to Calvin, who placed it under the fourth wire and up around the sixth, pulling it tight so that the lower wire stretched up toward the top of the fence. Calvin tied a knot at the top, leaving a nice gap above the fallen soldier.

"That should do it." Calvin bent down, crawled over the dead guard's body, and slid through the wires. On the other side, he rolled clear and signaled for them to follow. Once all three were through, Calvin reached back and retrieved the rifle and their backpack.

Kun-Woo motioned for them to hurry forward.

"You up for double time, Calvin?" Chris asked.

"Hell, I'm up for anything. Let's book it."

Chris smiled to see Calvin so energized. Apparently being a hero was good for him.

They moved quickly, with Calvin swinging his leg in a limping run until they reached a short, sandy path leading down to an isolated cove. Kun-Woo held up his arm and motioned for them to stay still. He used his flashlight to emit three quick bursts of light toward the sea. Three short lights answered them almost immediately. Chris crouched down, surprised the lights came nearly from shore, and realized a small flat boat waited just yards from the beach.

Kun-Woo signaled them onward, so they scrambled across the short beach and into the frigid water, wading nearly waist deep to reach the skiff. Chris couldn't help shrieking when the first cold wave hit him. He felt embarrassed, afraid he might have been heard, exposing all of them.

Calvin hoisted the AK-47 over his head, and Chris did the same with his backpack until they could hand them aboard. Strong arms reached down to help lift all three men out of the water, starting with Calvin and ending with Kun-Woo. The man pulling them aboard looked small and appeared to be well past middle age, but his rough hands and sturdy arms testified to his lifetime of hard physical work.

With the heavy lifting done the sailor had his first chance to view his new cargo. Eyes went wide when he realized these weren't the usual Korean refugees he usually charged to smuggle. He looked at Calvin, the first black man he had ever seen face-to-face, and then at Chris, a tall, blond-haired, light-skinned man, and immediately began yelling at Kun-Woo. He flailed his arms, gesturing forcefully indicating they would have to leave the boat. Kun-Woo whispered vehemently back, and a long argument ensued. Kun-Woo opened his backpack and acted as if he begrudgingly had to offer its contents to the old man. He pulled out a bottle of vodka and two red and white cartons of Marlboro cigarettes, holding them out at arm's length for the man to accept. There was a long pause while the sailor studied the bounty and finally reached out to accept them. He cursed at Kun-Woo, motioned for him to sit, then sat himself and glared as he picked up his oars.

He rowed out a hundred yards to pull alongside a modest fishing boat, then hurled a rope line up, which was caught by a woman who pulled the boats together, tying the rope securely around a cleat. Now she expressed shock, shrinking back as the Americans came aboard, sharply questioning the captain. He mumbled to her in a brooding fashion and motioned that she should go below. The woman backed away, cursing him under her breath.

The captain gave them a bundle of fresh clothes and urged them below to a cramped sleeping compartment that would keep them out of sight. He rapidly worked a set of ropes, winched the rowboat closer, and tethered it to the side of his ship, then hurried to take the helm and start the engine. He turned the boat toward the open sea, casting frequent glances back at the shoreline, in fear of being detected.

While the captain made way for open waters Kun-Woo went below, tossed another envelope onto a cot, and left them alone. Both men shivered uncontrollably, shedding their wet clothes for the ones the captain provided. Christopher's hands still shook rapidly as he picked up the note:

Christopher,

You have done well to come this far. Your captain has been paid twice his normal fee to smuggle you to safety. He has done this for many years but you will be a surprise. If he refuses, my friend will offer inducements. If he still refuses he will be shown his risk of being exposed. Your destination is Japan. He is with you in the hope of meeting me in South Korea. I beg you to arrange his safe travel to Seoul. It is all I ask in

exchange for your escape. Please understand my shame and know I wish you happy reunions with your families.
Soon Yi

Calvin read the note over Chris' shoulders. "I guess she's sincere. What'd you do to her that she's suddenly helping us?"

"I didn't do anything. She's either wants redemption or is just fed up with everything about this hermit kingdom. Whatever it is, I hope she's okay."

"Yeah. I got to hand it to her. She's a gutsy lady."

The boat gathered speed with a steady rocking motion front to back, waves picking up strength.

Chris nodded toward the door. "I don't trust the captain. You rest. I'm going up to make sure he isn't planning on turning us in somewhere."

"Good idea, thanks."

Staggering along the narrow passageway toward the ladder, Chris looked down, startled to see a small boy's face peering at him from behind a curtain. The head quickly darted out of sight, and he heard a short shushing sound. Chris stopped, extended his arm, and slowly parted the curtain using two fingers. The woman he'd seen above deck sat on a cot facing him with the boy held securely in her arms. A cloth bag at her feet held their meager possessions. Chris had assumed she was with the captain but now realized the mother and her son were escapees as well. He smiled in a way to convey he understood their situation and that he meant no harm. He let the curtain close again on his fellow refugees.

In the narrow passageway, the smell of rotting fish and damp wood competed with oily engine fumes. Chris grabbed the railing at the foot of the ladder and looked straight up into the stars overhead. *Calvin would know which way we're going just by the stars,* he thought. He climbed onto the deck and walked forward to the small cabin where the captain steered the boat, apparently consumed with navigating, while Kun-Woo stood quietly at his side smoking. For the first-time Chris felt optimistic that the captain was cooperating.

222

He tapped Kun-Woo on the shoulder and pointed at him, then raised his voice to be heard over the chugging and clanging of the engine. "You go South Korea?"

"Yes. South Korea. You take?" Kun-Woo pleaded.

"South Korea and Soon Yi!" Chris shouted.

Kun-Woo smiled broadly "Soon Yi!" He nodded vigorously.

The American laughed, and patted him on the back. "Soon Yi, yes," he smiled.

Chris looked back and realized he couldn't see the shore. The thought that North Korea now lay behind him hit him with a sharp rush of exuberance. He clenched both fists and shot them into the air like Rocky Balboa celebrating a victory. Exhaustion quickly overtook him, as though his short celebration had drained all his strength. He needed sleep and felt confident enough of Kun-Woo's motives to know he could leave him and the captain alone. He went below deck where Calvin was already asleep and joined him in the next tiny bunk.

Calvin's little cot was empty when Chris awoke. He climbed topside, squinting with the flash of daylight, to find Calvin and Kun-Woo sitting on a low wooden bench along the starboard railing. The captain gave him an annoyed look before turning his attention back to the horizon. As Chris approached, Kun-Woo signaled for him to stay low.

"He wants us stay down, patrol boats and planes monitor these waters constantly. He doesn't like us on deck at all," Calvin said.

"Got it. How far do you think we've gone?"

"Not very. From what I can tell we're sailing back and forth along fishing lanes so we don't raise suspicion. I gather the real break occurs tonight."

"Great! So, we're just sitting out here?"

"We're easing away from Korea. If we make a bee-line for Japan, all hell will break loose."

The captain started yelling and waving his arms. He pointed at Calvin and then at the deck. He stamped his right foot and then yelled again pointing at the sky.

"He's pissed we're up here. Worried a plane will spot us. Demands we go below."

Chris nodded and the two of them headed back down the ladder.

"We can't stay cooped up down here," Chris said. "Is there any food on board?"

"Some. They gave me a bowl of fish soup when I woke up. You know about the other guests?" He pointed toward the curtain.

"Yeah, saw the boy last night." He knocked on the wall next to the closed curtain, and it opened almost at once. The boy stared up at them wide-eyed. His mother quickly stood behind him with her hands on each of his shoulders, looking defiantly at the Americans. *A mother bear protecting her cub,* Chris thought.

He bent down to his knees and smiled at the boy. He thought about Joey and wanted to hug the child, but didn't wish to frighten his mother. Instead, he turned his head sideways and crossed his eyes making the funniest face he could. The boy didn't react at first, but then tilted his head, put an index finger from each hand into the corners of his mouth, pulled them wide, and stuck out his tongue. They both burst out laughing.

Chris looked at the floor around him and picked up a small piece of rag. He balled it tightly, placed it in the palm of his left hand and showed it to the boy, then slowly shifted it from one hand to the other, letting it float so that the child could easily tell which hand it landed in. He gradually moved the process higher until his hands rose just above the boy's line of sight and then silently tossed the rag ball behind the boy's head. Chris closed both fists and held them out, encouraging the boy to choose which one held the cloth. The boy chose the left hand. Chris opened it to show it was empty. The boy immediately tapped the top of the right fist.

224

Chris smiled and slowly opened his empty hand. The boy's eyes opened wider and his eyebrows shot up, suitably surprised, leading to more laughter.

Chris rubbed the child's head, smiled at his mother and said, "Great kid."

She seemed to understand. Her posture relaxed and she offered a slight smile that conveyed relief more than anything else.

"Cal, did you say fish soup? I've gotta get something to eat. It doesn't even have to taste good, as long as it's food."

"Well, in that case you won't be disappointed. Let Kun-Woo know you're hungry. He'll fix you up."

Chris grunted and climbed up the ladder until his head rose just above deck. He called to Kun-Woo and pantomimed eating. Their guide understood and went into the cabin at the back of the boat. Five minutes later Chris sat on the top step eating a thin soup with bits of fish and rice. It tasted bitter, but he asked for more, and Kun-Woo obliged.

The Americans spent a fitful, impatient day below deck planning what they'd do on shore in Japan, imagining what it would be like being back with their families. Chris thought about protecting the counterfeit plate so it wouldn't be taken before he could deliver it to the proper authorities. Calvin talked about his two sons and his wife, but then fell silent, staring at the floor, and quietly saying, "I killed a man."

"You did. You saved us! If you hadn't we'd be in prison or dead by now."

"He seemed young."

"Calvin, you can't think about it. You saved us. I owe you my life. My family, your family ... imagine if you hadn't protected us. You didn't have a choice."

"I guess." He looked at Chris, offering a weak smile.

"When I get home, I'm never leaving San Diego again. I'm just gonna hold Marla and my boys. I'll spend every day thanking the Lord for my family."

"Yeah, I know. My wife and Joey are all I think about. I've missed too much of Joey's life already. He's got to be close to kindergarten now. Maureen's done everything by herself. I've no idea what she's thinking at this point. But once I get home, I'm never leaving them again." He wondered if she was already done with him, if she was with someone else. The thought caused a physical shudder, but he quickly pictured squeezing the idea into a tight ball and throwing it away.

Their captain set nets, periodically winching them in and catching a fair number of fish. He and Kun-Woo labored to empty the nets into the hold and recast the lines. Calvin and Chris were suitably impressed, as the fish glistened in their nets and the haul grew larger. At mid-afternoon, the captain gutted and fried enough fish for everyone. It had been a long time since either American had smelled food cooking. They savored the aroma and cherished each bite.

In the late afternoon, heavy gray clouds rolled across the sky, slowly cloaking them in darkness. Their boat made wider sweeps, getting farther from land with every pass, while the captain calculated timing for a straight run to Japan. No other boats were in sight. No surveillance planes were overhead. He decided to wait a half hour to let the last bit of darkness shelter them.

The captain came below deck, bringing each passenger a canteen of water, and something else they hadn't expected. First, he instructed the woman and her son to move to their cot away from the curtain. To their surprise, he slid a wooden panel across the opening and snapped it in place so the room was now undetectable. He did the same for the tiny room Chris and Calvin occupied. Anyone coming down the ladder would see only one door leading to a small room where the captain slept and another door opening to a crude head. If someone opened that door, the strong odor of urine and human waste would encourage a speedy exit. They were now invisible in the bottom of an old fishing boat on the western edge of the Sea of Japan.

The ship's engine picked up speed, straining under the pressure of a full throttle. Calvin and Chris smiled, realizing the sprint toward Japan had started.

226

They lay on their bunks trying to rest, but the excitement of their escape pushed away any chance of sleep. The boat chugged ahead, rising and falling with the waves. Chris thought of Soon Yi and said a silent prayer of thanks for all her help. He pictured home and what it would feel like to hold Maureen and Joey again.

46 A VISIT AT SEA

Kun-Woo and the captain sat at the wheel drinking vodka and smoking Marlboros. They laughed and talked with growing animation. Kun-Woo felt the glow of vodka warming his insides and began to hum before breaking out into loud, off-key, singing. He sang about a young girl in springtime falling in love, but Kun-Woo substituted crude remarks and profanities over the original verse. The captain swayed back in forth with the rhythm, laughing and poking fun at Kun-Woo. He lit another cigarette from the end of the one he was finishing, then turned his radio on to pick up a Japanese station, blasting a rap tune to drown out Kun-Woo.

They didn't hear the speedboat approaching. It was a large North Korean patrol vessel skimming the water at full speed with lights out. It sliced up to the fishing boat, spun sideways, and flashed an intense spotlight onto the deck.

The captain leapt to his feet as Kun-Woo fell backwards onto the planking. Someone on the patrol boat threw a grappling hook to the rail of the fishing boat, pulling the two vessels tight together. Korean sailors quickly climbed aboard, shouting orders and flashing lights across the deck. One of them turned off the engine and silenced the radio. He grabbed the captain and threw him to the ground, yelling questions while three other sailors pointed weapons at Kun-Woo and the captain.

The captain got up, shaking his head protesting vigorously. He extended his arms wide with his palms held upward to indicate he hadn't done anything wrong. Kun-Woo stood and yelled that he was a soldier in the Korean People's Army. He summoned all his courage and demanded to know how they could be attacking a simple fishing boat in this fashion.

The sailors lowered their weapons a bit and began to talk in more modest tones. Kun-Woo's courage grew. He explained that the captain taught him navigation skills he would use to train other Korean soldiers. The sailors became more constrained but watched him with suspicion.

It seemed they might accept his explanation until one of the sailors looked toward the captain, seeing two cartons of American cigarettes and a bottle of vodka on a shelf by the wheel. He grabbed the cartons, waving them high in the air in front of Kun-Woo while screaming questions at him. The captain tried to speak, but a fist struck him hard across the face and he fell back against the wheel. The lead sailor shouted an order, and the others quickly began searching the boat. They descended the ladder to the lower deck and burst into the small captain's quarters. One yanked a thin mattress off the bed while another pulled everything apart looking for any signs of treason. Finding nothing, they burst into the head with its gagging stench, then quickly retreated to the passageway before climbing above deck.

Once topside, they looked at their commanding officer and shrugged: nothing found. He screamed and motioned for them to guard Kun-Woo, then stared at the captain, pushing a carton of cigarettes up to his face and barking questions at him. The captain shook his head, crossing his hands in front of him, waving them back and forth to indicate nothing was going on. The sailor nodded calmly, took a step backwards, and fired three shots into the captain's chest. The dead body spun and fell face down on the deck. Kun-Woo leapt back and gasped for breath. The sailor turned on him and demanded to know what he was up to. Kun-Woo's only thought was of Soon Yi. He clasped his hands together as if in prayer and begged for understanding. "Please! I'm not doing anything wrong." He decided to betray the Americans.

It might be his only chance. Before he could form the words, bullets shattered his head.

The lead officer calmly picked up the vodka and cigarettes. He handed them to another sailor and ordered everyone back to the patrol boat. While they disembarked, he went to the engine compartment and opened its hatch, studying the engine for a minute before reaching down, disconnecting the fuel line and sniffing it. As with most North Korean vessels, the engine had been converted from diesel to cheap wood gas. Gas sputtered from the line and dribbled onto the engine. He lifted the line and let fuel spread over the deck as he glanced back at the two dead bodies, then at the pooling gasoline, before taking a box of matches from his pocket. He struck three of them together, held them upside down to watch the flame grow and then tossed them at the edge of fuel. The deck burst into flame and burned toward the engine, where it flashed into a roaring blaze.

Chris and Calvin had heard the commotion when the Koreans boarded, and listened anxiously as footsteps clomped throughout the boat. Calvin kept his AK-47 pointed toward the enclosed doorway while Chris positioned himself to the side, ready to jump anyone who discovered their hideaway. The footsteps had grown louder just outside the passageway, then subsided and retreated above deck. The Americans exchanged glances, began to relax their tense bodies, and moved closer, pressing their ears to the door. A brief silence was followed by gunfire: three shots, a pause, and then two more. Calvin bent down to one knee, shouldering his gun and preparing for anyone approaching the cabin. Four minutes of silence were followed by the sound of a boat's engine revving and moving away.

Chris placed both hands on the door again, listening at the panel. He looked back at Calvin and shook his head "Nothing," he whispered. "I'm opening it."

Calvin nodded and steadied the gun tighter on his shoulder. Chris pressed firmly on the panel until it popped free, making a sharp cracking sound that caused them to freeze. Calvin held out the palm of his hand, directing Chris to stay still. He swung into the passageway ready to fire at anything that moved. He stared into the empty corridor, halted a second as his eyes adjusted, and then signaled for Chris to follow.

They approached the ladder cautiously climbing the stairs, one tread at a time, as quietly as they could. Chris noticed for the first time that the engine had quit. The silence was unsettling. Calvin poked his head above the deck and gasped. "Holy shit. We're on fire!" He rushed above deck swinging his AK-47 in a wide arc as he surveyed the boat from every direction.

Chris followed him topside. The engine compartment was raging, in full flame and spreading fast. He turned, rushed back down the ladder, and banged on the panel hiding the mother and her son. He felt along the top of it, pressed his fingers into a slim crease, and pried it free.

The frightened mother cradled her son beneath her on the cot when Chris burst in. She whimpered in terror, clenching her child tighter.

Chris grabbed her shoulder, pulling her around so that she had to look up at him. He gestured for her to get up.

"Quick!" he ordered. She looked confused. Chris gestured more forcefully. "Fire! Come now." He yanked her off the bunk and she rose with her son still in her arms. Chris pulled one of her hands free, gripping it tightly as he led her into the passageway. She hoisted the boy up to one shoulder with her free hand while screaming something in Korean.

They climbed the ladder, Chris nearly dragging her across the deck toward the rowboat. Her eyes went wide when she saw flames leaping from the engine, spreading across the deck. Calvin already stood at the starboard side, ready to lower the ropes holding the small skiff. As they approached, Calvin gave Chris a warning look and nodded toward the bodies of Kun-Woo and the captain. Christopher followed Calvin's gaze and felt his throat go dry as he realized their guides were both gone.

He pulled the mother and child onto the little boat and jumped aboard behind them. Calvin started lowering the ropes when Chris yelled, "Wait!" He leapt back onto the deck and ordered Calvin to "wait five." He rushed back across the deck toward the ladder feeling the heat from the flames, knowing he might not have enough time. He reached the ladder, spread his feet to either side, sliding down quickly, hitting the floor with force and turning back toward his cabin. Rushing inside, he grabbed the backpack with one swift motion, spun and headed back to the ladder.

The upper deck had become fully engulfed in flames. Black smoke streamed above hot red flames, forcing its way into his lungs and blocking his vision. He held the knapsack up to his face, lowered his posture like a football player rushing through the line, and ran headlong through the flames. At the other side, he could barely make out Calvin holding the last rope supporting the escape boat.

"Go on!" Chris screamed. "Lower it. Now!"

Calvin let the rope slide through his hands, sending the boat and its two passengers down into the water with a loud splash. Christopher's eyes were burning. He bounded to the Calvin's side and yelled, "You remember how to rappel?" Calvin nodded, grabbed the other rope, and rappelled down the side. Chris followed almost on top of him, and they landed heavily onto the small boat.

"We've gotta move before the whole thing blows!" Calvin shouted as Chris gained his balance, climbed over the woman, and grabbed one of the oars. He forced the end of it against the side of the fishing boat and pushed with all his strength to separate the two crafts. The child screamed with fright. His mother glared at Chris.

Calvin worked his way to Christopher's side, staggering with the motion of the waves. He reached behind Chris, pushed the tiny outboard engine so that it pivoted and its propeller splashed into the water. Calvin pulled the starter cord twice, and the little outboard coughed into life.

"Come on, come on!" Calvin muttered, urging the rowboat forward. Progress seemed achingly slow, but they gradually picked up momentum, steadily separating the two vessels.

"If that blows it could take us down with it! We need more distance."

They were making progress when the fishing boat exploded, lifting into the air, then slamming down hard into the water. Flaming debris rained around them. Their small boat nearly capsized with the blast. Their ears rang with the sound, completely covering the screams of the mother and her child.

The four of them sat, silently watching the charred and burning debris, not talking, feeling powerless, and dreading what might come next. After several minutes, Calvin tried to tell Chris something but his words literally fell on deaf ears. He put a hand on Christopher's shoulder to get his attention and then pointed toward the sky while mouthing, "Constellations."

Chris looked up and realized they needed stars to guide them. Few were visible; more than half the sky was covered in clouds. He looked at Calvin and shrugged. Calvin mimicked drawing a sword from his belt and raising it to the sky. He opened his hand and slid it back and forth across his belt while mouthing, "Orion's Belt."

That would be their guide. If they could locate the Orion Constellation and follow the line from Orion's Belt, Calvin would know which way to steer. He had already concluded they were more than halfway to Japan. With the right bearings, and if the little engine would hold out, they had a chance to reach land in about seven hours, assuming they didn't freeze first. They located their constellation, and steered the right course, but the engine sputtered on its last fumes in just over an hour, leaving them motionless as the first fingers of light began to nudge the horizon.

There's a warm current in the Sea that flows northwest in a large circular pattern heading directly to Japan. It's the only reason Vladivostok isn't blocked by ice in winter. Their little boat flowed with the current and the strenuous rowing of two Americans. It was a desperate effort; they all knew they couldn't survive a full day and night in the cold.

At mid-morning, they heard the distant roar of a large plane off to their right. They searched the sky shielding their eyes from the sun until they caught a glimpse of it far off their starboard side.

"That's one of ours!" Calvin said. All four passengers began waving wildly and screaming as if the pilots could miraculously hear them. The plane seemed to dip a bit, but then droned on out of sight, leaving deflated spirits adrift on the sea.

"It's AWACS—state of the art surveillance plane, and it can't even spot the four of us," Calvin complained.

Chris grunted, his hearing mostly returned but his resolve now nearly exhausted.

The sun reached its height in the sky, its burning rays masked by brisk salty winds. The wind and sun competed to do them in before they could die of thirst. Chris sat hunched over. His eyes caked closed, his tongue thick and swollen behind chapped bleeding lips. The woman lay sheltering her son. She woke to realize the rowing had stopped. The little boat bobbed like an open coffin on the waves. She reached out her foot and kicked Calvin's leg, cursing at him, her rasping voice almost gone. Calvin was in worse condition than Chris, but he stirred, giving the woman a weary nod of his head and picking up the handle of his oar. He nudged Chris, and together they dipped their oars and resumed rowing, staring straight ahead in silence.

Forty minutes later a patrol boat appeared on the horizon. The woman started to wave, but Calvin urged her to be still. Whatever it was, it wasn't an American ship, more likely the same boat that boarded them last night. They watched intently as it approached. Even from the horizon they could tell it was headed directly toward them. It couldn't have seen them yet, it might just be bad luck, or it may have been working from GPS coordinates. In either case, it spread panic to Calvin and his crew.

"They've seen us," Chris said quietly through clenched teeth, the patrol boat nearly on them. Its engines slowed and the boat turned slightly sideways revealing three crew members on deck. Two held machine guns, another sailor held binoculars while signaling others to join him on deck. One of the sailors aimed his gun directly at Chris.

"Jesus Christ, Cal, I'm sorry. I really thought we'd make it."

"Hush! We did what we could. At least we're done rowing."

"Yeah, we're done."

The patrol boat came within forty yards of them, then cut its engine and arched further sideways. That's when they saw the bright red and white Japanese flag flying behind her.

"Holy shit. They're Japanese!" Chris and Calvin exchanged looks of amazement and relief, high-fived each other and laughed.

"Oh, my God. We did it!"

Chris grinned at the woman and pointed to the patrol boat, "Japanese. Japanese!"

She hugged her son and cried.

Lieutenant McCarty stood stiffly, waving at the boat and shouting, "Americans. We're Americans."

Calvin started singing Stevie Wonder's "Signed, Sealed, Delivered [I'm Yours]," while waving both arms back and forth. He flashed a broad smile and burst out laughing.

Once on board, warm blankets and hot tea helped relieve their shivering bodies. They were told the AWACs plane had indeed spotted them and relayed their coordinates. It had been assumed they were refugees from North Korea and that the Japanese would want to intercept them.

Japanese sailors had a hard time comprehending what two Americans were doing in a tiny boat in the middle of the Sea of Japan and why a North Korean woman and child would be with them. Their captain suddenly approached Chris with a look of recognition.

"You, American traitor. You defect!"

"No. I prisoner," Chris responded in broken Japanese. He pointed to Calvin. "We were prisoners." He held his wrists together as if in handcuffs. "Prisoners."

The captain eyed him suspiciously, turning his head slightly but keeping his eyes locked on Christopher's. Calvin spoke in basic Japanese, indicating the US Navy would want to see them right away.

"We will see."

He radioed shore, talking briskly, never taking his eyes off the Americans, then paused and asked Chris and Calvin to state their names slowly. They complied and he repeated their names clearly over the radio. It became obvious someone in Japan was contacting US military authorities, and that orders were being relayed. Suddenly the captain hung up the microphone, giving a sharp order to one of the sailors who threw the engine into high gear. They were racing toward Japan. Chris clenched the backpack to his chest, then slid it behind him as he sat on wooden bench.

Their boat arrived on Japanese soil to a contingent of military police and intelligence officers. A marine colonel greeted them as they stepped off the boat.

"Lieutenant Christopher McCarty, I assume."

Chris nodded, and they exchanged salutes.

"I'm Colonel Hodges. Is this Chief Warrant Officer Calvin Jackson?"

"I am, Colonel, and damned pleased to be here." Calvin's eyes smiled.

The Colonel signaled to a soldier, who handed a bottle of water to each of the new arrivals.

"Well, don't expect any ticker tape parades. You gentlemen have a lot of questions to answer."

"Of course. Do you think you could take care of this woman and her child first? They're refugees with us."

"I know, our Japanese friends are making preparations for them."

"Thank you. One other thing, any chance we can get some food before the debriefing? We're starving."

The colonel laughed. "I'm sure that can be arranged, Lt. Jackson. You gentlemen might like some American food. We're just outside of Akita. They've got a couple of McDonalds here. We can afford a quick stop on the way."

Calvin and Chris looked at each other. "Bless you, sir."

"Only the drive-thru. From there we head directly to Yokosuka and the Seventh Fleet, where every branch of Intelligence has questions for you."

"Do you have a cell phone, sir? I want to call my wife."

"Sorry, Sir. No calls. At least for now."

"But someone will let our families know we're okay, that we're free?"

"In due course. There's a lot to sort out first."

"Our families are all right, though?"

"As far as I know they're just fine. Be patient, it won't be long."

Chris held up his hand and raised his voice. "Before we go, I have something I want everyone to see."

He slung his backpack around to the front of him and began to unzip it.

Five marines immediately drew weapons.

"Whoa! It's a *good* thing. Everyone stay calm. It's something from North Korea. I just want everyone to witness it so I can formally deliver it to the US Navy."

"Drop the bag! Now! And step back."

Chris shrugged. "It's not a weapon. It's a counterfeit plate that Kim used to make hundred dollar bills. I just want everyone to know about it so it doesn't suddenly disappear."

He lowered the pack to the ground in front of him, and backed away.

"You can take it out, sir. I just want to be sure everyone sees it and there's no question it's here."

The colonel knelt and cautiously unzipped the bag. He opened it wide, staring in rather than plunging his hand inside.

He looked up at Chris and Calvin. "Is this for real?"

"Real deal, sir."

237

The officer extracted the plate and examined it in the light.

"Can you hold it up, Colonel? For everyone to see?"

He stood and held the plate above his head, turning so everyone could see it.

"I'm officially taking custody of this article on behalf of the United States Navy. It is now the property of the American government."

"Yes, sir. Thank you, sir."

They were quickly ushered into the middle van of a three-vehicle convoy. Two motorcycle officers with flashing lights guided them into traffic, while two others followed in the rear. They drove at a steady pace without conversation. Calvin and Chris focused on life outside their windows. Traffic was picking up, far more than they would have seen in Pyongyang; the roads were wide and modern. People were busy with life, buildings had lights, and stores looked stocked with goods. They were drinking in civilization, treasuring their escape.

As promised, the motorcade rolled into the parking lot of a McDonalds in Akita. Chris craned his head against the window looking up at the sign. "I never thought I'd be so excited to see the Golden Arches." He nudged Calvin's shoulder. "Looks like home." Calvin gave him a fist bump.

The other vehicles idled while the van holding Chris and Calvin pulled into the drive thru. Their driver ordered for them, and handed their Big Macs, fries, and Cokes back before rejoining the convoy. Calvin unwrapped his burger, holding it close to his nose and inhaling deeply. He turned slightly toward Chris, raised his eyebrows, flashed a satisfied grin and said, "America!"

Chris held up a bag of fries and said, "At last." They touched the food together like a champagne toast and laughed like guilty schoolchildren.

A ten-minute drive took them to an airfield, where a Navy Seahawk helicopter waited. They had just gotten situated when Calvin broke into a joyful grin. He raised his arm, swinging it in a circular motion imitating the chopper's blades. "It's good to see the inside of one these again. Thank you, Lord. Thank you!"

During the thirty-minute flight to Yokosuka, Colonel Hodges peppered them with questions about their captivity. He had obviously seen the footage out of North Korea showing Christopher as a happy, cooperating defector who had turned his back on America. He leaned in until he was face to face with Chris and shouted above the roar of the rotors.

"I don't see how the two of you—looking like you do, could just waltz out of a military dictatorship, especially North Korea. Excuse me for being skeptical, but if you're some kind of Manchurian Candidates we'll find out."

Chris realized their interrogation would take longer than he'd anticipated. He also understood that Colonel Hodges wasn't the most receptive person to hear their stories. He assumed a more open audience would be found among his Naval Intelligence colleagues at the base.

If he and Calvin expected a public welcome with international press coverage, their expectations evaporated quickly. The chopper set down just outside a large hangar with Marines guarding the entrance. As soon as the Seahawk rolled inside the hangar, doors were closed behind them. Chris and Calvin exchanged confused looks.

"Right now, you gentlemen are Top Secret. We need to get a clear understanding of this, and we're going to take it one step at a time. Let me be clear: you'll have no communication with anyone on the outside, including your families, until we get some questions answered."

"In that case, Colonel, we'd like to start our debriefing now."

"Exactly our intention."

They were hustled into an SUV with blackened windows and driven out the back.

Yokosuka Naval Base is a city unto itself, and a familiar place to Calvin and Chris. Home to the US Seventh Fleet; America's most vital facility in the Pacific and the world's most advanced naval operation outside the United States. It houses 23,000 military personnel and civilians on 568 acres at the entrance of Tokyo Bay.

Everything about the base resonated comfort: The sight of Americans in uniform and civvies, signs written in English, a basketball court filled with activity, the sight of the US aircraft carrier *Kitty Hawk* at dock, and the bustling activity of a well-run, well-disciplined Naval operation felt like home.

They were driven to a long, flat building at the edge of the base. Their SUV pulled up tight against a side entrance, where they were escorted inside and ushered down a set of stairs into a small grey room resembling a waiting room at a military medical office.

A single doctor took their vital signs and gave them each a quick physical before certifying them dehydrated, but fit for questioning. They each had a saline drip inserted in their arm, then waited nearly an hour with nothing to look at, nothing to read, no means of communicating with the outside world, and no idea what was taking so long. Their conversations centered around seeing their families again.

In a room across the hall Bob Morgan listened to every word and watched each move on a wide-screen monitor. They'd been silent for the past ten minutes. Calvin had just fallen asleep sitting up. If Morgan hoped to discover anything from their interaction, he was disappointed. He picked up his phone, punched a button and said, "We're ready now."

Two intelligence officers joined him as he entered the room. They removed the saline tubes and told them to stand. Calvin was directed to follow one of them to a separate conference room, while Morgan motioned Chris to join him at a small metal table. He slapped a thick file in front of Chris and said, "There's a lot in here about you. But there's a lot more you need to fill in for us."

"And you are?"

"Robert Morgan, Naval Intelligence. I'll be conducting your initial debrief." He smiled. "I'm sure you understand. We're all very curious about your time in the Hermit Kingdom."

"Of course, sir. Before we get into that, there's someone we need to protect. A woman helped us escape. She's a mid-level officer in the North Korean military. Her name's Soon Yi. She served as my interpreter at first, but then worked with Kim to torture Calvin and keep me in line. I'm not sure why, but somehow, she turned. She helped us get out, and she's the one who gave us the counterfeit plate. I don't think she meant that as a gift; I think she took it to hurt someone: a general by the name of Moon. You probably have intelligence on him. Anyway, we wouldn't be here without her, and I doubt she'll survive very long without our help."

"Yes, the woman in your videos, very pretty. I can see why you want to help her. We've lots of questions about her. In fact, let's start with her."

Calvin was given a similar greeting in another room with a similar thick file in front of him. A video camera rested on a tripod aimed at him, and a microphone sat on the table next to a green can of Mountain Dew.

"Thought you might be thirsty. We can always get you coffee if you prefer."

Both men were questioned for hours. Timelines were developed; questions were asked, and repeated with slight variations to see how the answers might change. A series of questions centered on their impressions of average lifestyles in North Korea, a more protracted set focused on every detail Chris could recall of Kim Jong Il, while another homed in on every fact that could be remembered about military equipment and capabilities. Finally, they were asked to reconstruct their escape, detail by detail, and then to repeat it again, in reverse.

Three hours later, their interrogators switched places. Bob Morgan took a new tack with Calvin.

"We think you were set up, that you're the patsy here. Most of Intelligence is convinced McCarty defected willingly and that you had no idea what he intended. Let's start over so we can get to the truth and you can get back to your family."

Calvin shook his head in frustrated disbelief. He spread the fingers of his hands wide, placed them in front of him on the table, clenched and raised them as if about to slam them down, but stopped mid-air.

"Lt. McCarty is an America hero! He saved my life—we saved each other's—and I'll tell you whatever you want. But the truth is he's not a defector, and neither am I. You people are as bad as the North Koreans who interrogated us."

"You mean the ones who gave you that nice little cottage with the vegetable garden? Tell me about them. Were they soldiers, intelligence officers, party leaders, who?"

Calvin drew in a deep breath to calm himself and began to describe his captors again. He told them about a woman who appeared to be an officer in the North Korean Army and how she had escorted them out of captivity. He explained that she seemed to hate Chris at first, but that she had handed them off to Kun-Woo. He told them of the train, their night in an abandoned building, and their experience at sea.

Hours of questions designed to trip him up were being repeated to Chris. Every detail was dissected, questioned again, refuted as illogical or contradictory, and re-phrased.

After five hours Chris, with elbows on the table, cradled his head in hands, stared down at the file in front of him, closed his eyes and said, "Enough. I'm done."

"Good. So now you'll tell us the truth."

"No. Now I'm done. I get that you have to do this. I'm Naval Intelligence, too, but I'm exhausted, so's Calvin. We've told you everything. Please. Can we finish this in the morning?"

The two officers exchanged glances, one shrugged slightly.

"We'll see."

One left to consult Morgan, who agreed they were getting nowhere and a fresh start in the morning, after studying the tapes, might be productive. Usually he'd have insisted on keeping them up all night to fully exhaust them, but he could see they were already well past that. Given their time at sea, which the North Korean woman and her boy had verified, they probably hadn't slept for at least thirty-six hours.

Calvin and Chris were escorted to separate quarters for the night, a marine stationed outside each room. The next morning, they were awakened early and given civilian clothes to wear.

"I think I'm entitled to my uniform," Chris said.

The marine who had delivered the clothes simply said:

"Not my call. You're having breakfast delivered in ten minutes."

Chris thought it odd they would deliver breakfast rather than take him to a mess hall or to one of the fast food places at the base. Then he remembered: he was Top Secret. He and Calvin weren't to be seen in public.

"Before you go, can I use your cell phone for a minute? There's a quick call I need to make."

"Nice try, sailor. As far as I know, you're not authorized."

Chris fumed until breakfast arrived. He stared at it when it came. Scrambled eggs, bacon, potatoes, toast, orange juice, and coffee were savored slowly until he felt his stomach would burst. His thoughts turned to Maureen and the first breakfast she'd made him, just before their first shower. He thought of Joey, remembering him in his highchair at his first birthday when he made a sleepy face-plant into the frosting of his cake. An intense wave of homesickness washed over him. He rose quickly and lurched for the door, eager to get away, too frustrated to sit in an isolated room seven-thousand miles from home. He grabbed the doorknob and twisted hard. It wouldn't move. His shoulders slumped. He raised his right fist to pound on the door, but stopped and gently pounded his forehead instead.

Chris wanted to talk with Calvin, but had a feeling that wouldn't happen today. He was right. An hour later, he was escorted back to the interrogation room. Robert Morgan arrived, accompanied by two men Chris hadn't seen before.

"Lt. McCarty, these gentlemen are with the NSA and CIA. They've a few questions for you."

243

Those few questions were still being asked four hours later, with particular interest in how he came into possession of the counterfeit plate. Morgan sat across the hall monitoring every word and taking notes, often typing questions appearing on a CIA laptop where Chris was questioned.

When they broke for lunch, a soldier delivered a tray to Chris with tomato soup, two grilled cheese sandwiches, and a Dr. Pepper. Afterwards, he was left alone for forty-five minutes. He curled his arms on the table, nestled his head on them, and fell asleep.

The loud slamming of the door woke him. This time Morgan and each of the intelligence officers were standing in front of him.

Morgan snapped, "We've been patient, but let's review some things, shall we? You show up in North Korea in 2007; in July 2007, North Korea test-fired seven new missiles, including one capable of hitting Alaska. In October of 2007, North Korea set off a nuclear device, and suddenly four months later, you and Jackson miraculously find your way back here. Seems a little too convenient. We have to wonder if you've been indoctrinated—if you've been turned."

"Turned? Give me a lie detector! Do anything you want, but let's get this done. I don't know anything about their weapons or plans. Kim doesn't consult me on military operations. Are you kidding about Alaska? They can't even keep lights on in Pyongyang."

"What's interesting is that you boarded a boat at Chongjin. That's only 60 miles from their underground nuclear test at Kilchu. In fact, that train ride you talked about goes right through Kilchu. Let's talk more about that."

"I've never heard of Kilchu; I don't know anything about missile tests or nuclear explosions. We were prisoners. It feels like we still are."

"Okay. Let's start from the beginning." He nodded to one of the agents who withdrew briefly and returned rolling a television on a metal cart.

"Let's look at the pictures again, Lieutenant."

Christopher groaned, slumped in his chair, tilted his head back staring at the ceiling and said, "Oh, Christ. Just let me see my family."

Another hour labored on, reviewing every piece of footage: Chris at the state dinner, Chris waving to a theatre audience who gave him a standing ovation, Chris eating with an Admiral on the captured USS *Pueblo* and, later, Chris smiling with North Korean officers reviewing a military parade.

"I don't believe *prisoners* are treated this way," Morgan said. "Let's go over this again."

A forensic psychologist sat across the hall in front of a screen, watching every move, studying Chris for signs he was lying. He focused on the eyes. Were they moving up and to the right? Did they move up and to the left? Did his legs subconsciously indicate a desire to flee, or that he'd become defensive? Did his hands fidget at some questions but not others? He would study the tape over and over but, for now, he thought Chris was either telling the truth or extremely well coached.

Calvin and Chris each passed lie detector tests; their stories backed each other without sounding rehearsed, not too perfect. A consensus grew that they were telling the truth.

The next day Morgan sat at the end of a conference table surrounded by representatives from every branch of US Intelligence. Each was asked to report his or her conclusions. Some were uneasy about certain facts; some voiced skepticism that they could have escaped when too few true North Koreans could accomplish the same feat; most concluded Calvin and Chris could be believed. Some argued they should be hailed as heroes, and that the press should be called in to record their courageous story.

Bob Morgan nodded thoughtfully, and then turned to the man in civilian clothes sitting behind him to his right. He looked back at the group.

"Some of you know Milton Conrad. He's been sent here by the White House and speaks directly for the President. Mr. Conrad ..."

Milton still carried himself with a military bearing, demanding respect, if not fear. He'd been monitoring the developments of Christopher McCarty and Calvin Jackson from the first news release out of Pyongyang and had been among the first to learn Chris wasn't alone in captivity, that an American pilot was also imprisoned. In fact, he had been tasked with making the whole McCarty affair disappear. And it would have if Calvin hadn't been a sudden surprise.

He stood and looked across the conference table, purposely locking eyes with each participant.

"These gentlemen are telling the truth. We had a doctor in Pyongyang who verified their situation. The fact that they got out is a hell of a miracle. But let me be clear. No one is to know they've escaped. No one in this room is to breath a single word of it. Am I understood?"

Their response was a mixture of agreement and confusion.

A Lt. Colonel began cautiously, "But, Sir, this could be a great propaganda coup: a real embarrassment for Kim, and a show of American resourcefulness. Shouldn't we be announcing this from the rooftops?"

"That's the whole point. Let me spell this out. If Kim's embarrassed, what do you think he'll do with those missiles he's been testing, who do you think he'll take it out on? Suppose we announce his prize possessions have landed safely on Japanese soil? If Kim can hit Alaska, he can damn sure hit Japan. He could also retaliate with a strike on Seoul— a significant one. We're already picking up reports of major realignments among his senior officers. Repression is escalating. Even the Chinese caution us that things are destabilizing."

Heads slowly nodded in agreement as people began to understand the implications.

"And don't think we're taking these gentlemen back to the States to parade them around like heroes. The fact is, everything would have been better if they'd never escaped." He paused and again locked eyes on each participant. "As far as the world is concerned these men never left North Korea. Your careers hinge on keeping them secret. Am I clear?"

The nodding accelerated and a general murmur of consent rose around the table.

"Very well. Morgan and I'll handle this from here. You're dismissed."

47 MAUREEN'S RENEWAL

Maureen sat in her small sunroom watching the snow accumulate in her backyard. It didn't seem to snow as much as when she was a girl. She remembered how fun those days had been: free from school, sledding with her sisters, always followed by her mom's hot chocolate and whipped cream. Now, she was the mom, and Joey was experiencing his first official snow day. She would make hot chocolate for him when he came in; maybe they'd bake cookies together, if she had the energy.

The snow storm had started lightly overnight but grew rapidly, settling down just before noon. Large moist flakes twirled and fluttered like feathers meandering their way to the ground. She watched a cluster of flakes dance and drift to the top of the swing set. Her thoughts drew back to the upstairs room of an Annapolis restaurant, watching snow tumble softly among sailboats in the marina and then, looking down, staring into a sparkling diamond ring. She had said no. Maybe she should have stuck to her decision, trusted her instincts. She would have enjoyed life as a young single woman in Washington, DC, maybe moved into a quaint brick townhouse in Georgetown, dating young successful professionals.

But when she saw Joey, bundled from head to toe, making a snow angel, everything felt worth it after all. She'd gone back to using her maiden name and was working at Fairfax Hospital as a patient care advocate. It was far from her dream job, but it had its moments. Mostly she liked it because

248

people left her alone; no one seemed to recognize her, so she could develop her own strategies to foster patient satisfaction. It boiled down to communication. Patients want to know what to expect, what rights they have, who they can turn to, and that they're not abandoning control by being in a hospital. Technically a non-essential employee, she wasn't expected in when the roads were frozen.

Maureen started toward the door to call Joey in when the phone rang. Colleen spoke so rapidly Mo wasn't sure what she was saying.

"Our Education program's taking off!"

"Our what's doing what?"

"Your idea, the software we developed for teaching! You know, the eight schools we've had beta testing it? They love it. Students and teachers! The Montgomery County District just confirmed they'll make it available to all their middle and high schools next year!"

"That's great! Now all we need is about a thousand more to sign up."

"I think they might just do that! I'm taking it to the national education convention in Houston next month, and two of the teachers who tested it are coming as well. You have to be there. We could develop real momentum around this."

There hadn't been any real news about Chris for nearly six months. He hadn't shown up in videos, there weren't any follow-up stories in the press to raise issues all over again. Her constant appeals to the Navy, the State Department, and her Senators had yielded nothing. Maureen had become resigned to life as a single mother, helpless to solve any of this.

At some point, Joey should have a man in his life. He didn't deserve to have Korea hanging over him the rest of his life. Often, late at night, she lay sleepless, envisioning children being cruel to Joey. Anger and shame welled within her. What if Christopher never comes home, and Joey is left to bear this? Twice, her mother suggested divorce. Maureen flared in anger each time. She couldn't begin to think about doing that to Chris. Still, it would be nice to feel loved again, to feel pretty. Maybe if her software program did take off she could the start a new life. She tried not to think about it, but moved more lightly on her feet, feeling her world suddenly more open.

She would call Joey in soon before he got too cold, but first she had some hot chocolate to make. She wondered what ever happened to Bosco. That's what her mother always used. Now she wasn't sure they even made it any more.

48 CALVIN'S ASSIGNMENT

Calvin sat stiffly in a black leather chair with curved wooden armrests. He wore his uniform for the first time in months, surveying his reflection in the glass trophy case across from him in Morgan's office.

Apparently, Morgan had been a boxer and, judging by the number of trophies, a damned good one. If Calvin had attended the Academy, he would have heard the stories of Morgan's winning the Brigade Boxing Championship all four years. A gold disk gleamed in front of a picture of Morgan clenching his large fists and flashing a menacing glare.

It wasn't the picture that captured Calvin's attention. It was the reflection of his own face, far older, thinner, and more wrinkled than he could bear. His hair had nearly all grayed out. He thought of Marla, and his boys, growing urgently impatient to see them, but what would they think of him now? He wasn't the same man they knew anymore. Old and tired, with a permanent limp, and probably done with the Navy. He wasn't sure what he could offer them now. His focus shifted through the glass to the trophies and he sat straighter, resolving to fight his own battle. He would get past all of this.

He rose quickly to attention when Colonel Morgan entered. Pain shot up his leg and he nearly buckled.

"Sit down, Chief Warrant Officer."

"Yes, Sir."

Morgan sat on the corner of his desk staring down at Calvin for several seconds without saying a word, holding his hands together as if in prayer, letting them wave up and down before pointing them toward Calvin.

"Here's the thing, Calvin, what you did was remarkable, truly heroic. But you can't tell a soul. You know better than anyone else what a nut job Kim is. If he knows you're here, he'll retaliate. And If he learns you're stateside with your family, he'll come after all of you."

"What are you saying?"

"I'm saying we need to protect you; not forever, just until Kim's gone. From what we can tell, his health's pretty fragile. Once he checks out, you're in the clear. In the meantime, how do you feel about Italian cooking?"

"Sir?"

"Italy. Ever been?"

"No, sir."

"Well, you're being reassigned there. Your family will join you in Naples. You'll be assigned as support to the Sixth Fleet. The public has no idea you were ever held in North Korea. You won't mention a word of it. You'll maintain a very low profile.

"Your family won't be permitted to mention your captivity to anyone. In fact, they'll be flown to Naples without any chance of telling friends and neighbors where they're going. We're planting a cover story that they've joined Marla's mother who's in a Texas hospice. It's too damned easy for North Koreans to enter the States. If Kim can't find you, he'll look for them. We won't leave a trail for him to follow."

"Italy, Sir?"

"Italy."

"When can I see my wife and sons?"

"They're being briefed when the sun comes up stateside, and we'll have them on a flight within thirty-six hours. Your son at Duke's a bit of a problem. We're arranging for him to attend The American University in Rome for at least a year. It means his basketball dreams are on hold for now. But you'll all be safe."

"When do I leave?"

"Now." He picked a folder from his desk and handed it to Calvin. "Oh, and you're using your middle name from now on. Officially you are Antoine Jackson."

Calvin rose, took the folder and saluted Morgan.

"Thank you, Sir."

"You deserve our protection. Oh, and one other thing: Lt. McCarty will have no idea where you are, and you won't know his whereabouts. It's to protect each of you."

49 SUPER BOWL SUNDAY 2008

February 3rd was Super Bowl Sunday. Chris remained isolated, but Morgan arranged for a television to be wheeled into the Lieutenant's room.

It wasn't until the pregame show that he even realized which teams were playing. The New York Giants—his Giants—were contending for the championship. Chris hated sitting in a cramped bedroom watching television. He wanted to be home. But it helped that his Giants were playing.

From what the announcers were saying, New York hadn't won a playoff game in seven years. Now they had a chance to be the first NFC Wild Card team to win a Super Bowl. Not much of a chance; they were playing the Patriots, and Eli Manning wasn't nearly as consistent as Tom Brady. Chris had been provided with popcorn, Skittles, and a six-pack of Budweiser. It was 0730 Monday morning in Japan, but, given his mood, not too soon for a beer.

Late afternoon on the east coast, Maureen and Joey were getting ready to watch the game at her parent's home in Bethesda. The set's stereo flowed through the new surround sound system her father had installed after their robbery. He sat nursing a Jack Daniels and absorbing every pre-game statistic, thinking of the not-so-friendly bet with his brother in Milton, Massachusetts. If the Giants won, Ben would turn over his beach house on the Cape for a full week. If the Patriots won, Brad would host his brother for a week of golf at Congressional Country Club. Just the thought of it made him cringe.

Joey sat on the sofa next to him, holding a juice box with two hands and imitating his grandfather. He tried to put his feet up on the coffee table, but they wouldn't reach. As the teams lined up for kickoff, Joey studied the screen, puzzled. He looked up at his grandpa and asked, "Which blue team, Papa?"

His grandfather showed him the difference in their uniforms, explaining which team was which, and why the Giants deserved to win. Joey nodded as if accepting great wisdom. The ball had barely left the kicker's foot when the doorbell rang.

Brad turned to his wife with a look that conveyed, "*I'm* not getting up."

The bell rang again as Karen rose to answer it. Brad let out a "For Christ's sake!" Someone's fist began knocking as Karen approached the door. Slim glass panels framed each side allowing her a narrow view of the porch and the street below. What she saw filled her with apprehension. Two Lincoln Town Cars were parked out front, and whoever stood at the door wore a military uniform. She took a deep breath and turned the knob.

Three solemn men stood in front of her, the one she had seen in uniform and two others in civilian clothes with long heavy coats.

"Yes?" she brought one hand up to her necklace while keeping the other firmly planted on the edge of the door.

"We're here to speak with Maureen McCarty."

"What's this about?"

"We need to come inside, ma'am. We shouldn't be seen on your porch. It's important."

Karen studied each face for a second before slowly opening the door wide enough for them to enter. The uniform turned toward the street, signaling the drivers who pulled quickly away from the curb.

"Is this about my son-in-law?"

"We really need to be addressing your daughter first."

Maureen's curiosity had already pulled her from the family room into the front hall. She stopped cold as she realized this wasn't a neighbor on a social call. This had to be about Chris.

"Mrs. McCarty?"

A quiet "yes?" with a slow questioning nod.

"I'm Captain Emanuel; these gentlemen and I are with Naval Intelligence. Are there any persons in this house who are not family members?"

"No."

"Good we need to talk with each family member, but only after we've briefed you."

"Oh, God. Please. Just tell me about Christopher."

Emmanuel smiled. "I'm pleased to tell you he's fine. He's free."

Maureen let out an involuntary shriek, clasped her hands in front of her, and then asked quietly: "He's free? Did you really say he's free?"

"Yes, ma'am he is." Taking off his gloves, he continued, "We have a number of details to go over."

She hugged the captain and shook hands with the other two repeating, "Thank you. Thank you. Thank you."

"I have to tell Joey." She turned to go but tallest of the three men, pulled her back by the arm.

"He can't know yet. Soon, but not yet."

Maureen looked puzzled and suddenly suspected they'd lied to her. Who were these characters anyway? They hadn't shown any identification, if this turned out to be some kind of cruel trick …

Emmanuel sensed her concern. "It's okay. Your husband really *is* safe. Precautions need to be taken to keep him that way. I think it's best if your mother keeps your son occupied while we talk."

Karen and Maureen exchanged looks. Her mother nodded and headed back to the family room. Brad sat, still enjoying his Jack Daniels, absorbed in the game. She reached a hand out to Joey and said, "Come help Nana make popcorn." Brad didn't take his eyes off the TV.

Maureen sat on the edge of the living room sofa, clasping her hands in front of her and looking expectantly at Captain Emmanuel.

He walked her through a summary of Christopher's escape without mentioning Calvin at all. Christopher had escaped. He remained on a military base somewhere in Asia, and she would see him soon. He went on to explain that North Korea's Kim could be very hostile and would seek to retaliate if he knew for sure that Chris had gotten out of the country. He hesitated and then explained that Kim might come after her and her family if he knew Chris had been successful and remained alive.

"We're going to reunite you with him, but we have to play a bit of a shell game first."

At that point one of the two coats explained that if she and Joey suddenly disappeared it might send a signal to Kim that they had found a way to join Chris somewhere. Any unexplained disappearance might spark interest by the press and raise red flags all the way to Pyongyang. She would be offered a job with a hospital consortium in Texas and would turn in her two-week notice at Fairfax Hospital, say her goodbyes to friends and co-workers, put her house up for sale or rent. The Navy would handle the transaction, pack her belongings, and help them out of town.

A woman bearing a close resemblance to Maureen but who, in fact, worked for Naval Intelligence, would report to her new job in Texas and stay there a few months.

She and Joey would soon be flown to meet Christopher, with the understanding that only her parents, and Christopher's mother, would know he'd escaped. Their parents could know he was safe, but they wouldn't know where. When Kim was out of power, the Navy would return her husband to the United States and proclaim him both a victim and a hero who served his country honorably throughout.

In Japan, Christopher had lost interest in the game. New England held the lead in a low-scoring contest with no real spark from his Giants. Watching it only heightened his need to be home. His frustration grew, fueled by every play and each commercial. Seeing the United States from afar, sitting alone in a small room staring at a screen depicting everything bright and exciting about America, filled him with a restless urgency. He realized that, while his whole life had turned upside down, apparently, everything at home remained exactly the same.

The fourth quarter was winding down when Colonel Morgan rapped twice and pushed himself through the doorway. Christopher sat on the end of his bed; it took a second to realize he should stand.

"How's the game?" It was perfunctory. Morgan didn't care about football in the least.

"Discouraging, Sir, I appreciate being able to watch the Super Bowl, I'm grateful for the snacks and beer, but I've got to get out of here. I have to see my family again."

"Will three weeks be soon enough? Hand me a beer."

"Three weeks? Are you serious? I'll be home in three weeks?"

"Not exactly. It'll cost you that beer."

Chris took two cans of Budweiser from the small cooler and handed one to Morgan.

"What does not exactly mean?"

"It's all good. It means you'll be with your wife and son in three weeks, just not in the States."

"They're coming here?"

"Not exactly." He popped the tab and took a long slow draw on the beer. "Down Under."

"Sir?"

"Down Under. You leave for Australia in five hours. Your family will meet you there. They should be finding out just about now. Officially you're not here and officially you won't be there. You're being assigned to US Naval Communication Station Harold E. Holt, otherwise known as North-West

Cape. It's a listening station spread over 60 miles with the largest, most sophisticated monitoring devices outside the States. The VLF antenna array alone covers a thousand acres. The base hosts the tallest tower in the Southern Hemisphere.

"You'll be tasked with interpreting chatter from North Korea and parts of China. We're sending you there as Patrick Madigan. It's temporary. Once Kim is dead or ousted, you'll be free to return home. The Navy will declare you a victim who staged a heroic escape. You and your family will have your lives back, after the press is through with you, of course. Hell, they might even make a movie out of you."

"Yes, Sir, and my family, when ..."

"February 24th. She and your boy will arrive in Perth at 2200 hours. Your smiling face will be there to meet them. You'll have ten days to enjoy the beach before reporting, Lieutenant Madigan." He held out his beer can for Chris to touch with his. "To a new start."

"New start. New life! Thank you, Sir. And Calvin?"

"Calvin will disappear as well. When this is all over we'll help you find each other. In the meantime, neither of you will know the other's location. But he's safe. He's actually with his family already."

Chris suddenly realized the Super Bowl had ended, and his Giants had pulled off a last-minute win. He felt giddy, ecstatic.

50 DOWN UNDER

Lieutenant Madigan paced back and forth just outside customs at Perth international terminal. Wearing his full-dress uniform, he cradled a bouquet of flowers in one arm and a large stuffed kangaroo under the other. He was following a regular route: once around the five rows of seats, then back to the glass wall where he searched the sky for two minutes, checked his watch twice, and repeated the process.

Ensign Margaret Flanders stood watching him with bemusement. She had never seen anyone so impatient. Flanders was one of only three people in Australia who knew Christopher's true identity; she'd been assigned to accompany him to the airport. She also had a surprise for the family once they were reunited.

"All that pacing won't get them here any sooner."

"I know, but I can't sit down. It's clouding up out there. Might even be a storm building. If their flight's delayed ..."

"Relax. The forecast is fine. They'll be here soon. But if all that walking and squinting at the sky makes you happy, go for it."

The plane touched down at exactly 2200. Chris shot a quick glance at Lt. Flanders. "How do I look?"

"Like an over-anxious puppy. Calm down, sailor!"

When Maureen and Joey finally appeared, Chris burst into a broad smile; his eyes fixed on hers, his hand with the flowers rose involuntarily over his heart, and a joyful tear traced a path down his cheek. His gaze shifted to his son. He was stunned to see how much Joey had grown. Chris bent down and held his arms open wide for his boy. For his part, Joey felt apprehensive, not sure how to react. He let go of

Maureen's hand but, instead of rushing to his father's arms, pulled back behind his mother. Maureen reached around, clasped his shoulder, and gently directed him to Chris, who swept him up and sailed him twice around the room before giving him a major hug. Looking over Joey's shoulder, Chris beamed a bright smile at Maureen and mouthed, "I love you."

He put Joey down gently and embraced her. "Hello, Christmas." They spun and laughed, as if getting away with something deliciously naughty. A long kiss, and then flowers for Maureen. Chris turned to Joey, bent down on one knee, handing him the stuffed kangaroo.

"You know what they call a baby kangaroo here in Australia?"

Joey shook his head.

"It's *joey*. They name all their baby kangaroos after you!"

Joey laughed, looked the kangaroo in the face and said, "Hi, Joey. I'm Joey too."

Lt. Flanders approached Maureen, extended her hand, and introduced herself.

"I've been assigned to watch over your son for the next few days so you two can have some alone time together."

Maureen and Chris looked at each other.

Chris said, "Sometimes the Navy overthinks things, Lt. Flanders. I appreciate the offer, but I'm not letting either of these two out of my sight anytime soon. What we need is family time, all three of us. As far as I'm concerned, you can take the next few days off." The ensign looked flustered, but understood. She drove them to their hotel and left the family on their own.

The next afternoon they lay on beach towels, watching Joey pat damp sand on the castle he'd patiently built. Chris had started the project, showing him how to use his red plastic bucket to form towers at the corners. Joey continued, creating an intricate network of walls and turrets, surrounded by a moat with its own bridge of popsicle sticks. He used seashells to decorate the arch at the edge of the bridge.

Chris smiled at Maureen, truthfully happier than he'd been in his entire life. He rested a hand on her knee and scrunched closer, nodding at Joey.

"I think we may have an architect in the family. You've done a great job with him. I still can't get over how tall he is.

"Mo, I know I keep saying it, but I'm so sorry about all of this. I should've known right away not to trust anything in North Korea. I went into Intelligence because of what happened to my family, and that decision nearly cost us ours."

"We're together now ..."

"But my reputation's still ruined, maybe for life. We might never be welcome in the States again. How do you feel about staying in Australia?"

She sat up, leaning over to kiss his shoulder. "I wanted to tell you something. Joey and I weren't exactly idle while you were gone." He sat up, feeling apprehensive.

"I started a new business. Joey's my Vice President of Hugs. Colleen helped me develop educational software, and we're selling it together. More schools are using it all the time. It's doing much better than breaking even. We can make a nice living from it, and can operate it from anywhere in the world. You can be stationed anywhere, and I can keep my business running from there."

"You mean I'm superfluous?"

"Not completely." She kissed his forehead, handed him the sunscreen tube, and turned her back. "I know you can't leave the Navy until your name's clear. But that'll happen. After that, you can decide whether to stay in the service or not. If you do, just know it's not a financial consideration. We'll be fine."

She turned and took his hand. "I love you more than koala bears."

"I love you more than seashells."

262

51 A GOOD CALL

Kim Jong Il died on December 17, 2011. Chris knew it nearly a full day before the rest of the world, a benefit of working intelligence in one of the world's largest listening posts. He wanted desperately to get home to Maureen, but was quickly swamped with duties.

Every nuance of communiqués and messages into and out of North Korea had to be scrutinized, interpreted, and passed up the chain. First, however, he made sure Milton Conrad heard the news. He called the number in Washington that Conrad had given him to use only in emergencies.

His work kept him there until after midnight. He couldn't sit still. Every few minutes he was up, staring out the window or heading to the door, nearly reaching the knob, wanting nothing more than to yank it open and rush home to reclaim his life. Maureen and Joey were sound asleep by the time he got there. She'd probably spent most of the day on the computer with her sister.

His news would have to wait until morning. He crawled quietly under the covers, softly kissed her forehead, and lay staring at the ceiling, thinking what it would be like to be home.

He was still awake when Conrad called at 0600 to confirm that he and Calvin would get their lives back.

"As soon as this gets out, the press'll undoubtedly show footage of you and Kim in North Korea. They'll dredge up the whole thing again. We think it's best to get the news out about you, to get you exonerated, while North Korea is still distracted with grief. I don't have details yet, but you and the family should prepare to be stateside within days."

Maureen padded barefoot into the kitchen, yawning as she headed toward the coffee.

"You were late last night."

Chris smiled. He took her into his arms, lifting her off the floor and giving her a playful kiss.

She stepped back, surprised. "You're feeling frisky this morning."

"Wake Joey up. I've got good news!"

Her eyebrows went up. She cocked her head in a questioning look. He waved toward Joey's room with the back of his hands twice. "Go. He needs to hear this."

As she turned, Chris picked up the phone, dialing a number he knew by heart. It was seven o'clock in the evening Connecticut time.

"Mom, it's me, Chris. ... Yes, it's really me. I know, Mom, I'm safe. It's okay. We're all safe. I'll explain everything to you soon. Mom ... I'm coming home. We all are."

A glimpse of Kevin's next book follows:

KEVIN'S NEXT BOOK

A TIME OF CHAOS

1 A NEW BEGINNING

Light snow had fallen overnight but ended just before the new president's arrival at the Capitol. By mid-morning, clouds had cleared and a bright sun shone on Inauguration Day. Washington, DC, in its winter splendor, had rarely looked better.

The large crowd at the West Front of the Capitol, those lucky enough to have tickets, chatted excitedly while shaking off effects from last night's festivities. They rose in unison when the ceremonies began. From the call to order and opening remarks to the benediction, readings of poems, and the swearing in of the vice president, the crowd grew restless, eager to see the president sworn in and to hear her Inaugural Address.

She spoke with confidence for the country's future. Her message stressed that change was occurring far more quickly than anyone could appreciate. Change in every fabric of our lives. "It's not happening in a straight steady line," she said, "rather it's happening exponentially. Advances in computing, medicine, energy, communication, transportation and technology are advancing beyond all expectations. More will be accomplished in the next eight years than in the last one hundred."

The new president emphasized that America deserved a government capable of responding to those developments. A government agile and responsive to its people would preserve its place as the leading nation of the twenty-first century. She promised a more efficient Washington, one that harvests the power of that change, listens to its people, streamlines its programs and serves as a true agent of progress for its citizens. It was a safe, optimistic message.

Secret Service agents had carefully secured the Capital and its grounds. They'd traveled every inch of the parade route several times. Manhole covers were sealed; dogs had frequently walked the route, sniffing for explosives. Government snipers held their positions on rooftops, while police helicopters circled overhead. Surveillance cameras covered every inch of the route from the Capitol to the White House. Agents watched the crowd through banks of monitors, while others mingled with onlookers along the sidewalks.

As far as Secret Service agent Rick Barker was concerned, there were too many different agencies and too many people involved in the process. A ten-year veteran of the presidential detail, he had been through this drill before. Everything had been considered, checked, and re-checked, but Barker's intuition told him something had been missed.

After her speech, the new president and her husband held the traditional lunch with the outgoing first family. They exchanged tense pleasantries and said their goodbyes before the former first family boarded a helicopter to take them home. Finally, the new first family took their place in the presidential limousine, all smiles, for the slow parade to the White House.

A thin man with short-cropped black hair stood at the front of the crowd just west of the Old Post Office Building on Pennsylvania Avenue. As the motorcade approached he slipped the glove off of his right hand and reached into the pocket of his dark grey overcoat. He fingered a small plastic box and felt along its edge for a metal switch, drew a deep breath, counted slowly, and then nudged the switch into position.

On a rooftop two blocks away a tiny green light blinked on the underside of a drone. A metal plate slid away from what appeared to be a rooftop air conditioner and the craft's engine sprang to life. The drone rolled out from under its cover, taxied the length of the flat tin roof, and lifted into flight. It was over the parade route in less than 12 seconds, immediately acquiring the presidential limousine. A single missile flew from its underside, finding its target. The president's car exploded violently, bounced off the pavement, and burst into flame, leaving no chance for survival.

Screams were followed by stunned silence as the crowd stood in disbelief. Nine seconds later, the drone self-destructed over the Potomac River.

2 A MOONLESS NIGHT

Seven thousand miles from Washington, DC, at the North Korean border with Tibet, a young woman crept quietly along the frozen ground. She flattened herself before the barbed wire and lifted the first coiled link to slide below it. Using her arms and elbows, she scrunched forward, lifting each coil as she went. Every ten yards another curling snare of spiked wire would have to be conquered. She had barely crawled thirty yards when her hair caught in the barbs. The woman reached up, but stopped when the high-beam of a floodlight flowed over her.

She knew what the guards would do. They would laugh and place bets on her. The first bet would be to shoot her in the legs. The next would be her buttocks, finally, they would bet on splitting her skull with a final kill shot. She breathed uncontrollably, her heart pounding fast, as if she'd run a marathon, lying still, waiting for the worst. The light slid over her, and continued forward. She remained motionless for nearly four minutes, then placed her right hand on her stomach. She felt the tiny heartbeat, and began to cry. Going back wasn't an option; there was no choice but to go forward. She started sliding, but her hair was still caught on the wire. She froze again, caught her breath, then yanked forward, leaving a clump of hair behind. She squealed involuntarily and lowered her face into the mud; if she had believed in a god she would have prayed. Instead, she silently promised her child a better life. The woman squeezed her fingers into the frozen mud and pulled herself forward again.

Two hundred yards away the Tibetan border offered freedom. If she didn't make it, then nothing would matter. If she did, her baby would have a chance. She knew the stories: Tibetan farmers patrolled the border, looking for escapees they could capture for handsome bounties the North Koreans were happy to pay. But it was a moonless night. She might be able to escape into the darkness.

ABOUT THE AUTHOR

Kevin Kelley lives in Boulder, Colorado, with his wife, Ronda, where he works as a Financial Advisor, and Ronda develops educational software. He is active in several non-profit organizations, and cherishes the time he can set aside to write.

Kevin can be reached at: kevinkelleyis@gmail.com

Made in the USA
San Bernardino, CA
20 March 2017